THE Mommy Tree

MARGARET
GRAVES

DISCLAIMER: This book is a work of fiction. Names, characters, places and incidents are products of the author's imagination or are used fictitiously. Any resemblance to actual events or locales or persons, living or dead, is entirely coincidental.

Copyright © 2008 Margaret Graves
All rights reserved.

ISBN: 1-4392-0236-2
ISBN-13: 9781439202364

Visit www.booksurge.com or www.Amazon.com to order additional copies.

DEDICATION

For Yuri, Reino & Austin
with all my love

CHAPTER ONE

I'm about to tell you a story about a tree, a very special tree. Okay, I know. Who cares about a tree, right? Yes, but like I said before, this was a very special tree—not your average, run of the mill brown thing with branches. This tree was so special that it changed the lives of four very different women in the span of one year. The four women affectionately called it the "Mommy Tree."

How did a tree change these women's lives? Let's just say that there are no wizards, elves, or magical beasts running around in this story. And no, the tree is not some alien being from another planet looking to return home like on the TV show *Star Trek*.

Before I go any further, allow me to introduce myself. I'm Missy Danvers, just your normal (well, my husband might say that's debatable!) everyday soccer mom who is one of those four women I just mentioned. I start the story with me since, well, I know me the best and I know how the Mommy Tree changed me. As for the other ladies, I can only guess how the Mommy Tree changed them. One thing is for sure though: we all changed. But I'm getting ahead of myself. Let's start from the very beginning from the first time I saw the wonder that was to become the Mommy Tree.

It all began on a hot August day in Las Vegas, Nevada, 2003. Picture a scene of total confusion and chaos. There were little clumps of adults holding children's hands, walking every which way trying to reach a cement building. Some of the children were scared, crying and tugging on their parent's hands to turn back. Some of the adults, mostly the women, were crying, too. A mishmash of cars were parked everywhere along a narrow, two-lane road. Car doors were slamming, children were running and chasing each other, and some parents were yelling. I remember seeing cars circling around and around like a pack of sharks waiting to attack any available parking spot. I heard the low hum of children's voices, screams and laughter echoing off the buildings like ghosts in the air. There I was, trapped in the middle of it all driving my 1998 green Dodge minivan with my two sons, Ray and Allen, strapped neatly in the rear in their car seats. You may have guessed where I was by now. I was trapped in the horrors of the parking lot on the FIRST DAY BACK TO SCHOOL. Cue the horror music... duh,duh,duuuuuh.

My husband, Eric, had decided to park our other car in the bus-loading zone at Polk Elementary School. I noticed that he was waving frantically for me to pull over and do the same. Well, I can tell you that with my ex-officer-in-the-military-thou-shall-follow-all-lawful-rules background, breaking the sacred traffic rules of the yellow bus-loading zone, which was clearly marked and posted, was just not going to happen. I frantically shook my head at Eric and rejoined my fellow car sharks in the circling pool. I continued to look for a parking space around the block behind the school. After a quick glance at the clock, I suddenly realized that I only had five minutes to get Ray to his classroom. A slow, cold knot of anxiety rose from my stomach to my throat. RAY WAS GOING TO BE LATE FOR HIS FIRST DAY OF KINDERGARTEN, AND IT WAS MY FAULT!

Let me explain a little of my panic here. For starters, I am rarely late for anything. I am an ex-Air Force officer and it was expertly drilled into my brain and body, by a thousand push-ups, that being punctual is important. My drill instructor used to bellow out while we sweated out our umpteenth lap around the building, "You can't be late for the battle or you'll miss the war." For some reason, this little punctuality quirk stuck with me the most through the endless hours of mind-numbing training.

I can only recall about five times in my entire life that I was late for anything, and I can honestly say that most of those times weren't even my fault. In fact, even the births of my children were early, for goodness sakes! I pride myself on my planning and time management because that is what the key to being punctual is all about. I'm a bit of a control freak, and time is that *one thing* I have a little control over in my life. Now, I was actually going to fail in one of my very well planned out mornings to get Ray to kindergarten on time. In failing him, I was failing myself and losing my all-important *control.*

Desperate times called for desperate measures. I decided right then and there that I was going to break a traffic law! Oh yes—this is something else I have never done before. I have never broken the law, and that includes not even one little speeding or parking ticket. I ignored the nagging voice of my conscience as I decided to follow Eric and park in the *yellow bus-loading zone!* Gasp! I imagined loud, gigantic buses trumpeting like a herd of elephants at me to get out of their rightful loading zone. I imagined the angry stares from the other parents scorning the "One Breaking the Yellow Bus Loading Rules." Thankfully, none of that happened. No, the only thing causing some people to stare was the wild waving and yells from my husband Eric standing on the curb.

After jumping out of the van and quickly scanning the scene for "school cops" (who I was sure were coming to arrest me right away for parking illegally), I quickly undid Ray's and Allen's car seat buckles and ushered Ray out of the van. Meanwhile, Eric frantically ran over.

"Missy, why didn't you just park here in the first place? I know you saw me," he barked. The four of us started a hurried walk through a big metal fence towards another fenced-in playground where the other kindergarten children were going into their classrooms.

"I was *not* going to park there. It is a yellow bus-loading zone. It's illegal. It's for *buses*, Eric," I snapped back.

"Oh, okay, so you would rather make your son late for his first day of school than park illegally for five seconds?" Eric hissed. "That's ridiculous."

He stopped and knelt down to Ray, all sweetness and smiles. "Okay, big guy, let's take a few pictures. Smile!" And Ray gave one of his classic smiles. It was the kind of smile where I could tell he was just posing and faking a genuine smile. I just loved how kids, when they reached around five years old, put on the silliest fake grins for the camera. They look like they had just smelled something rotten and are grimacing from the fumes. I affectionately call these kinds of smiles "cheesy grins."

Still angry with Eric for yelling at me, I sarcastically said under my breath, "Oh yeah, and stopping six thousand times for pictures and videotape is not going to make him late either." Eric frowned at me and continued to focus his camera on Ray.

Just as Ray was giving Eric one of his best cheesy grins for the camera, a metallic, computerized chime sounded. It was the bell that indicated that school was about to begin. Ray was going to be tardy! I quickly grabbed little Ray's hand and whisked him through the playground gate to his classroom. Eric and Allen were slightly behind us, desperately trying to keep up with my Olympic runner's pace.

The classroom door was blue-jay blue, and when I opened it I immediately smelled the familiar old smells of a classroom: white Elmer's glue mixed with melted wax crayons, chalk, and old socks. It sent me back many years to my own kindergarten classroom. Ms. Taguishi, Ray's kindergarten teacher, approached me. She was a small Asian lady with dark eyes and flowing black hair as smooth as velvet. Her airy manner vaguely reminded me of a cotton ball or maybe a cloud. She was soft spoken and smelled like fresh laundry. Ms. Taguishi gave me, and more importantly, Ray, a warm, sincere smile as she welcomed my son to her classroom.

Breathlessly, I apologized for our tardiness and blamed it on the horrible parking conditions all the while vowing silently to myself that this was the last speech of this kind I would ever make again! Ms. Taguishi nodded her head in understanding and motioned for Ray to come forward into her classroom. Then, very gently, she smiled and began to close the door.

Eric and I blew kisses and called out words of encouragement to Ray as the door slowly shut him out of our view. Ray stood quietly near the door dressed in his red striped T-shirt and khaki shorts, wearing his new Hulk tennis shoes with a brand new Spiderman backpack that was almost as big as he was. His copper penny hair shone, since I had slicked it down with hair gel that morning to make sure he did not have bedhead on his first day of school. My son's big auburn eyes were blinking rapidly as he looked at us. It looked as if he was trying not to cry, but there was a little bit of excitement brewing there, too. Ms. Taguishi gently took him by the shoulders and turned him around to walk him away from the door. Right before the door shut all the way, Ray quickly spun around and gave us his best ever cheesy grin. Click. Now *that* was the picture for *my* memory book.

I knew lots of mothers who cried and were sad on their child's first day of kindergarten. Kindergarten meant that their baby was leaving them for school, taking that all-important first step to independence. However, at the moment when Ms. Taguishi finally closed the door, I wasn't really sad...yet. My sadness would come later. What I initially felt was a little *relieved* because for a few precious hours I would have some time to myself for a change and some quality time with Allen, who was sometimes lost in his big brother's shadow.

I am not a woman who likes to wear my emotions on my sleeve, either. So, crying in front of other people-in public, for goodness sakes—was out of the question for me. I know that goes along with all the stereotypical "Military Woman, GI Jane" stuff that I told you about earlier, but for me it was true. My yearbook picture today would read, "Missy is an independent thinker who is something of a loner and gets her feelings hurt a lot, but you would never know it." I am three people fighting inside one: the "ex-military officer", the "now-military wife" and "the mother." I am often crying inside from being frustrated and overwhelmed by life's little stresses, but I never let those feelings out. I don't feel comfortable with everyone seeing my weaknesses. I am overall very happy with my marriage, my children, and my life, but I don't fit in to the typical "Mommy baking cookies" mold. I don't belong in that circle. I am insecure. I am strong and weak at the same time. I am Woman, hear me roar. No, just kidding. I threw that in there for a joke. I am really nothing special. I am just good old average me.

So, why did I first feel relief and not sadness at Ray starting kindergarten? I think it goes back to the time before he was born. Eric and I had been married for about two years and I had just left the Air Force because I was pregnant with Ray and wanted to be a stay-at-home mom. We were stationed in New Orleans, Louisiana, at the time, and New Orleans was a few thousand miles away from any of our closest family members. After Ray was born, I was very much alone for the trying times of the "newborn stage." Those mind numbing, sleep deprived first few months of Ray's life rattled around my mind like a hazy fog. Between the bottle-feeding, diaper changes and constant colic crying, I don't even remember taking a shower for three months! My life was completely dedicated to this baby and its needs before my own.

We found out later that Ray had a few minor health problems to boot. Nothing serious, thank goodness. Just the usual—and I say that sarcastically—baby stuff like ear tube surgeries, pneumonia coughs, acid reflux disease, rotavirus, the flu, croup, colic, etc., etc. I saw more of my son's pediatrician and the local hospital staff the first year of Ray's life than I did my own husband! I was lucky that Ray's medical problems were really not too serious, but they were serious enough to make me a total stress ball for at least a year.

However, the first few months of Ray's life helped me to appreciate what my mother had done for me. I was clueless as to how special and how self-sacrificing motherhood was until I became a mother myself. I can very distinctly remember two instances where this point really hit home for me.

Ray was about two months old at the time and I was a total walking zombie mess. Eric wasn't much help to me at this time with the nighttime feedings and all the "newborn baby fun" because he had just been transferred to a new billet (that's military talk for job position). He was in training working long overtime hours. Here I was, a college graduate and successful career woman, completely overwhelmed and humbled by this tiny, two-month-old being. I felt so alone and I was losing it big time. It was then that my mother, Sheryl, planned a trip to come help me out with baby Ray.

My mother had a sweet, calming presence that I desperately needed at that time. In the wee hours of the night feeding Ray, I pictured her soft, beautiful brown eyes looking into mine and giving me strength. Her inner warmth radiated from her and drew people to her like moths to a flame. Her short, brown hair was streaked naturally with gray, which only enhanced her already elegant facial features. I've always thought my mother was the perfect model of conservative stylishness. She instinctively knew how to dress appropriately but with flare for any occasion. I've always tried to emulate her classy presence but to no avail. So, when my mother offered to come and help me, I yelled, "Hallelujah, amen, and thank God she's coming!"

It was a hot, muggy evening in New Orleans the day Mom was to arrive. I packed up little Ray in his car seat and set out for the airport about two hours early (don't like to be late, remember, and I couldn't wait for Mom!) As I sat in the hard plastic airport chair under the harsh sterile lights, I anxiously kept looking at my watch waiting for her plane to arrive.

Little Ray was a trifle fussy in my arms and whimpered softly. But soon, Ray's whimpering escalated into piercing screams, and people stared. My mind felt like a rubber band that was stretched too tight around the newspaper, ready to fling off in all directions at any minute. "Please, please, Mom, get here soon," I chanted over and over in my mind to keep from crying.

I got up from my chair and did the "Making a Martini" dance. I held the baby in cradle position in my arms coupled that with a back and forth hip and arm swing. Swish, swish, swish. I looked at my watch again. Swish, swish, swish. I walked to the front counter to check the arrival screen. Swish, swish, swish. I walked to the window, frantically searching for the plane. Swish, swish, swish. All this swishing and martini shaking started me thinking about how good a real martini sounded about then! After what seemed like an eternity, you can imagine the music to my ears when I finally heard "Flight 1356 from San Francisco will be arriving shortly at Gate 54." *Gate 54?* I thought, swish, swish, swish. *I'm at Gate 45!*

Sleep deprivation at its finest was my only explanation for mixing up the gate numbers. I grabbed my diaper bag, which weighed about 103 pounds by now with all the stuff I shoved in there. I mean did I really need three extra baby outfits, four bottles, a container of wipes, six diapers, diaper cream, three rattles, two bibs, three spit-up cloths, two blankets, two pairs of socks, and two Barney teething books? No, but you never know when those extra pair of socks will come in handy, right? So off I ran through the terminal like a rabbit on fire carrying Ray and my ridiculously heavy diaper bag.

After running for about five minutes, my swish, swish, swish had turned into a juggle, jiggle, bounce, and Ray's screams let me know he was not happy with the ride. Gate 46, Gate 47, Gate 48, juggle, jiggle, bounce. Gate 49, Gates 50 through 53, juggle, jiggle, bounce. Finally, I reached Gate 54. I was a sweaty, stressed out, sore, mess, and Ray was red-faced and crying. My lower back throbbed like there was a red-hot fire poker stuck in it. I was breathless and soaked in a fine layer of sweat, but whew, I had made it and Mom was here!

I searched each passenger's face as they debarked, looking for my mother. I looked like a crazy person standing there inspecting everyone in a frenzied rush. Then, I saw her. She walked through the arrival gate fresh and new like an early spring morning. She had a huge smile on her face as she reached for the sobbing Ray. As the brick weight of him left my arms, I felt my heart swell with love, gratitude, and appreciation for my mom. I felt as though God had sent me my own personal angel and I was not worthy. All the horrible things I had said to my mother in anger as a teenager filled me with shame because at that moment, I understood what all mothers go through for their children and how deep a mother's love can be.

My mother even after thirty years had come to help me. I understood at that moment what it meant to love someone so deeply that you would dedicate your life to them forever. I knew I deeply loved Ray, too. No matter how frustrated and hopeless I felt as a mother, I still loved my son more than anything in the world. My mother had given me all of the same late night feedings and diaper changes, and now here she was thirty years later, still drying my tears. A mother's love, what can I say? It's unforgettable.

That was only the first time that my mother came to save me from the insanity I was feeling during the first year of Ray's infancy. There was one other distinct time where she came to my rescue. As I said, Ray, Eric, and I were living in New Orleans during the first few months of Ray's life. When Ray was about nine months old, I had finally settled into some sort of daily routine that actually included a shower, if you can believe that! Eric had settled into his new job and had some more time to spend with the family. By now, Ray's pediatrician visits for his various medical issues were starting to taper off to once or twice a month instead of once or twice a week. Things were moving along nicely when old Mother Nature decided to throw us a curveball with her son, Hurricane George.

If you have ever lived in the Deep South, then you will know the panic I felt when I saw that little tiny red spiral on the Weather Channel indicating that a hurricane was making a beeline straight for New Orleans. I guess Hurricane George (pronounced the French way, *zheorzhge,* like the actress Zsa Zsa Gabor) wanted to spend a little time in the Big Easy. We were told that we had about three days before Big George would arrive. You might as well have called *me* Hurricane Missy the way I tore through the house packing up photo albums, clothes, baby items, etc. You name it—I crammed it into the minivan. Old Hurricane George had nothing on me based on the speed I was going. Yep, I was in full panic mode.

I was glued to the Weather Channel, listening repeatedly to how New Orleans was going to be completely devastated in a few short days. Flooding was going to be the biggest problem. That night, Eric got home late from work, and even though it was nine o'clock we decided to drive inland north to Jackson, Mississippi. When I went to get the sleeping Ray out of his crib, however, I noticed that he had a runny nose and his familiar croupy cough. Of course he was getting a cold; I mean, it had only been a few weeks since his last one! I didn't have time to worry about it, so I filled little Ray up with some baby cold medicine and pain reliever and off we went for our three-hour car ride north to safety.

I watched the rain pelting the car window in large, round drops. The wind was making the car sway slightly back and forth on the road, which glistened like glass in the moonlight of the wet storm. Ray's little chest wheezed slightly with each breath. I prayed that we would get to the hotel quickly and safely. We finally arrived at the Econo Lodge and I never thought I had seen a more wonderful sight. The red, neon blinking letters of the Econo Lodge looked like beautiful, welcoming rubies to me blinking in the night sky. We had made it and we were going to be safe!

By the time we settled in for the night at the hotel, I was exhausted. My muscles ached from the packing and my nerves were frazzled. I kept thinking about how we might lose everything that we owned except for what I had packed in the minivan. Ray let out a fussy little moan in his play and pac makeshift bed, and I went to comfort him. Even as tired as we both were, Eric wordlessly switched on the Weather Channel and we both listened to the TV as I fed Ray his bottle. Eric made a few phone calls to his parents and my parents to let everyone know where we were and that we were safe. A few seconds after making these calls, however, the phone rang: Eric was to report back to New Orleans for hurricane duty. *What about family duty?* I wondered. But I already knew the answer to that one, and I understood. In the eerie, white fluorescent glare of the TV, I searched for comfort in Eric's soft green eyes.

"Are you going to be all right with Ray in the hotel here alone?" he asked.

"Of course," I lied. I mean, I didn't really lie that I wouldn't be *all right;* it's just that I was scared, worried and didn't want to be alone. But I didn't want Eric to think that I couldn't handle things without him, and I didn't want him to see my panic either. I knew his duty was important and I didn't want to be an extra burden. When you marry a military man, you marry the military, too. I knew that and I was going to follow the rules. Following rules, remember? It's what I do best.

The phone rang again. "I'm sure it's for you. You might as well get that," I said. Ray was startled by the phone and started his barky croup cough, so I hustled him into the bathroom for a quick hot steam treatment and to give Eric some quiet. After calming Ray down, I went back into the small bedroom. Eric was looking at me.

"So, was that your commanding officer calling again?," I asked quietly swaying Ray to sleep on my hips. Swish, swish, swish.

"No, actually, it was your parents. You are not going to believe this, but they have bought you and Ray plane tickets so that you can go stay with them until the hurricane blows over. What do you think?" Eric asked.

What did I think? What did I *think?* I thought that that was the most wonderful idea I had ever heard. I was so grateful for a second that my heart actually stopped and skipped a beat. I felt a huge wave of relief wash over me like a warm shower. I was going to go home to the safety and comfort of my parents' love and home! Hurray! I was not going to have to be stuck alone in a tiny hotel room with a croupy baby watching a storm take any earthly possessions I had left behind. I also knew that deep down Eric was relieved to know that I was going to my parent's house, too, because then he could concentrate fully on his duty and not worry or feel guilty about leaving us.

Looking at Eric's face etched with anxiousness and worry, I replied, "I think that is the best idea I've heard. When do we leave?"

With that, I called my parents and all the arrangements were made for Ray and me to leave first thing in the morning.

Of course I was thankful for my parents at that moment—but wait, my story gets better. This lesson about motherhood is not quite finished yet. Really, it didn't start until the airplane ride home the following morning.

About forty-five minutes into the plane ride, Ray decided to let everyone know that he was not a happy camper anymore and that his croup was making him cranky. He let out his first wail—and that wail continued all the way from Jackson, Mississippi, to Phoenix, Arizona! Oh yes, we were the hated passengers on Flight 603. The worst thing was that we still had another two hours to go until we reached our final destination of San Francisco.

I tried everything I could to calm him down: pacifiers, stories, songs, walks up and down the aisle, bottles, and toys. You name it, I tried it, but nothing worked. Ray was working himself into quite a state and after a time I was in quite a state as well. After about four hours of his fussiness and crying, the other passengers were giving me dirty looks and mean stares. One old woman actually snapped her head around the seat and spat these angry words at me: "I can't even hear my husband speak with that baby crying. Can't you get him to shut up?"

Well, honestly, no, I could not get him to "shut up." Everything I had tried had failed. The only sympathetic looks I saw were from other moms or grandmothers who seemed to understand my plight. Little did they know that I had had less than two hours of sleep the night before and was about to lose everything we owned to a hurricane. I was falling apart inside and silent tears pooled in my eyes. I bit my trembling lower lip to keep from crying

Then I felt a soft tap on my shoulder. I turned around and looked into the soft, chocolate eyes of a very large black woman. Her melodious southern drawl filled my ears as she said to me, "Honey, I've raised four babies of my own and I am a grandmother of ten. Believe me, child, some say I got the magic touch when it comes to little ones. Why don't you hand that there baby over to me for a spell so you can get yourself a bite to eat and a little break?" She sensed my apprehension about handing my child over to a total stranger. Her pearly white teeth shined as she gave me a huge smile. "Don't you worry now, honey. It ain't like I'm going anywhere. Just me and this baby are goin' take a little stroll up this ol' aisle. Get yourself something to eat. I promise he's in good hands with me. What's his name?"

She stretched out her arms, waiting to take my baby. I told her his name, and then handed the screaming Ray over. "Sssh, hush there now sugar," she said to him in her velvety voice as she hugged him close to her bosom. Ray looked up at her with his big brown eyes and his face washed over with curiosity and a little apprehension. He instantly stopped crying.

"Mmm hmmm, I still got it, I still got it. There ain't no baby that I can't calm down, mmm hmm." She winked at me, nodded her head, and gave a hearty chuckle.

She strolled away from me talking and humming to Ray, who was entranced by the power of her rich, soothing voice and the comfort of her plump arms. He was finally quiet.

I could almost feel the silent cheers of joy from the other passengers. I think I even heard a few claps of applause.

The flight attendant rushed over to me with a large plate of food, from first class no less, and a small glass of red wine. "I thought you would need this," she said. With tears of gratitude in my eyes, I thanked her and hungrily attacked the food in front of me.

I watched as the southern woman walked Ray around the plane. She was introducing him to the other passengers saying, "This here is little Ray. Oh yes, he's the little one making all that fuss y'all been hearing. He's not goin' fuss no mo' for me now. I promise you that. Mmmm hmmm." Up and down she walked, and I watched amazed by her presence. I felt so stupid for not being able to calm my own baby. I felt like a failure.

Ray had finally fallen fast asleep in the woman's warm arms when she quietly handed him back to me. I thanked her again but all she did was smile and say, "Mmm hmmm, I still got it." I realized later that I didn't even ask her what her name was. I think I would have liked to have sent her a card or something. She'll never know how much her kindness meant to me that day.

When we finally arrived in San Francisco, I saw my parents waiting for me at the terminal. I literally flew off the plane and handed Ray to my mother, who cooed and fussed over him like he was the sweetest angel in the world and not the fussy devil that he had been on the plane. My dad gave me a huge hug, and at that moment, I felt like a little girl again, safe and protected from the world in Dad's big arms. Both of my parents could see the exhaustion and stress in my eyes of the last twenty-four hours.

Luckily, as ol' Hurricane George threw his tantrum, we only suffered minor flooding damage while Ray and I ended up having a great little vacation out of the deal staying with my parents.

So, yes, after all those trying times, maybe that's why I wasn't so *sad* about having someone else take care of Ray for a little while. Although I may not have been sad, however, I was definitely *worried* about him and how he was going to adjust to his new school environment. Goodness knows the preschool experience had been a disaster at first!

Ray was not like most five-year-old boys who jumped around and drove their mothers crazy all day. He was a very quiet and shy boy, a lot like me at that age, who enjoyed playing computer games and looking at books. Loud, screaming kids running around a small, cramped room was just not his style. Also, he did not adapt well to change. His "separation anxiety" fits, as they were labeled by the so-called "experts," were still fresh in my mind. It was awful having Ray clinging desperately to my pant legs, bawling his eyes out and hysterically sobbing "No, Mommy no, don't go," as I tried to quietly duck out of the room. All the while, I was calmly saying, "It's okay, sweetie, Mommy will be back soon," but inside my head I was screaming and bawling, too! It is a horrible feeling to leave your child with strangers when he is so upset. But the caregivers, whoever they are, all give you that "you should be going now" expression, so you bravely turn around and walk out the door.

I can't even count how many times while Ray was at preschool that I would wonder how he was doing. Was he still crying? Was he sitting alone in some corner? Was he okay? I got to the point where I thought it was probably better just to keep him at home than to go through this daily torture for the both of us! And don't get me started on the worry I felt that he was the only child crying hysterically while everyone else's kids were quietly playing or waving and blowing kisses goodbye to their parents. I always second-guessed my mothering abilities with Ray. I wondered, *What have I done wrong?*

The so-called "experts" are quick to point out that in cases in which a child has severe separation anxiety, it could be because he or she has not been "socialized" properly at a young age (read in bright, bold, red, neon blinking letters: MOMMY FAILURE). Ray was only four years old, for goodness sakes! What did he know about "social" issues? On the other hand, those same "experts" who are so quick to slap labels on everyone's kids also say that a child's hesitation to change and cautiousness displayed at unfamiliar settings can be recognized as a sign of great intelligence. Being Ray's mother, I happen to agree with the second diagnosis, of course!

It's not as if I didn't prepare myself for the preschool experience or the whole motherhood journey. After all, I had been a professional career woman, and I had nine months to research the whole "motherhood" thing. I devoured child-rearing books, like the very informative *What to Expect the First Year*. What I expected, however, was not what I got at all! I certainly didn't expect the tiny little being that was completely dependent on me for *everything* from changing its poopie diapers to cutting its soft fingernails.

Call me naive, but I somehow believed those first few months would be as easy as my childbirth preparation class made it out to be. I mean, heck, I did a bang-up job changing the diapers on the plastic baby dolls! I even got the whole procedure down to thirty seconds flat. Nothing to it: strip, wipe, flip it up, strap it on, and whammo, I was out of there. I honestly expected my real baby to lie there quietly and wait, even eagerly, for the diaper change. I was not prepared for the wiggle, squiggle, kick, cry, and almost roll off the changing table routine! And just for added fun, both my little boys squirted pee pee on me the minutes their little "guns" hit the air. I think if my plastic baby doll from childbirth class had "wee weed" on me, I might have asked for a refund and called the whole thing off.

So now, as Eric and I were anxiously listening at Ray's closed kindergarten door, we expected to hear our son's usual wails and screams based on our preschool experience. But we heard nothing. Silence. We flattened our ears to the door. Still nothing. No screams. No wails. Ray was all right! Inside my mind I was shouting, "Hooray, thank God, and uh oh, Ray isn't upset at not being with me anymore!" I was obviously having one of my "schizophrenic moments," as I like to call them. On one hand I was extremely glad that Ray was happy in his new environment, but on the other hand I was a little hurt because he wasn't upset at not staying with me anymore. Can you ever win as a mother? I think not sometimes. They should write *that* in the child rearing books!

Slowly, we started to leave the schoolyard. I clutched Allen's little hand. He was just two years old and had at least one more year until preschool. I looked down at Allen's tiny head covered by fine, blondish baby hair, and then I looked into his wide hazel eyes. I could see his jealousy about not being able to go to school yet. I smiled at him and playfully ruffled his hair. He gave me a cheesy grin back.

Looking at Allen reminded me of when Ray was his age. It seemed like just yesterday when I was holding Ray's hand the same way and looking into his big doe eyes. Soon, I would be dropping Allen off for his first day of kindergarten. Time was passing too quickly. I surprised myself by choking back tears.

I thought to myself how sweet Allen had looked just then while we were walking and how precious Ray had looked standing in the door. I also wondered how it was possible that I had given birth to two children that look nothing like me. And I do mean nothing. I have short, dull brown hair that I have highlighted with auburn streaks. I am such a rebel, ha! Whereas Ray's hair is reddish copper and Allen's hair is dishwater blond. I feel left out sometimes when people comment on how much Ray looks like Eric. Is it wrong to feel jealous of my husband and this special "physical looks bond"? I guess so. I think so. But, I share this because maybe I'm not alone in these feelings—or at least that is what I tell myself. It just seems unfair to me. I made the children with my flesh and blood, so for goodness sakes you would think some little part of me would show up in them, that's all. I mean we don't even share the same "parts", what with both of them being boys. Silly, I know. But to me it is sort of like a mother's reward to hear, "Oh, how precious, he has your eyes" or "There's no mistaking this child is yours; he has your chin." Nope, no rewards here for me.

Okay, I can hear the violin pity music playing so I'll stop here. I should be and am just thankful that I have two wonderful children with no serious deformities or physical problems. So many other mothers deal with real problems in this area. Here I am feeling sorry for myself for no reason. I wonder if something is wrong with me that I think the thoughts I do sometimes.

Eric, Allen, and I slowly walked back to the bus-loading zone (don't get me started again because I was still looking for "school cops" out of the corner of my eye). As we walked, I noticed that all the confusion and chaos of the previous five minutes was completely gone. Everyone had eerily vanished! The schoolyard looked and felt like a deserted ghost town. There were no children with backpacks looking like an army of midget campers. No parents. Nothing. In the distance, I could see and hear the last few cars pulling away. We were actually quite alone.

Eric took Allen's little hand from me and they walked slowly ahead of me towards the van. I watched the two of them for a moment and smiled at the so-obvious contrast in stature. A big man holding a little boy's hand that will someday become a big man's hand, maybe holding another little boy's hand. Elton John's "Circle of Life" from *The Lion King* swirled in my head and I smiled a little more at how corny I was at times. But genuine sadness filled me as tears swelled in my eyes and blurred the vision of father and son. Wham! Bam! I realized at that moment that my oldest boy had just begun his own "circle of life" by leaving me and starting school. Ray had just left me for a new beginning that I wouldn't actually be able to share with him every step of the way. Kindergarten was his first step towards independence and our first step to eventual separation. Our circle of life.

The tears trickled softly down my cheeks as I quietly mourned the end of Ray's toddler-hood. I was somewhat ashamed of my blatant expression of feelings. I thought the military had hammered the "Thou shall have Repression of all Feelings in Front of Other Civilians" lesson a few thousand push-ups ago. Quickly, I got a hold of myself and glanced around to see if anyone had seen me crying. I wiped my nose on my sleeve and took a deep breath.

Then I opened the minivan door and waved a hurried goodbye to Eric, who was about to get into the driver's seat of his own car. I was still upset with him for yelling at me earlier, but we would talk and work it out later. We always made up. Eric looked at me with a puzzled expression and then slowly got out of his car. He had seen my blotchy face and puffy eyes. Wordlessly, he pulled me into a big, warm hug. After a few moments, I pulled away and smiled at him. He always seemed to know the right thing to do at the right time to make me feel better. Eric winked back at me and got into his car, waving as he drove off for work. Aw, all was forgiven.

I turned from the van and looked in the direction of Ray's classroom, checking one last time to see if he was running out crying for me. Thankfully, he was nowhere in sight—but that was when the Mommy Tree first caught my eye. It was a magnificent looking oak tree with a weathered blue bench circling around it. It stood alone in the middle of the schoolyard like a proud, stiff soldier keeping watch at a fort. The tree was so beautiful that I was momentarily mesmerized by its enchanting branches. The practical side of me took over at some point and I thought, *What a perfect place to wait for Ray later this afternoon. The tree has great shade and a good place to sit. Perfect.*

I shook off any more thoughts of the Mommy Tree at this point and I buckled Allen into his car seat in the back. I drove off for home. That was the end of my morning, but little did I know that it was just the start of a new beginning for me in the year to come.

CHAPTER TWO

I think I mentioned that we lived in Las Vegas, Nevada, during this time. Yep, Sin City, home of the cheap, tawdry, glitzy and glam. Did I also mention that it was late August when school began? Let me just say this. It was hot that day. Hotter than Hades. Hot as hot can be. So hot you could fry an egg on the sidewalk. Even the locals joke that Satan himself leaves Las Vegas in August for cooler stomping grounds. Hot. Hot. Damn hot—just another typical summer day in the desert.

When I think back on that year, I now realize why the beautiful oak tree mesmerized me so much the first time I saw it in the empty schoolyard. Let's put it this way: you just didn't see that many oak trees in the desert atmosphere of Las Vegas! It was unusual to see an oak tree at all, let alone one as distinct and grand as the one towering proudly in the schoolyard. Palm trees and sand, sure. But an oak tree? Well, that was just unusual.

But there it was. That magnificent tree just stood there and prospered, outwardly defying the blazing sun and dry, desert climate. I immediately respected it and silently cheered its defiance.

It was around high noon when I arrived at the school later that same day to pick up Ray. Since the kindergarten classes only met for half days and the other grades met for full days, I found the parking situation had vastly improved. Plus, with my quirk for punctuality, I was about fifteen minutes early. I was literally the only car on the street. I was the first one there. Hooray!

I parked my minivan, which I hate to park because it feels like a huge bus to me, unstrapped Allen from his car seat, and we slowly started walking up to the gate to where Ray and the other little ones were to be let out for the day. I took a deep breath and felt the dry, oven air scorch my lungs, as I looked around for a quiet, cool place for us to sit. It was then that I remembered the great oak tree with a bench.

By the time I reached the oak tree, I could feel drops of sweat dripping down my back and down my chest. I thought *Ew, great, now I am going to stink.* These small drops of sweat reminded me of my awful "smelly" story.

Nothing is more disgusting to me than that sweaty guy, or girl who has that very distinct smell of HBO and I'm not talking the cable show here. It's that all-powerful, all-pungent Human Body Odor. We have all smelled it and we have all even stunk up the place a time or two ourselves.

My favorite place to exercise at the time was at a recreation center with full gym equipment and air conditioning—a huge plus in Las Vegas. My exercise weapon of choice was the treadmill, which some find boring, but I happened to like the "mouse on the spinning wheel" effect. I found it peaceful to be walking without really going anywhere.

One day as I was walking along my treadmill just enjoying my workout, I suddenly had a whiff of a very *ripe* person. It was the kind of smell that resembled a wet dog who had just rolled in garbage and vomit and farted. Just flat-out gross. It was just my luck that the owner of that "dog/garbage/vomit/fart" smell stepped on the treadmill right next to me and proceeded to jog. He was a younger man in his twenties, and I don't think he had *ever* washed his workout clothes. Little crusty brown spots marked his underarms and his jogging suit actually looked stiff from crud. I quickly muffled a gag and tried to continue my own workout. It would have been obviously rude if I would have stepped off my treadmill immediately after he got on his. So, I just continued with my pace, trying to breathe through my mouth and not my nose.

After about ten minutes of this torture, I started to feel little drops of moisture bouncing off my legs. I looked down, thinking that this was an odd place for me to sweat. I felt another drop then another. *What is this?* I thought. I looked over at Stinky Man, as I had nicknamed him by now, and saw sprinkles of sweat flying off of his hair! He was his own smelly sprinkler system! *Ohmygod!* I shouted in my head. Enough was enough. This was absolutely the grossest thing that has ever happened to me. I mean, even my own kids had pooped, puked, and peed on me, but I had never been sweated on by a foul jogging Stinky Man before.

I completely freaked out. All manners cast aside at this point, I literally flew off the treadmill like a crazy woman on fire. Inside the ladies restroom, I wildly danced around, flinging my hands like I was doing some sort of weird tribal "gross out" dance. I started grabbing fistfuls of paper towels and washing my legs in one of the stalls. I felt so dirty, so *unclean*. It took me a good five extra pounds of weight gain as an incentive before I entered *that* gym again. To this day, I still keep an eye out for Stinky Man and his sweaty sprinkler hair.

While sitting on the blue, plastic bench that circled the tree thinking about Stinky Man, I waited in the serene silence of the schoolyard. Allen was happily looking at a tiny bug that was trying to escape the heat just like the rest of us. Looking around the schoolyard brought back so many memories from my own school experiences that I was gladly lost again in a sea of my thoughts for a minute or two. I fondly remembered the friendships I had made and the experiences I shared in the many different schools that I had attended. I was a typical Air Force brat who had gone to eight different schools due to the military moves required of my father. Like father, like daughter, I too joined the Air Force after college.

My first step towards filling Dad's shoes was to complete the seventeen-week training course at Officer Candidate School. Let's just say that Officer Candidate School was a slight *challenge* for me, big time. I was a mess—worse than a mess: I was a complete and total train wreck of a mess in that training environment. Nothing I did was right. After about two weeks of hell, I wasn't sure if I would even graduate. What a failure! All of that changed, however, after I met fellow Officer Candidate (OC) Eric Danvers.

I remember the first time I saw OC Danvers. I was sitting in class trying to concentrate on some sort of new leadership concept. I was too tired to keep my eyes open from having late night duty the night before, and I napped off and on during class. Out of the blue, OC Danvers stood up in class and made a very witty comment of some sort. I can't remember exactly what he said because I was too tired to care, but I do remember how handsome he looked saying whatever it was. My sleep fog instantly vanished. This guy was a bona fide fox in military clothing! I remember his cropped, brown hair and sexy hazel eyes. He had the face of a little boy with cute, smallish features. I watched as his sensuous mouth formed words, and all I could think about was what it would be like to kiss those sweet lips! He was stocky with a strong build. *Not too tall and not too short, just right*, I thought in my best *Goldilocks and the Three Bears* voice.

Slowly, out of my lust-induced fog, I started to listen to what OC Danvers was saying: "I think, sir, that females in the military can hold back a male in combat. The men will be too worried trying to protect the women instead of focusing fully on the mission at hand. Some females, and I stress *some*, have a place in the military, I just don't think their place is in combat."

I just stared at him. Uh oh! Was I hearing that right? Was my fox turning into a sexist pig? Oh no! After class, I rushed up to Eric to see if I had heard him correctly or if my brain was just shutting down from training.

"Uh, excuse me, OC Danvers. Did you just say that you are not sure that females should be in the military especially in combat?" I asked.

"Yes. I did." Eric turned away and started to talk to another male OC.

"Uh," I pursued, "excuse me, but I'm here and I'm a female. You don't think I can serve effectively in the military in combat?"

Eric laughed. "You said it. Not me." He turned back to his male friend and started to walk away. I was stunned. He had dismissed me just like that! My fox had just oinked.

Okay, so how did I end up marrying this guy? As time went by at OCS, the Christmas holidays approached and the OCs were given leave to spend the holidays with their families. My classmates and I were standing in the front hall of our dormitory waiting for our taxis to take us to our airports, hotels, or anywhere far from the base. As I waited for my taxi to pull up,

I turned to my friends to give them all hugs goodbye. Out of the corner of my eye, I saw Eric standing to the side by himself waiting for his taxi. I felt bad for him standing all alone so I walked slowly over to him and gave him my best cheesy grin.

I said, "All right, OC Danvers. I guess I can give you a hug too. After all, 'tis the season, right?" I giggled nervously because walking up and giving random hugs to guys was just not my normal thing to do.

I reached up and put my arms around Eric's neck. He put his strong arms around my waist, and I felt them squeeze me ever so slightly. And whammo, bammo! I fell in love right there on the spot. It was the best hug I had ever had in my entire life! Not too tight, not too soft, just right. Our bodies seem to fit perfectly with each other. My head rested comfortably on his shoulder. We fit like two pieces of the same puzzle. Neither of us let go.

Faintly, I heard my friends urging me to go when my taxi pulled up. I snapped out of my time warp. I let go of Eric, stepped back a few feet, tripped over my suitcases, and landed right on my rear end! Eric laughed softly and helped me up off the floor. He took my suitcases to the taxi and opened the door for me. I noticed that he really was a gentleman at heart, and that was the beginning of everything.

When we got back from the holiday break, training was back to its usual normal hell. This time, however, I had a new interest and a new friend. Eric. It was Eric who helped me when I was tired and couldn't do one more push-up. It was Eric who helped me shine my shoes until I could see my face in them. It was Eric who saved me from my own nagging self-doubt. He was my support, my own personal tower of strength. Over the next few weeks of training, we developed a great friendship. Friendship was the only approved relationship at Officer Candidate School. No physical fraternization between male and female OCs was allowed. I always objected to that rule wondering how the military could stop true love. Well, the military can't stop true love but it certainly can end a career. Eric and I had both worked too hard to let an inappropriate relationship ruin our military futures. So, at OCS, we were good friends and that was it.

Our courtship came later when we were both commissioned officers stationed together on our first tour. We could now move on from being just friends to a dating couple. Eric and I were married almost a year to the date after our OCS graduation. Although Eric never did really change his view about females in the military, I at least changed his view about *me* being in the military. Stick with me, and I'll keep trying, one female at a time!

Eric and I enjoyed a few years of freedom as newlyweds with no children to slow us down. We did the usual bed and breakfast romantic getaways. We slept in late and read the Sunday paper in peace with our coffee. With our double incomes and few responsibilities, the sky was the limit to us financially. We purchased lovely furniture and all the latest electronic gadgets, a gigantic big screen TV and up-to-the-minute computer equipment.

Eric and I slowly progressed as a couple from being footloose and fancy free to loving pet owners. We followed the natural chain of pet selection, each pet increasing with responsibility: from fish to hamsters to birds to finally our dog, a golden retriever named Randall. He was really our first baby in so many ways. I often wonder why so many couples take the pet chain of responsibility before having children. I think it is to test our primal parenting abilities with animals before we have a real human being to care for. Pets are that first step to having an obligation, something that depends on you for life. When I see young couples walking a dog, I know that soon I will see them walking little Junior in his shiny new baby carriage with the poor dog left sadly trailing behind on his leash.

Like many women in today's world, I later left the military when I became pregnant with Ray. Eric stayed on active duty and we were transferred shortly after Ray's birth from New Orleans to San Diego. I always made it a point to try to find something positive about each transfer and new duty station, such as making a nice new friend or loving my house. In San Diego, Allen was born, so my positive experience was easy to identify. After our tour in San Diego, Eric was transferred to Nellis Air Force Base in Las Vegas. That was pretty much my life in a nutshell up to the point where I first saw the Mommy Tree.

Looking back now, I know the warm, dazed effect I was feeling from my newlywed memories was because of the magic of the Mommy Tree. Peace and comfort are just two of her special powers we came to learn about.

I heard a car door slam and the peaceful silence of my thoughts shattered instantly. Looking up to see who had disturbed my few precious moments alone and with sweet Allen, in the distance I saw a plump woman with long dark hair pulled back in a ponytail cautiously approaching the kindergarten schoolyard. She was wearing a beige T-shirt that was a size too small and her ample breasts strained against the thin cotton. She was wearing basic blue jean shorts with an elastic band that she probably got from Target. I noticed that she walked slowly, without purpose, and I could see that she, too, was looking around for a place to escape the desert heat. When she saw the oak tree I could see the same look of relief and amazement cross her face that had crossed mine earlier. She saw me sitting there and shyly looked away, maybe looking for somewhere else to sit, I don't know. I decided to make eye contact with her and gave her my friendliest cheesy grin. It worked. She smiled her own cheesy grin back and started walking towards me where I was sitting. When she was close, she uttered a shy, "Hi."

"Hi," I said. "How are you?"

"Oh, okay." She said. She sighed and she sat down next to me on the blue bench.

I should have been more comfortable with new situations considering my countless childhood moves and military training. However, I am inwardly a very shy person and do not enjoy the usual fake, awkward conversations that everyone has when they first meet. I would say all the "Hi, how are yous" and "just fine, thanks" and then try to find some sort of common ground to keep the conversation flowing. In this case, I knew she was waiting to pick up a child so I decided to approach a conversation with her from that angle.

I said, "So, how did your first day drop-off go?"

She perked up and looked at me. "Pretty good," she said. "Eli, my son, didn't cry or nothing. But I couldn't find no parking this morning. That was a mess."

I noticed she spoke with a slight Hispanic accent. "Oh, I know, parking was a nightmare. We were almost late for our first day!" I exclaimed. I proceeded to tell her about my "illegal" parking job and my lateness panic, "school cops" and all, and she laughed.

"That's crazy. No, we did okay this morning," she said.

We sat silently for a few moments, which drove me nuts, so I turned to her and introduced myself. "My name is Missy Danvers. What is yours?" I asked.

"Ana Morales." That explained the Spanish accent. We shook hands. Hers were plump and soft and reminded me of a firm dough ball. "Is your kid with Ms. Taguishi or the other one, uh, Miss Manson?" she asked.

I replied quickly because I was thrilled that she was starting to ask me questions and not the other way around. "He's with Ms. Taguishi. I really liked her at orientation. Did you go?"

"Oh yeah, don't everybody have to go? Eli's got Ms. Taguishi, too. I liked her okay," she said.

Our conversation paused again for a moment but I decided to let the silence stand. We both turned a little when we heard another car door slam. "Here comes someone else," Ana said. We both watched as a skinny, muscular woman with bleach-blond hair grazing past her shoulders got out of her car. She wore a white mini tank top that showed her flat stomach, and short, short blue jean cutoffs. She opened up the door to her back seat and leaned so far into the back seat that her short cutoffs revealed two tiny tan moons of butt cheeks. She huffed and finally pulled out a big black leather handbag. The bag looked too large for her slim frame, but she heaved it up onto her shoulders and slammed the door. Then she glanced around the schoolyard and spotted us by the tree.

She trotted towards us slinging the large bag along with each bounce. I thought for sure she was going to topple over from its weight. She didn't fall, though, and finally reached the tree. "Hey, do you mind if I join ya?" she asked directly.

No cheesy grin from her. Both Ana and I made the same "oh, no, not at all" speech and slid over a bit to make room for her on the bench. As she sat, her big bag made a loud thump on the ground. There was a slight red mark on her shoulder from its weight. Ana and I silently stared at the mark, not wanting to look directly into her eyes.

"I'm Tammy Lewis. How are ya doin' ladies?"

Again, I was relieved because we were getting back to the "standard first conversation" mode. "Hi, I'm Missy Danvers. How are you? Are you picking up your little one, too?"

"Ooooh yeah. You know how we do the 'mom' thing," Tammy replied, making air quotation marks with her fingers.

She turned to Ana and looked her up and down. Tammy's blue eyes peeked over the top of her sunglasses as she expertly scanned Ana's plump figure and overall frumpy appearance. Mentally, Tammy was sizing her up as nothing special and definitely not a Threat with her one look. I don't blame Tammy for her judgment of Ana; I was doing the same thing myself to Ana and Tammy, too.

See, judging is just something women tend to do, and I have no explanation for it except that judging each other is a primal instinct. It's not a nice instinct, but neither is going to the bathroom and we still instinctively do that. Women deep down know that they have to compete with each other for the attention of males. So, naturally, women will divide out the Threats from the Non-threats and go from there with how they want to interact.

Threats by my definition are usually very confident women who usually have to-die-for bodies, but they can really be anyone that makes you feel insecure about yourself for a number of reasons: physical, emotional, whatever. Non-threats in contrast are those women to whom you are a Threat to. It's as simple as that.

Ana was definitely a Non-threat in the looks department to both Tammy and me, and all of us sitting around the tree knew it. I judged Tammy as a physical Threat to me. She had a perfect, slim body and I had my little fat bulges here and there. Why wouldn't I consider her a Threat? What Tammy in turn thought of me, I didn't know. I'm guessing a Non-threat in body figure but a slight Threat for leader of the pack.

Ana shyly introduced herself to Tammy and looked towards the kindergarten building. She fidgeted uncomfortably with her T-shirt, pulling it away from her chest. It was almost as if she was trying to stretch it out or something. I don't know what she was trying to do but it started to make me fidget with my key ring. The awkward silences were killing me. Jingle, jingle, stretch, stretch. What a pair we were.

Tammy dug in her bag, and Ana and I turned our heads to stare once again. I heard clanking noises and a few shuffles that sounded like paper being crunched. Lord only knew what she had in there! Finally, Tammy pulled out a pack of Marlboro Light cigarettes and a white lighter with the words "Viva Las Vegas" written on the side of it.

"Hey, do you guys mind if I smoke?" She was already putting the cigarette to her mouth.

She flicked her lighter, preparing to light her cigarette, when Ana piped up. "Yes, actually I mind. I'm allergic to smoke." Ana averted her eyes from Tammy's face. Stretch, stretch.

Tammy let the cigarette droop from her lips and peeked again at Ana above her sunglasses. Ana had just moved to Threat.

Good for her, I thought. I, too, would have minded if Tammy had smoked but I was too worried about being polite to say anything. Move my place to loser Non-threat.

Tammy stuffed her cigarettes and lighter back into her enormous bag. "Whatever," she said, and she took off her sunglasses and began to chew on the ends.

I noticed a hardened look to Tammy's blue gaze. These were no spring chicken's eyes. This chick had been around the henhouse a few times, and probably with lots of different roosters to boot! Deep worry lines crossed her forehead like a road map of Texas, and a tangle of crow's feet surrounded her eyes. She looked weathered and slightly reminded me of a dried-out carrot that you find after cleaning the vegetable drawer in the fridge. I could tell that she wore contact lenses because her eyes had that fake "too blue" look to them. The lenses were probably called "Caribbean Sea Blue" or "Ice Crystal" or something like that. Real eyes never looked that blue. It was odd. She wore black globs of mascara and eyeliner that looked like two spiders perched on her lids. As I looked at her, I slowly began to put her in the physical Non-threat column. How easily we women changed our minds.

A few more car doors slammed in the meantime. The three of us were not alone anymore. Slowly all the parents were arriving to pick up their children. It looked to me like a scene from the movie *Night of the Living Dead*. The parents walked zombie-like in the heat, glazed looks in their eyes, all creeping towards the one gray building. I could hear a low mumble of voices from those parents who already knew each other. As I looked around, I saw that to the side of us people were scattered around, either restlessly fidgeting or looking bored. Some introductions and handshakes were being made, but for the most part, everyone just quietly stood by waiting as other "zombie" parents arrived. Only Ana, Tammy, and I seemed to be having any real conversation, and no one else seemed interested enough to approach the tree to talk to us.

Imagine my surprise when I felt a hand tap lightly on my shoulder. I turned and saw a woman with soft, brown hair with reddish highlights and large, round green eyes wearing tiny black spectacles. "Oh, hi," I said turning away from Tammy and Ana and starting the "standard first conversation" with our newest person.

"Hi. Do you mind if I sit here?" she asked.

I motioned for her to sit down and moved a little closer to Ana to make room. The lady smiled sweetly at me and continued, "Thanks. I have multiple sclerosis and it is sometimes painful for me to stand for a long time. Thanks for moving over. Not everyone moves sometimes."

I smiled back but didn't really know what to say to her admission. I know there has to be some sort of social thing to say and do when someone shares that they have a disease, but maybe I missed that in my socialization as a child. Awkwardly, I introduced myself and the others. "My name is Missy Danvers, this is Ana Morales and Tammy Lewis."

With short nods and quick hellos, Ana and Tammy shook hands with the newest lady at the tree.

"I'm Gina McClosky. Whew, it is so hot today. Is it always this hot?" she asked.

Hot, hot, damn hot popped into my mind but I kept silent. It was Tammy who answered her in an abrupt manner.

"Well yeeaah, this is a desert. Hellooo." She had obviously put Gina in the Non-threat category or her answer wouldn't have been so sarcastic.

Embarrassed, Ana and I looked at each other and then looked away. Tammy quickly jumped in again. "Oh hey, I'm sorry. That was totally rude of me. I'm just a little on edge. You three have no idea about the night I've just had. See, I slop drinks down at Caesar's Palace. Take it from me, bein' a cocktail waitress in this town is not as glam as everybody makes out. I have had such a crazy night workin' two shifts and they've got me booked for a double tonight, can you believe that? Plus, my boyfriend Rick is drivin' me nuts. He's always demandin' this and demandin' that. I mean, does he really think I want sex after workin' an eight hour shift bein' on my feet with a bunch of gamblin' drunks all night? And my other sons, Johnny and Jason ain't no better. Johnny, he's the oldest, is always bringin' home his friends and they are all eatin' me out of the house. I can't afford to feed him and his lousy friends. And it's not like the boy's deadbeat dad is any good. No child support for the last ten years. Bastard." She took a deep breath and looked at us dead on. "So, yeah, to answer your question, Gina, it is always this hot here." An awkward silence filled the air. None of us really knew what to say after all that.

Now, it has always seemed to me that when people get *that* personal *that* quickly they are just asking for attention. Tammy was not just asking in this case, she was screaming for it.

After waiting a beat to make sure she was done spewing out her life problems to everyone, Gina replied, "Oooh-kaay." A beat. "We just moved here over the summer from Idaho."

Tammy's "Caribbean Blue" eyes scanned Gina for a moment and she questioned, "Idaho?"

Gina smiled and a slight twinkle shone in her green eyes. "You da ho? I thought I just said I da ho. Get it? I. Da. Ho. Like, 'I'm the ho!' I just love that." She emitted a soft, rich chuckle at her own joke."

Ana and I couldn't help but smile slightly at that one. Even old cranky Tammy cracked a smile and shook her head lightly. "Yeah, yeah I got it. Why the hell would you move from 'Farmville' to here?"

"For school. My husband, Gary, is attending UNLV. He's trying to get a better education to get a better job. He's working on a bachelor's degree in history and hopes to go to law school after graduation."

"Well, I've been livin' here in Las Vegas for about fifteen years. That makes me as local yokel as you can get in this town. You'll see soon enough that everybody is just about from everywhere *but* Vegas here, so you'll fit in just fine, honey. How many kids you got?"

"Just the one, Ethan, and today was his big first day. What a day, huh?" Gina asked nodding at Ana and me. We both shook our heads yes. Ana and I filled Gina in on our kids' names and teachers, and she peered at us over the top of her black glasses. "So, do you work or do you stay at home?" she asked, looking directly at me.

It was my turn to be a joker now so I said, "Well, I do work but the pay is lousy. I work as a stay-at-home mom. Get it? No pay but all work?" I cracked myself up over that one.

Gina smiled and appreciated my lame attempt at humor. "Me too", she replied. "I think I have the same boss with the same lousy pay." She smirked, and I thought to myself that she and I were going to get along just fine.

Ana perked up at that moment. "Yeah, me three." Tammy, Gina and I looked quizzically at her. Ana continued, "You see? You say 'me too' so I say 'me three.'" A hearty, throaty laugh enveloped Ana and her whole body shook like a bowl of Jell-O. She was having a grand time with her joke! We all, including hard-hearted Tammy, started laughing now since Ana was working herself up so much over her joke. It really was a funny sight. The more she laughed, the more we laughed at and with her. Her laugh was infectious! Ana's laugh was like a spider and we were caught in its web, powerless to stop ourselves.

The whole thing was quite silly, actually. It was if we ladies had changed into the schoolkids now instead of being the parents. Here we were, virtual strangers, sharing a special bonding laugh. It was pure childlike silliness and fun. Laughter. The magic of the the Mommy Tree.

I felt the cold stares of the other "zombie" parents as we laughed under the tree. They were just jealous of our giddiness and our quick friendship with each other. Slowly as if sensing the disgust of the "zombies," the four of us got a hold of ourselves. Ana wiped away tears from her eyes with her little stretched-out T-shirt. Gina's face was red and sweaty and she was holding her sides taking deep breaths. Tammy put back on her sunglasses and sifted through her humongous bag all the while trying to stifle a few snorts of laughter. I, like Ana, wiped away tears from my eyes. *Damn*, I thought, *there goes my mascara.*

The metallic bell that I had heard that morning chimed and broke the air of silliness. It was back to "Mommy Time" and the four of us rose from the bench to approach the gate where our little ones would soon be coming to greet us.

Like a row of tiny soldiers, the children poured out of the blue classroom doors in single file lines. I immediately spotted Ray and watched him for a few precious stolen moments before he saw me. He looked so mature standing in his line behind the other little people. I watched as the other children's faces lit up like light bulbs, their tiny hands waving at their parents as they spotted them from outside the gate. The "zombies" seemed to come to life at the sight of their own kids. The other parents cooed, "Hi, baby," and, "Hi, sweetie," from behind the wire metal fence. I watched as Ray's big doe eyes anxiously searched the crowd of parents looking for me. I was touched by his obvious eagerness to see me. My heart felt like someone had reached in and given it a tug as I was filled with love for him.

A mother's love is such a strong, all-encompassing love that is kind of like when little kids squeeze baby chicks to death. Have you ever heard about a little child that finds a nest of baby chicks and knows that they aren't supposed to touch them? But the child is so curious that he has to pick up just *one*. After picking the baby chick up, the child feels the soft, downy hair and smells the chick's sweet smell and is lost in his love for it. The child then squeezes the chick, just a small hug, but he doesn't know that that hug crushes the fragile bones of the chick's body. The child doesn't realize that he is too strong for the chick and by loving it so much has actually killed it. That was how I felt at that moment watching Ray. Like I just wanted to smell Ray's hair, feel his soft skin, and love him so much that I could almost squeeze too hard without knowing it.

Ray was finally released and ran over to me with his oversized backpack swinging back and forth behind him. I hugged him hard, but not too hard! He was excited and told me about the craft projects he had made that morning. Allen was jumping around him with excitement and envy splashed across his little face. I smiled at my sons and gently herded them back towards the minivan. Gina shouted a quick "Goodbye and see ya' tomorrow!" I think I said something stupid like "Yeah, same bat time, same bat place." Ever the jokester, I was.

When Eric came in the door around dinnertime that night, he grabbed Ray and swung him around the room. "Hey, big guy, how was your first day?"

"Good," answered Ray. When Eric put him down, he picked up his Gameboy and continued to play his Dragon Tales game. Eric leaned over and kissed Allen, who was engrossed in setting up his train tracks. Then my husband sat down on the couch and proceeded to ask Ray about his first day.

"Did you have fun today?"
"Yes."
"Did you like your teacher?"
"Yes."
"Did you meet any other nice kids?"
"Yes."
"Did you like it?"
"Yes."

Eric smiled at Ray and playfully ruffled his hair as he got up off of the couch. Ray was obviously a man of little words.

With the third degree over, my husband came into the kitchen where I was cooking Ray's favorite meal, "Pirates Goulash," which is really just meatloaf and rice. "Mmmm, smells good, me hearty," he joked in his best Long John Silver imitation. I turned from the stove and gave him a quick kiss. I asked Eric how his day was and made some small talk, but I was dying to tell him about the ladies I had met.

As soon as Eric had gotten through the basics of his day, I said, "I met some really interesting ladies today while waiting to pick up Ray." I was draining some peas. "You wouldn't believe what this one lady, Tammy, was saying to all of us. I mean she was talking about her *sex life* and all! Then, there is this other lady, Ana, who is Hispanic and really sweet so far. Oops, dropped a pea. Anyway, she was kinda shy but you know how that is. And this other lady, Gina, was very nice. I liked her a lot. I think we might be friends. She just moved here from Idaho. Talk about culture shock for her. She's got multiple sclerosis and I'm going to have to go on the Web to find out what that is all about."

Steam rose from the sink and blinded me for a second and I stopped my chatter. Eric was sitting on one of our kitchen chairs listening to me. He looked so handsome in his uniform that I forgot what I was blabbing about for a second. Unlike Ray, I was obviously a woman of many words, often too many words.

Eric nodded to indicate that he had heard me describing the ladies and rose to leave to go change for dinner. On the way out of the kitchen, he stopped and gave me another kiss on my neck. "Glad you met some new friends. They sound nice. I'll be back in a minute." He left the room and left me with a serious blush. Even after almost ten years of marriage his kisses on my neck still gave me the tingles.

Dinner was eaten and the plates were cleared and washed. The boys were bathed and dressed in their PJs. Teeth were brushed. Books were read. Prayers were said, and stories were told. The boys were tucked in and finally asleep. Eric and I breathed a sigh of relief. The nighttime routine was done. It was our time now.

I went into the kitchen and poured my nightly glass (and often two glasses) of red wine. I can't even begin to describe how much I sometimes looked forward to those glasses of wine at night. Talk about medicinal value! I didn't see anything wrong with a few glasses at night to relax the body and soul. After my first, I felt the soft, warming liquid helping me to finally let my "mommy guard" down for a bit. For the first time that day there were no little people running into the room screaming, tattling, hollering or—my favorite—*demanding* things from me during that precious first glass of wine. By the second glass, I had evolved, from the worn out "Mommy Caterpillar" whose tiny feet and bulbous body absorbed and met all of her family's desires and needs that day, into a colorful, fragile "Butterfly Woman," the person I used to be before children. This miracle juice let me be *me* again to soar proudly, beautifully, with uninhibited freedom for just a few hours a night. A Butterfly Woman whose freedom wings tear in the morning waiting for the whole metamorphosis from caterpillar to butterfly to begin again.

Okay. I know it sounds like I am already well into that second glass of wine right now telling you all that crazy stuff. But I'm not drinking now. It's just how I feel, corny and all.

Speaking of butterflies, it has always fascinated me how when I touch the wings of a butterfly my fingers are left with a little bit of chalky substance on them afterwards. I named this substance "butterfly dust." As a little girl, I used to imagine that butterfly dust was a magic powder that could solve all problems and dissolve all hurts in children only. In my innocent mind, I wished that I could bottle this magical dust and sell it to the world in tiny glass test tubes capped with cork tops. I imagined setting up a huge, wacky factory like the one in *Charlie and the Chocolate Factory* and just cranking out these tubes by the millions, but all the while never hurting the butterflies in the process. They would always be set free again to make more dust. With this dust, maybe I could have stopped all little kids from falling down and scraping their knees, bumping their heads, being teased, getting colds and the flu, breaking their bones, having cancer and other incurable diseases, being born with deformities of the mind and body, being abused by adults. Being killed. Butterfly dust. There's something to it. I shouldn't have stopped believing in a way to bottle it.

It was late now. All of the reality TV shows about people looking for love, eating bugs, and living in the wilderness trying to win millions of dollars were long over. My two glasses of wine were finished. It was time for bed, time for the whole process to start all over again. Good night, free Butterfly Woman, hello Caterpillar Mommy.

CHAPTER THREE

As they say, time marched on. The first day of school jitters and excitement had passed, and everyone had basically settled down into their own comfy routines. Part of my routine was to always be the first one at the Mommy Tree in the afternoon. As the school days passed, I found myself anxiously waiting for those few precious moments with Allen by myself to get lost in my thoughts. Ah, heavenly bliss in its finest form. To have an uninterrupted thought without the phone ringing or children needing something or the dryer going off—that was the kind of bliss I meant. Don't think that I was sitting there pretending to be Plato or Socrates or someone like that working out the world's most complex philosophical questions. Oh no, it was much simpler than that. I would just make a list in my head of the things I needed to buy at Wal-Mart that week or the next birthday party I was planning or what to have for dinner that night. That's as complicated as it got with me. Every once in a while I would have some sort of deep thought. But those were few and far between. I just enjoyed the few moments of uninterrupted peace each day.

Allen would always find some part of nature that fascinated him for a while and kept him quietly amused while we waited each day. The past week it had been a collection of sticks and tiny stones to create mini-forts for a group of ants. That kept him busy and happy. I think he enjoyed these few precious moments to himself, too.

I don't know when exactly, but in a weird way I started to look forward to seeing the other three ladies each day. That was just the start of what the Mommy Tree had planned for us. The school year was still relatively fresh, so our friendships were basically in the awkward "get to know you phases" where conversations were still pretty shallow and guarded. After a few weeks, we all knew our husbands' names, kids' names, where everyone worked and lived, and what our hobbies were. I call this phase the "gathering" phase of every friendship. We were gathering as much information on each other as we could to ascertain whether or not it was worth pursuing a deeper level of friendship from each other. The exception to this sharing of general information rule was, of course, Tammy, who every week seemed to air some sort of dirty, *very personal* laundry right off the bat. Last week she had shared how her oldest son was sleeping with a bar slut and that she had the misfortune to walk in on them in her own bed! This week it was how she was starting to notice a few of her pubic hairs turning gray. Eww. I put that little tidbit in the TMI column—Too Much Info. Tammy was like a car wreck. I couldn't help but be horrified by the scene but I was compelled to look at it anyway. I'd been shocked each week by her outlandish tales, but I couldn't wait for the next week's crisis! She was definitely interesting, to say the least. Of course, I always had to check to see that Allen was well out of earshot whenever Tammy began her tales.

What confused me the most at this time was that the person who seemed the least fazed by Tammy and her wild, real-life-waiting-to-be-a-reality-TV-show stories was Ana. I had derived from my "gathering" that Ana was a shy, timid woman who might have led a sheltered childhood in the barrios of some little town in Mexico hardly on the map. I had imagined her as the stereotypical Mexican little girl who mashed corn for fresh tortillas while wearing a brightly multicolored skirt, a white peasant top, and black slippers for dances around the family sombrero at night. I even went as far as imagining her father as the friendly and polite coffee advertisement character, Juan Valdez, with his donkey and all! How ignorant I was at that time about Ana and her experiences.

Whereas Gina and I on the other hand would sometimes look down at our feet blushing or giggling in embarrassment after a TT (Tammy Tale, as Gina and I came to affectionately call them), Ana would merely shrug and say, "Well, that's the way the river flows," or, "That's how the cookie crumbles," or some other childish adage that seemed to fit the Tammy crisis of the week. However, if the story was in the least bit funny, then all heck would break loose with Ana. The same infectious laugh from the first day of school would entrap all of us. Every time. No fail.

Gina and I had a special bond right from that first day of school. The more I "gathered" from her the more I saw just how much we had in common as far as life situations and past histories. There are some people in life you bond with right away and Gina was one of those people. I can't tell you exactly when I became closer to Gina than the other ladies at the tree. It just happened. No problem here with moving on to a deeper level: Step Two of the Friendship Stairway. It was Gina whom I decided to invite for a playdate.

"Hey Gina," I asked, taking her arm and gently leading her away from Ana and Tammy. "What are you and Ethan doing after school today?" I spoke softly so that Ana and Tammy couldn't hear us. I really just wanted the playdate to be between Gina and me.

Gina turned to me and said in a not-so-soft voice, loud enough for Ana to hear, "Oh, nothing. Do you want to do something?"

Ana had heard Gina's question and thought it was directed at her and not me. She turned around, looked at Gina, and said, "Sure. I'd love to do something. You wanna go to lunch or something?"

Gina answered Ana with a flustered, "Uh, okay." She turned and looked at me with her wide eyes full of apology. Then she meekly asked, "Do you want to go with us, Missy?" and let out a "hahaha" to cover her mistake.

I smiled at Gina to let her know it was okay and played along with the game to help cover her goof. I said, "Sure. Thanks for inviting me." (Who says I'm not a little sarcastic, huh?) "So where to?"

Well, by now, Tammy had been alerted to the action and, not wanting to be left out, promptly invited herself. "Hey, ladies, let's go to McDonald's. They have a great indoor play place there. We can let the boys run off a little steam."

A small groan escaped my lips. The mere mention of the word "indoor play place" sent shivers down my spine. Those places were just a doctor's visit waiting to happen. With all the germs floating around on those plastic slides multiplying in the moist, stale, enclosed areas even Typhoid Mary herself would run away screaming. So I have to admit that it was with a bit of trepidation when I heard myself saying to Tammy, "Sure, Mickey D's it is."

The metallic chime sounded and the boys bounded towards us. Ana and her son Eli were going to ride with Tammy and her youngest son Jeremy while Gina and her son Ethan were going to ride with Ray, Allen, and myself. We all boarded our respective minivans and headed to the nearest Mickey D's that had an indoor play area for the kids.

In the car on the way to the fast food joint, Gina turned to me and said, "Oh, Missy, I am so sorry. I didn't realize until it was too late that you just wanted it to be us at lunch today. I can be so dense sometimes, ya know?"

I smiled at her. "It's okay. No big deal. Ana is okay, but I just didn't know if I wanted to eat my burger with a side order of pubic hair stories." We both started laughing at the ridiculousness and the awful truth to that statement. "Anyway," I continued after getting control of myself, "it's fine. We'll do something else just us two some other time. I do have to tell you, though, that I hate these indoor play places. They give me the willies. I swear if I hear one kid with a hacking cough or see someone with a snotty nose, I'm outta there!"

Gina chuckled. "Oh, me too! It is so gross how slimy some of those places can be, but we just don't have any better options especially when it is one hundred degrees outside in the summertime. I took Ethan to the playground this summer when it was one of those really hot days and he actually burned his butt going down the slide!"

I smiled and thought to myself, *Hot, hot, damn hot.* I responded with sympathy, "Poor thing! But I know what you mean. I don't know, maybe it's me. I am such a snotaphobic. I mean, I just don't like to be in places where I know there are going to be a lot of germs. If someone sick just even *looks* at Ray, he'll catch it for sure, and then it's off to the doctor's office and lots of nights with no sleep for me."

"It's the same for Ethan, too. And, please, Missy, you are talking to the original snotaphobic right here." She giggled.

I glanced at her and smiled. "Do you know that I actually carry antibacterial hand liquid in my purse everywhere I go? I've used it so often that the boys automatically 'assume the position' by sticking out their hands after every place we go. They know the drill by now."

Gina's eyes twinkled. "Well, I'll see your antibacterial hand wash liquid and up you a can of Lysol sitting in my purse right now. I spray it everywhere we go. So be prepared to inhale some fumes, girlfriend, if you want to hang out with me." We both laughed again. I was glad I had found a kindred soul in my snot and germ obsession. It was nice not to be alone with my neurosis.

We finally made it to the nearest McDonald's and piled out of my minivan and went into the restaurant. The minute we hit the line to order our food, my boys started anxiously tugging on my legs jumping up and down like water beads on a hot skillet, begging me to let them loose to run around the play area. "Just a minute," I growled at them while turning to order and pay for our food. Ana and Tammy had arrived and ordered ahead of us, so their boys were already playing.

Gina waited back with Ethan, who was almost pulling her pants off by the leg, too. She and I exchanged wearied glances and with one swift wave of my hand, I let my boys go to wait for me in the play place. Like a quick flash of lightning, my boys and Ethan took off. I swear I could see the hair of the other customers blow back gently from the hurricane of the boys making a beeline for the play area. Gina and I softly chuckled and began the juggling act of carrying our full trays to our table.

I don't think I mentioned in my earlier complaint about play places to Gina that another reason I disliked them so much was that invariably some little girl was always screaming at the top of her lungs. Well, that was the first thing I heard as Gina and I found Ana and Tammy at the table in the play place area. I cringed as I heard the primal screech of this little girl pierce my brain.

"Don't you just hate these places?" Gina asked Ana and Tammy as she winked at me.

"Oh my, yes," Ana sarcastically replied.

I sat down and set out the food from the boys' Happy Meals and squirted the ketchup out from the tiny packets.

Gina looked at me and smiled. She said, "I don't know which is worse for screaming kids and chaos, those pizza places for kid's birthday parties or these fast food play area places."

I grinned and nodded that I understood while stuffing my mouth with a french fry. I have to say that although I hated the play areas, I did love McDonald's french fries. I've tried all the fast food joints and I can honestly say that as far as french fries go, Mickey D's was the best, but that's just my opinion, for what it's worth.

It was at this point that I noticed the weird thing Ana was doing with her food. She was leaning over the table and very meticulously arranging her food into neat little piles. First, she unwrapped her Big Mac. Then, she smoothed the wrapper into a one flat, square sheet almost like a placemat. But that was not what was weird. I mean, lots of people make little placemats out of the burger wrappers. Right? No, what came next was the weird thing. Ana picked up each individual french fry, examined it, and then placed it very precisely into the far left corner of the placemat/wrapper into one of two neat rows. She continued placing each fry until her carton was almost gone. The fries looked like little yellow, salty soldiers all lined up for battle. I glanced over at Gina and Tammy to see if they had noticed Ana's quirky habit.

They had. Tammy's face was scrunched up like she had just sucked on a pickle and she was staring at Ana like she was from the planet Mars. Gina had a quizzical look of disbelief on her face. When Gina caught me looking at her, I covered my laugh by pretending to cough. The whole thing was hysterical really.

It was Tammy who finally said the one thing that was on all of our minds: "What in the *hell* are you doin', Ana?"

A little embarrassed and caught off guard, Ana dropped her fry and looked around at us. "What?" she asked.

"I said, what in the hell are you doin' with those french fries?" Tammy asked rudely.

"I'm just lining them up," Ana said, waving her hand at Tammy like Tammy was some annoying fly.

Tammy shook her head. "*What?* Why?"

"Oh, I don't know," Ana replied. "I like the way they look. I like to feel and enjoy my food before I eat it."

"'Feel and enjoy' your food? Where do you think we are, at Chef Hoity Toity's place? It's McDonald's, sister. They are just french fries, for Christ's sake," Tammy said still with that pickled look on her face.

"Okay, I know. It's just that when I was little my family was *muy pobre*, you know? Very poor. I like to really look at my food and just be happy that I have food. I like to save some of it and just eat it slowly, no? Sometimes, we just didn't even have food in my house and we didn't have running water. We were *muy pobre, amiga. Muy pobre.* You have no idea. I always think it is strange how most Americans who are used to having lots of food just wolf down their food without taking time to really enjoy it. Or how you say? Appreciate. Yes, they don't *appreciate* the fact that they even have food. They just don't know what it is like to be so poor that you have to go hungry for days. Okay,

I do this little thing with my fries. I like looking at how many I have."

After she finished speaking, Ana looked down shamefully and fiddled with her shirt. Tammy's face relaxed a bit as a little guilt splashed into her eyes. I could see that she actually felt bad for being a bit harsh with Ana.

"Ya know, it is a little weird thing that you do, Ana, just plain ol' weird. But, hey, if that's what floats your boat, more power to ya, Okay? Hell, I sure ain't one to judge no one. I didn't grow up with lots of money either, ya know. Let's just say that my ol' man put the word *trash* in trailer trash, ya know? There was more beer in our fridge than bread, and that didn't make for an easy life for my mama and me. So, yeah, okay, so I'm not linin' up my french fries and *appreciatin'* my food like you do, but I do know where you are comin' from on that. And that's okay by me."

Tammy reached out and stopped Ana's hand from pulling on her shirt. Ana looked up. Her eyes were slightly moist and she smiled and took Tammy's hand, too. After about two seconds, Tammy dropped Ana's hand like it was a hot potato. A bit flustered, she cleared her throat and said, "Uh, okay. All right. Let's just eat."

I looked over at Gina who was eating her Big Mac, and then quickly scanned the play area for the boys. All was well in the plastic dome o'fun. I decided to change the subject and try to get to know Gina a little better.

"So, you and Gary decided to move here from Idaho so that he could go to school and finish his bachelor's degree? That must have been hard for you to leave your family and come all the way here to start over."

Gina gulped down her bite of Big Mac and thought for a minute. "Yes," she said, "it was a hard thing for us to do, especially for my parents since we were taking their only grandson so far away. The good thing is that with Gary's night school schedule he is home during much of the day, which is a big help to me especially on those days that I am not feeling all that well."

I agreed with her on that point as far as having her husband at home to help. I was feeling a little uneasy though because I was still pretty ignorant about her disease and all. I had good intentions to look up some information on the Web but I just never found the time to do it.

Ana jumped in. "It must be hard for you to not feel well and still have to take care of Ethan. I'm sorry for not knowing, but what exactly is multiple sclerosis?"

Gina peered at us over the rim of her glasses and her eyes glazed over with a bored look like she was about to say what she had probably said a million times already. I could tell that it was her standard stock speech for this subject.

"Well," she started, "where do I begin? I get asked this all the time, and ya know, even when I talk about it I still can't believe that I have it. Basically, MS is a disease of the nervous system. What happened to me was that a few months after giving birth to Ethan, I woke up one morning and couldn't feel my legs. It was if someone had chopped off the lower half of my body. I couldn't walk and I couldn't feel anything. It was the weirdest, strangest sensation, and boy, was I scared to death. So after that, I went to the doctor and a series of tests were run on me, but they couldn't find what was actually wrong with me. Finally, I had a CAT scan that took a picture of my brain. Let's put it this way: a normal brain is a solid, formed mass. My brain looked like a bowl of popcorn with all these little polyps on it. It was then that the doctor said that I had a disease of the central nervous system called multiple sclerosis."

Gina took a deep breath and continued, "The central nervous system is basically your brain and spinal cord. My doctor told me that all of our nerves have a protective covering around them called the myelin sheath that helps the nerve signals from our brain travel to the parts of our body and vice versa. Well, my myelin sheaths are wacky and have formed scar tissue. The scar tissue destroys the nerve. That's why my disease is called multiple sclerosis or MS. MS basically means multiple scars. Since I have this scar tissue on my nerves, my brain can't signal messages to other parts of my body well and my body, in turn, can't signal messages back to my brain. That's why I sometimes have trouble walking and seeing and even speaking. My brain can't process the signals fast enough to those parts to tell them what to do."

Tammy studied Gina's face as she spoke. Then she asked, "So, let me get this straight, because I am not so good with doctor mumbo jumbo. Are you basically sayin' that you got some sort of disease that kills your nerves so that your brain can't talk to your arms, legs, whatever; and that your arms, legs and whatever can't talk back to your brain?"

"Yep, that's about it in a nutshell, Tammy," Gina replied indifferently.

Ana peered sympathetically at Gina. "Tell me, amiga, isn't there some sort of cure for this, uh, this, MS?"

Gina stared directly into Ana's eyes and replied, "No. No cure. Yet." She took a sip of her coke but her eyes never left Ana's.

"What does all this mean, amiga?" Ana softly asked.

"It means I have an incurable disease that will someday leave me completely disabled, possibly without my vision, my speech, or use of my legs. It will eventually take my life—that is, if I am not hit by a bus in the meantime," Gina replied with a weak laugh.

There was no hint of self-pity, anger, or sadness in her voice. She was so matter-of-fact about the whole thing that her nonchalant attitude left Tammy, Ana, and me speechless for a second. We all felt as if a brick had just fallen from the ceiling and landed smack dab in the middle of our table. We were all thinking the same thing. What if it had been one of us? What would we do? Would we be able to talk about our disabling disease over lunch at McDonald's like it was just another head cold or the flu or something? I sincerely admired Gina's courage at that moment.

I sat there and chewed a bite of my hamburger and processed all that Gina had shared with us. I realized that maybe I was taking my own motherhood martyr mentality a little too far. Okay. Let's face it, I didn't have a disease or anything. So maybe I was a little sleep deprived, a little stressed, a little anxious about messing the whole motherhood thing up at the beginning. And so what if Ray had cried in preschool? I at least had a clear brain and could feel my legs! This was a huge reality check. I felt a little attitude change slowly wash over me.

"Wow," Ana said. "My family was poor but at least we had our health and stuff. I feel so bad for you, Gina."

Gina was a little taken aback and replied slightly defensively, "Oh, please don't feel bad for me. I absolutely hate that. I really don't want to be pitied."

Ana quickly jumped in. "Oh no, Gina. I no pity you. Oh no. Please no think that." Her accent had thickened a bit. It seemed that whenever she was upset or nervous her accent became stronger. "I don't always say the right words," she continued. "All I meant was that I just feel bad for you that you had to go through all that. *Lo siento.* I'm sorry. I hate when people pity me because I was poor. I know how it feels to be pitied and I would never do that to you."

Gina's face softened a bit. She was so strong, and it was the first time that I could see that inner strength in her. "It's okay, Ana. I didn't mean to jump all over you. It's just that once everyone knows about my MS, they start to treat me differently. I am not different. Well, yes, I mean, I *am* different because I sometimes use a cane to help with my balance and I do sometimes have trouble with seeing because of double vision; but I can still do *almost* everything that you ladies can. Now, I might not be able to say that in ten years, or maybe even sooner, who knows? But for now, I am fine. And until that day comes when I am not fine anymore, I am just going to try and live my life just like everyone else, and my MS be damned!" Her face flushed with emotion.

Tammy hooted. "Whoo, you go, girl! Good for you." We laughed. Tammy reached over and picked up one of Ana's soldier fries from her placemat. She gave Ana a wink and ate it. Ana gave Tammy a crooked half smile and reached over and picked up one of Tammy's fries from her red carton. She raised the fry as if in a toast to Tammy. She winked back and promptly replaced her missing soldier fry in her neat row. Tammy's eyes crinkled in amusement and both she and Ana chuckled softly to themselves. I think Tammy would have said "touché" to Ana at that point, but I was pretty sure she didn't know the word.

My gaze shifted from Gina and the table for a moment. I scanned the restaurant like the robot Arnold Schwarzenegger played in those *Terminator* movies. I scanned very slowly and deliberately, very focused. In my scrutiny, I noticed that there were tiny clumps of other mommies at the other tables. Most were engrossed in their adult conversations, completely oblivious to their children, who were running around screaming like they had their hair on fire. Some were laughing and shaking their heads in agreement at something their friends had just said. Others had sour looks on their faces and looked like they were griping about something or someone. Two guesses on who and what that could be! Yep, children and husbands would be my guess.

Which group did our little ragtag band fit into? I wondered, hoping it was the laughing scenario. But after our serious conversation just a minute ago about the harsh reality of poverty and living with an incurable disease, I didn't think so. Just like at the Mommy Tree, the four of us stood alone from the rest of the usual mommy crowd, which suited me just fine.

Gina took a big swallow of her Coke, not diet, I might add since she didn't need it, and smiled at us. "Now it's my turn to ask you all something. Do you mind?"

"Not at all, shoot," I replied with my interest fully peaked.

"Do you really like being a stay-at-home mom or do you find it really frustrating and even boring sometimes?" For some reason Gina was peering at me intently. I guessed that I was in the spotlight on this question.

"Well, on the whole I would have to say that the baby years were pretty rough for me. I mean, Ray basically had every minor illness in the book and I was pretty much on my own to deal with it since I didn't have any family close by because of our military assignments. But now that I look back on things, it wasn't *that* bad. It's like how they say, the mind forgets the bad stuff. That's kind of what happened to me.

"Let's put it this way, I have good days and bad days. On good days, I have everything under control. On bad days, I feel hopeless and weird. You know? I guess the hardest part is that I just didn't expect to feel so much *guilt* over everything all the time. I mean, for me, the guilt started right away because I didn't breast-feed either of my boys, for goodness sakes. I tried with Ray but absolutely hated it. I didn't even try it with Allen. But deep down, there is this nagging sense of guilt that my kids didn't get any antibodies or serious mother bonding like the books and doctors say, you know?"

"I completely know what you mean!" Gina responded. "Since I was diagnosed with my illness right after Ethan was born, I really didn't have the strength to breast-feed, and I had started a treatment program where the medicines would be transferred to the breast milk. I was also so worn down and was experiencing migraines, which are another wonderful side effect of MS. I mean, after that morning when I couldn't walk, you better believe I didn't feel like breast-feeding! But I know exactly what you mean about feeling guilty for that choice. You have all these other mommies blissfully breast-feeding because they are being "natural" and doing what's "best" for their child. And here I was barely able to take care of myself and my own child without falling down."

I smiled and started to get a little animated. "I am so glad that you understand what I mean! At least in your case, you had a legitimate reason for not breast-feeding. My only excuse is that I just didn't like the feel of it. I hated the way it hurt and the fact that Ray would get up every hour looking for food. I was a walking cow! Have you ever pumped? Ohmygod, the *mmmmaaaawmmmmaaaw* noises of the breast pump were enough to send me into a fit of tears every time. It was kind of degrading being pumped like that. Am I weird to think that? I mean, I didn't even like the fact that Ray was sucking on that area of my body. It was just weird and not at all natural for me. To suddenly have a baby attached there twenty-four/seven was creepy for me—and don't forget painful. I know some women think I am psycho or something for feeling this way."

Gina laughed softly. "You aren't psycho. You are perfectly normal. Besides, I'm sure other women have felt the way you did. I mean, you don't see any formula companies shutting down and going out of business, do ya? Obviously other women prefer bottle feeding, too."

"Wait, wait, wait a minute you two," Tammy interjected, emphasizing each "wait." She picked up a fry and leaned in closer to the two of us across the table. "Okay, Gina, *you* I get," she said waving the fry at her. "You at least had a legitimate medical reason for not breast-feeding. But you, Missy?" She wagged the french fry at me now. "I just don't get it, girl. Yeah, it's hard and painful at first. I mean, we all get chapped nipples." (*Eww*, skipped across my brain.) "We all feel that, but after a while it's wonderful, ya know? I breast-fed all three of my boys, Johnny, Jason, and Jeremy. It was the best thing in the world, not to mention the cheapest. My minimum wage job plus tips at the casino just couldn't cover the expenses of formula and my Mexican lady who took care of my boys. No offense, Ana."

Ana nodded that no offense had been taken.

I was definitely taken aback by Tammy's accusatory attitude towards me. I mean, I did understand that formula and childcare were expensive, especially in her single working mother salary budget. However, I felt that my view had to be explained further so that I wouldn't be labeled as the "bad" mommy.

"Well, Tammy, I don't want to belabor this issue," (yes, I did but I said it anyway), "but have you ever noticed how this bottle-feeding/breast-feeding issue really divides women? I can't stand that! I have been in some pretty heated conversations about it, and both sides argue that they are right and it always ends up with someone's feelings being hurt. My whole view on it is that women should do whatever feels natural to them and fits with their personal lifestyles. For me, I loved knowing exactly how much Ray was getting to drink. I even kept a journal of the exact amount of formula he drank per feeding. I also liked the fact that Eric could feed Ray and Allen. You know, he could have some father bonding time, too. I just think that being a mommy is hard enough without having to feel bad and having to argue this issue with other mommies."

Tammy rolled her eyes at me, let out a huge sigh, and leaned back fully in her chair. She bit the french fry that she had been using as a pointer at us in two.

"You are so right," Gina jumped in taking my side. "I think a lot of the hurt feelings come from the breast-feeding mommies knowing that they really are doing what is 'best' according to the doctors for their child so they try and make the bottle feeding mommies do the same thing. Deep down, the bottle feeding mommies know it isn't what's 'best' medically but maybe 'best' for them and their individual situations. Because of this, the bottle feeding mommies maybe feel a little guilty for their personal choice while the breast-feeding mommies maybe feel a little superior sometimes." Gina leaned back in her chair and took another bite of her Big Mac.

I took a swig of my Diet Coke and leaned back in my chair. "I'm glad I bottle fed because it turned out to be the best thing for *my* family. I was such a stressed out mess breast-feeding that I was not enjoying being a mother at all. I was slowly starting to resent Ray for making me feel like such a disaster and failure. I admit it. My resentment faded after I switched and I actually relaxed a little and started to enjoy those feeding moments of holding him in my arms in a comfortable manner. But, yeah, you're right about the guilty thing. Deep down, I do feel a little guilty."

"Oh, you shouldn't feel guilty at all!" Ana finally piped in. "Look how healthy and happy your boys are! I breast-fed Eli but only because I got so much pressure from all those breast-feeding support groups. Talk about a guilt trip, amiga! I was afraid they would take the baby away if I didn't breast-feed! They would call me all the time and stop by my house to tell me that I shouldn't give up breast-feeding and that I would be doing the wrong thing by giving formula. They told me not to 'let my child down.' Can you believe that? Believe me, I would have bottle fed in a minute if I wasn't so afraid of the breast-feeding people." Ana popped one of her precious fries into her mouth and smiled at me.

I nodded to her in agreement.

"Oh, Missy, you're just a wimp." Tammy stated. "There was really nothing to it. I'm tellin' ya, it was the best thing in the world and the best for the baby. But, yeah, if you were *anal* enough to where you had to log everything in a journal and you had a man paying for all your formula bills then bottle feeding was probably the best for *you.*"

And there it was. There were the hurt feelings that I had just mentioned. This time, the hurt feelings were mine. I decided to suck my feelings up in true military style. Wimp? Ha! Anal? Weeeell, yes, but was that a bad thing really? And why hold it against me if I was able to have a good marriage to a decent man with a job? I took the higher ground and actually managed to smile at Tammy. She smiled back, but when she did she looked just like a tiger does when it's about to eat its prey.

Thank goodness Ray, Allen, Ethan, Eli, and Jeremy breathlessly ran over to us at that moment and plopped themselves down at our table. Like a pack of hungry wolves, the boys began to devour their Happy Meals. Of course, I momentarily stopped my boys from eating and generously applied a thick amount of antibiotic lotion to their hands in my vain attempt to kill all the play place cooties. Gina wordlessly dug in her purse and handed me her can of Lysol. I smiled at her and silently acknowledged our private joke.

It was after that that I looked over at Allen and was amazed that he was actually eating! Allen was what they call a fussy eater. Basically he didn't eat any types of food at all except for junk food. He was the original junk food junkie. However, I refuse to include McDonald's French fries in the junk food category. I mean, French fries are potatoes after all, right? And doesn't ketchup fit in the food pyramid as some sort of fruit or vegetable?

So there was Allen blissfully devouring his little Happy Meal. I was so proud and relieved to see some sort of actual nourishment entering his body. Allen at this point was the skeleton man minus the black top hat and cane. He was complete skin and bones and probably weighed less than a wet cat. When I undressed him at night for his bath and looked at his little body, he reminded me of a freshly plucked chicken from the grocery store. He had just a bit of silky blondish body hair with a bluish-white skin tone, and I could count each of his ribs. He worried me to death! What does a mother do when her child won't eat? We can't force their mouths open and force the food in! I missed those days when he was a baby and I could control his nutrition content through baby food, and yes, even *formula.* Gasp!

I had tried every little trick in the book that I could think of to make Allen eat. I tried the making-the-food-look-more-appetizing trick and the let's-make-up-silly–names-for-the-food-trick (i.e., Pirates Goulash). Nothing worked. The more I tried to make Allen eat a decent, well-balanced meal, the more I failed. Being a failure was the only thing I seemed to be good at so far in this motherhood journey. Sigh.

Out of the blue, Ethan, Gina's son, reached over and grabbed Allen's Happy Meal toy. Allen, of course, let out his best protest whine. *Oh my, here we go,* ran through my mind. I waited a beat to see if Gina would say anything to Ethan about grabbing someone else's toy. She said nothing. It was a little awkward, but I felt I had to say something. "Ethan, that toy is not yours. Please give it back."

"No, I want to see it," Ethan responded. Again, I looked over at Gina. She slowly dropped her french fry.

"Ethan, that is not yours. Give it back," she said nonchalantly.

"Noooo, I said I want to see it. It's not like mine and I want it," whined Ethan.

Gina looked at me and shrugged her shoulders. Allen glanced at me with pleading eyes while Ethan gloated over his new prize. Okay, if Gina wasn't going to step up to the plate and fix this, than it was up to me. My mama-bear instincts kicked in big time.

"Ethan," I said in my best intimidating mommy voice, "Allen was playing with that toy first. Allen will share the toy with you, but you shouldn't just take it away from him like that. Please give it back...now!"

There was a moment there when I saw flecks of shock and surprise in Ethan's eyes, but that flickered away faster than a candle in the wind. I could feel him sizing me up, wondering what I could or could not do to him. We locked eyes. We stared. "Look, boy, I've stared down the vice presidents of major companies in negotiations, so don't think I can't handle you," my eyes said. Reluctantly, Ethan gave Allen the toy back. I smiled in triumph. After eating most of their meals, the boys ran back to the play area for more fun and germs.

Gina smiled weakly at me. "I'm sorry," she muttered. "He is such a headstrong boy and sometimes I just don't know what to do with him. He never listens when I tell him something. The only person he listens to is his father. I know I should have made him give the toy back, but there are some battles I just can't fight all day long."

I smiled at her but it was a hollow smile. Uh oh. Here was a point that Gina and I differed on immensely. I absolutely don't like it when parents stop being parents by not disciplining their children.

Tammy immediately jumped on this hot button topic. "What do you mean that Ethan only listens to his father? You need to stand up to that boy or he's going to walk all over you when he is a teenager! Take it from me, I know because I learned the hard way. Take my oldest son Johnny, who just turned twenty-one this year. Johnny's dad is a no-good loser who basically just planted his seed and split, ya know? I was eighteen when Johnny was born and completely on my own. Johnny had no father growin' up. I was it. I was the whole kit and caboodle. Ya know what Johnny did as a teenager?"

We all shook our heads no anxiously waiting for a new Tammy Tale to spin.

"Well, he had no discipline from me. He just ran around wild doin' whatever the hell he wanted because I had to work two jobs and I just didn't have the time to discipline him. Johnny ended up with some bad crowd and was busted at fifteen for smokin' doobies at school."

Ana gave Tammy a confused look, apparently trying to find the Spanish word equivalent for "doobies."

Tammy said, "It's marijuana, Ana. Johnny was caught smokin' marijuana, ya know? Weed, pot, doobies? Whatever you want to call it. He was in high school, for Christ's sake. Well, I'll tell you what. When that boy got home that day, I tanned his hide so bad that he couldn't sit for a week. Ya think he screwed up in school again? No way, Jose. Johnny to this day is workin' on his associates degree at Las Vegas Community College and works at Wal-Mart part time. He wants to be a computer specialist one day."

She proudly smiled to herself. Then her face changed back to serious mode and her blue eyes pierced into Gina's. "The moral of my story, Gina girl, is that if you don't step up and start puttin' the fear of you into Ethan now, it will be too late when he's a teenager. Believe me, I know. I'm takin' those steps now with Jason, my sixteen-year-old, and Jeremy that I didn't take with Johnny. It was almost too late for him. Now, both Jason and Jeremy know that if they step over the line, I'm gonna to be waitin' right there with my spankin' paddle in hand just ready to swing away." Tammy smugly shook her head up and down at Gina.

Gina stared straight ahead, dumbstruck. She took a deep breath and said defensively, "Tammy, I just don't like using physical punishment like spanking or paddling to discipline Ethan. I think that spanking can be a little abusive when taken too far, that's all. I prefer to talk and reason with Ethan or to put him in time-out if he disobeys. The problem is he just doesn't listen to me when I tell him to go to his time-out chair. He sometimes even laughs."

"Of course he laughs, Gina!" Tammy exclaimed. "He's walkin' all over you because a time-out chair just doesn't work. You need to spank that boy when he steps out of line. A little whack on the bottom is the only thing some children understand. You can't 'reason' with a five-year-old for Christ's sake." Tammy let out an exasperated sigh. She continued, "Ya know? I was at this playdate one day—"

Ana, Gina, and I all raised our eyebrows at her in disbelief.

"Oh stop it. I know, I know," Tammy said, "As shockin' as that is, I actually used to go to playdates with Jeremy. Anyway, here was this little holy terror on wheels just hittin' and takin' all the other kids' toys, ya know? All the kids were cryin' by now. So, what does his mom do? She decides to put him in time-out." Tammy sarcastically stressed the word *time-out* and used her fingers to make quotation marks. "So, she goes over to her child, who I'll just call little Billy, and she starts to pick him up. Well, of course he starts screamin' bloody murder and kickin' and the mom just drags him to an empty bedroom for a time-out." Again, Tammy sarcastically stressed the word with more finger gestures.

"By now, all of us other moms are just tryin' to ignore it and keep talkin' as if nothin' is happenin'. The mom comes back embarrassed and apologetic. We all tell her, 'oh, it's okay,' or some other crap like that. By now, though, Little Billy has really worked himself into a fit and starts kickin' at the door. Unbelievable, right? I have to tell you ladies that my spankin' hand was so itchy for some butt right then! So, anyway, the mom gets up, apologizes to us again for like the hundredth time, and goes to get Little Billy. She comes out holdin' and huggin' him tryin' to calm him down. Little Billy finally smiles and trots off to the other kids to start his crap all over again."

Tammy paused with her story. She leaned in closer to us and lowered her voice to a whisper for some sort of dramatic effect. "Now, I ask you, ladies. Who was really punished here? The mom who was embarrassed as hell in front of her so-called friends, or Little Billy who got hugs and kisses for kickin' at a door? Think about that one, Gina girl, the next time you put Ethan in a time-out." Tammy leaned back in her chair and dipped a Chicken McNugget in the sweet'n'sour sauce container.

On the surface of it, I had to admit that I agreed with Tammy on this issue. I definitely support spanking when necessary and even spanked my own boys when they were naughty. I even agree that time-outs are somehow not effective for certain personality types. Take Ray, for example, who actually enjoyed sitting in his time-out chair. I think he liked the peace and quiet of it all. It was not an effective disciplining tool at all for him. Spanking clearly worked with Ray. Allen, on the other hand, used to laugh at my spankings and said, "What was that, Mommy? That was funny." However, he hated to be taken out of the action, so a time-out chair worked for him. Go figure.

I also have to admit that Tammy's story rang true with me. I, too, had experienced similar "Little Billy incidents" at the numerous playgroups I have attended. However, it wasn't the issue that was bothering me at the table. It was Tammy and her so-full-of-herself attitude. I just didn't like the way she was verbally attacking Gina on this issue. She was being mean, and after the breast-feeding comments to me, I was in no mood for any more of her nastiness. Gina was upset and embarrassed, and that really bothered me. I decided enough was enough! I stepped in ready for battle.

"Hey," I said and took Gina's hand. "Don't worry about it. We all know that you are doing the best you can with Ethan under the circumstances. I mean, I do think discipline is important, but that doesn't mean that Ethan is going to end up on drugs like Johnny did because you didn't spank him for goodness sake. That's ridiculous! There were other factors as to why Johnny ended up on drugs."

Zing. My first arrow flew and hit Tammy directly between the eyes. She glared at me. I locked eyes with her and gave her my best cheesy grin.

Tammy's face flushed pink. She still glared at me and then she suddenly ducked under the table, rummaging through her black bag. So, I thought to myself, Tammy could dish it out, but couldn't take it, huh? Hmmm, interesting. I filed this little tidbit somewhere in my brain.

At this point, though, I was more concerned with Gina's feelings than Tammy's mean glares, so I continued, "I think that as mothers our role is naturally to be the nurturing supportive one while the daddies are natural disciplinarians. Daddies are stronger than us and of course our children are instinctively wary of them. You can see that in the wild with animals and the whole alpha-dog mentality. But I do think it is important that Ethan learns to listen to *you* as well as to Gary. However you want to accomplish that goal is up to you. Either you spank or give time-outs, whatever, but remember that whatever you do has to be an effective and meaningful punishment or Ethan could maybe get hurt."

Tammy let out a big snort under the table but I ignored it. Ana spoke up. "Yeah, yeah, I know what Missy means, amiga. You have to be strong with your kids so they know when you say something you mean it, or something bad might happen to them. Let me tell you this story, and maybe you'll see what I am talking about."

We all intently looked at Ana. She started, "I lived in Los Angeles about two years ago. My best friend there was a sweet lady named Consuela. Consuela has a little girl named Marina and she let Marina do whatever she wanted. Whatever Marina wanted she got from Consuela. Consuela did not believe in discipline. No spankings, no time-outs, no yelling, no *nada*." We all looked at Ana in disbelief.

She nodded. "I know, I know. *Loco*—crazy, no? So one day Consuela and Marina came over to my house to go swimming. Consuela noticed that Marina was starting to take off her clothes like she was going to go into the pool. Marina couldn't swim so of course Consuela yelled, 'No, no. Don't go in that pool.' Do you think Marina listened? No. She continued to take her clothes off, waved at Consuela and me, and jumped in that pool! Consuela jumped in after her and thank God Marina didn't drown."

Shocked, Gina asked Ana, "So what did Consuela do? Did she punish her for not listening?"

Ana let a puff of air out of her nose that was almost like a snort. "No. Consuela did *nada*. Nothing. She hugged Marina and said, 'Don't do that again,' but that was it." Ana leaned in closer to Gina. "You have to make sure that when you say something, Ethan gets the message or something like that could happen to him. Okay?"

Gina smiled meekly. "Okay. Geesh, I feel like everyone is jumping all over me. I'll do what I can to get Ethan to listen. I get that. I'm not stupid. It's just hard sometimes."

I gave her hand a squeeze. "We're not trying to jump on you, Gina, and we know you aren't stupid. We're just trying to help you. I know that this is hard for you right now. It's hard for all of us, too. We'll help each other, don't worry."

Tammy emerged from under the table holding a Hershey's Kiss. We all stared at the piece of chocolate in her hand like wolves staring at a fresh kill. "What?" Tammy demanded. "I've got to do somethin' with my mouth since I can't smoke around Miss Allergic here." She waved her chocolate at Ana.

There has to be some rule about chocolate that basically sends every woman into a greedy fit of need when they see it. We were no exception to this rule.

Ana smiled. "You got two of those, amiga?"

"Three?" Gina asked.

"Four?" I asked, testing the water with Tammy. It was time to call a truce. After all, the girl had chocolate! I was like Superman facing Kryptonite. I was defenseless.

"Oh for Christ's sake, what do I look like? The Candy Man?" Tammy said. Ana, Gina and I nodded.

"Oh, all right. Let me see what I got in here. Damn, you three sure are demandin'." Tammy rummaged once again through her large bag. Ana, Gina, and I watched in fascination as Tammy's bag clinked, clanked, and rustled while her fingers dug around looking for more chocolates. After a few minutes, she produced one other chocolate.

"There. That's for you, Ana girl. But I swear if you start breaking it into little pieces and lining them up or somethin' else weird, I'm gonna smack ya and then eat it myself."

Ana chuckled, peeled the wrapper and promptly plopped the entire chocolate into her mouth. "Satisfied?" she asked Tammy with her mouth still full of chocolate.

"Thank you," Tammy said and continued to rummage through her bag. After a few more minutes, she produced two other pieces of chocolate. One piece was fine but the other was half unwrapped and fuzzy with purse lint. It was slightly melted to boot, and a piece of long, blond hair was stuck to the side of it. Tammy offered Gina the good one and the fuzzy one to me. "Here you go, Missy," she snarled and chucked the candy at me. "I'm sure you don't mind a little fuzz considering you probably ate bugs and all after being in the *military*."

She spewed the word *military* like it was a dirty word. Zing, Tammy's arrow flew and hit me, but not between the eyes. It was more like in my arm or somewhere else not so deadly. Her comment was meant to be hurtful but all it did was show her ignorance, because it was such a silly thing to say. I actually felt sorry for her a bit. I decided right then and there that enough was enough. It was time to end our small feud. I mean, I really did like Tammy, after all. She certainly kept things interesting.

"Okay, okay, okay," I said holding my hands up in mock surrender. "I give up. I'm sorry that I offended you, Tammy. I didn't mean anything I said as a personal attack on you or anything, okay? I know you had it rough with raising those boys and that you are doing the best that you can with them. Okay? And for the record, I did not eat bugs. I was in the Air Force as a contracting officer. I had a desk job. I was not some marine running around and fighting in the wild jungles eating bugs to survive. Sheesh."

Tammy's piercing eyes scanned me up and down. I felt her sizing me up and assessing whether my apology was sincere or not. Finally, she took a deep breath, let it out, and said, "Okay. It's cool. Whatever." She waited a beat before continuing, "Ya know, I once dated this marine who would, like, eat anythin'. I mean, bark off of trees, grass, bugs. You name it, he ate it. I remember this one time he started to eat—"

Gina choked on and spit up some of her Diet Coke. She cut Tammy off and said, "Ohmygod, Tammy. I just ate lunch!"

"What? What's the matter?" Tammy grinned like the Cheshire cat, knowing full well what the matter was.

"I just don't want to hear it, that's all. It's bad enough I can kinda picture the marine eating gross things in my head now. And all I can say to that is *ewwww*." Gina grimaced. All of us at the table erupted into laughter, including Tammy.

While she was laughing, Tammy spoke out, "Well, Gina girl, then you really don't want to know about the time I went out with this Navy submarine operator who put a whole new spin on the phrase 'down periscope.'" More laughter from all of us as Gina's face turned bright red.

We started to pile our garbage on our trays and brought them over to the trash bins. Then we flagged our boys down who breathlessly ran over to us. We helped to put their shoes on, sufficiently de-cootied them, and all piled out of the restaurant and back to our minivans.

As I was stepping into the driver's seat, I felt a tap on my arm and whirled around and came face to face with Tammy. "Hey, Missy, ya lose somethin'?" she asked me, smiling.

Panic washed over me as I went through a mental checklist in my head: (1) Kids? Check. They were buckled safely in car. (2) Keys? Check. Used my keys to get into the van, duh! (3) Purse? Ohmygod, my purse! No, no, my purse was sitting safely there in the front seat. Check. My mind? That was it! Oh no! I had finally lost my mind! I always knew this day would come and here it was! The men in white coats were coming. Aggghhh!

Tammy grinned, knowing that I was in full panic alert mode, and stuck out her hand. I saw something tiny and wrapped in foil sparkling in the sunlight. It was a perfect Hershey's chocolate kiss. No fuzz. No hair.

Tammy gently tossed the candy to me, which I amazingly caught with one hand. Then she quickly turned around, blond hair flying, and headed towards her car. As she walked away, she yelled out over her shoulder, "You're welcome, girl!" I waved, but she didn't see it. I was still a little too shocked to speak.

As I buckled my seat belt, I popped Tammy's peace offering into my mouth and shook my head in amazement. I guess I would never figure her out. Gina glanced over and smiled at me. She had witnessed the entire thing. I shrugged my shoulders and put out my hands as if to say, "I don't know." Then I pulled away from McDonald's and headed back to the schoolyard to drop Gina and Ethan off at their car.

***

Later that afternoon at home, I said a silent prayer of thanks to God for my health, my family, and my happiness. Just when I thought I was weary and weak at times, I realized things could be a lot worse. I was pretty lucky with my health, financial, and marital situation. I hadn't appreciated it or even realized it until that afternoon at McDonald's. The Mommy Tree had opened up my eyes by bringing me new friends to see how difficult life could really be sometimes. Thanks, Mommy Tree. I promise I won't forget it.

CHAPTER FOUR

Fall was in the air. I saw and felt it everywhere. Burgundy, gold, and tan leaves drifted softly down from the outstretched limbs of trees. All around me I saw children jumping in crinkly leaf piles laughing and throwing the leaves at each other. The faint acrid smell of burning leaves permeated the air. Scarecrows, hay bales, and baskets of dried corncob stalks adorned porches of the neighborhood houses. Jack-o-lanterns grinned their wicked, toothless smiles as their candles flickered in the cool night air. The faint roar of a crowd cheering for their favorite football team was heard on Saturday afternoons. I curled up and nestled with my favorite blanket on my worn, comfortable couch and settled in to relax and read a book with a cup of warm apple cider as the cool breezes blew outside.

Okay. Wait a minute. Scratch what I just said. Let's go back to reality. I was living in Las Vegas, Nevada, remember? Plastic pumpkins with cracked tops and blue blinking lights littered front porch steps while gigantic blow-up Frankenstein monsters loomed eerily on front yards. That was more like it. No leaf piles, no hay bales, no scarecrows. Just a whole bunch of desert rocks and palm trees decorated with phony paper spiders and grotesque witches. No leaf piles to jump into here. Palm trees did not shed.

Most of the houses in Las Vegas didn't even have real grass in their front and back yards. Due to the shortage of water, most people, including our landlord, opted to put in "desert landscaping": tiny yard rocks instead of grass, a palm tree, and a cactus or two—and voila, instant "desert landscaping." I liked it, considering my desire to do yard work was basically zilch. I reflected on that point as I hung a taffeta vampire monster windsock over my front door and placed a large, inflatable pumpkin squarely in the center of the yard.

It was a pleasantly low seventy degrees now, though, instead of the hot, hot, damn hot heat of summer. No cool breezes and no hot apple cider for me. Fall was in the air Vegas style.

I was getting ready for Halloween and enjoying my solid school routine when out of the blue I was called one morning by Lisa Jones, president of the Parent/Teacher's Association. I just loved the women who were active in the PTA. I really did love them. Maybe I was basically just a lazy person, but I did not want to run the popcorn machine at the next school function or sell school T-shirts at the local K-Mart. I had never felt this burning desire to run anything or to be really that involved in the PTA. I don't know why that was, but it was the way I felt.

The PTA at Ray's school was the glue that held everything together. They organized the Halloween Fall Festival, Winter Holiday Party, and the Spring Fling. You name it related to school, and PTA was right there organizing and fundraising all the way. Busy little bees, that's what those PTA ladies were all right. Well, I had just received a call from the queen bee herself, Lisa Jones.

"Missy? Hi, this is Lisa Jones from the PTA. How are you?" she asked. I noticed right away that she ended every sentence like she was asking a question and she sort of sang each word. I don't know how to describe it except to say that it was annoying.

I cautiously answered her because I knew what was coming next. "Hi, Lisa. I'm fine." And I cringed.

"Good," Lisa said, but she sort of sang it like "goo-ouuood." "Look, Missy, as you probably know, the PTA is currently working on the Halloween Fall Festival that is coming up on October 27th, and we could really use your help." Lisa giggled at the end of her sentence.

Oh boy, here it comes, I thought. I could already smell the popcorn. My brain frantically whirled trying to think of an excuse for being busy on that date, but I knew that Ray was looking forward to attending the Halloween Fall Festival, so Lisa would no doubt see us there. Plus, I just can't say no, so I plunged right in. "Sure, Lisa, what can I do?" I asked, slightly gritting my teeth.

"Oooh, I am so glad you asked. We are looking for volunteers to run a game booth at the Halloween Fall Festival for the kindergarten class. Would you be able to do that for us?"

Run a game booth? What in the world did that mean? Would I be swindling poor little children out of their hard earned allowance money? I could just see it now, me yelling, "Step riiight up. Just one quarter will win you this great prize," all the while knowing that the pins that need to be knocked down to win the prize were glued to the board they were sitting on. Oh, the horror of it all. Well, it was for the school and the PTA, for goodness sakes. I guess I could help and it might not be all that bad, right? My inner carnie giggled with glee! It sort of actually sounded like fun.

"Okay. What does that mean exactly and what do I have to do?" I asked.

I could practically hear Lisa beaming to herself, oozing her positive energy right through the phone line at me.

"Oh, it's not hard at all. All you will have to do is run the 'Jack-O-lantern Beanbag' booth for the kindergarten class. The kids will be buying tickets and will play the game. Every game is a winner so you will also have to give out small prizes. You will be working with another PTA partner. We're all about partnerships at the PTA!" A soft giggle here from Lisa. "Anyway, you'll collect the tickets and the kindergarten class will receive credit for the amount of tickets collected. You will have to be at the booth at six thirty and run it with your partner until about seven thirty. How does that sound?"

It sounded boring and wait, did I say *boring?* However, being the good martyr that I was, I said, "Great, you can count on me."

More giggling from Lisa as she singsonged, "I knew we cooouuuld. Oh, I almost forgot. Remember to dress up! This is a Halloween festival, after all. Thanks again and we'll see you there!" Lisa hung up.

Dress up? Oh no! My worst nightmare was coming true. What in the world did a thirty-something mother dress up as for a school Halloween event? With today's politically correct environment, lots of choices were cut for me. It was no longer PC to dress up like a witch because a witch symbolized devil worship and offended all of the God-loving folks. But wait, that would exclude me from dressing up as a vampire and all other monsters and scary creatures, too. And I don't know about you, but I think mature women who dress up as Dorothy from the Wizard of Oz or any other such cutesy characters like Little Red Riding Hood and company are ridiculous, not to mention a little weird.

So that left me with all the *adult* costume choices. The ones like the pregnant Virgin Mary or the sexy cocktail waitress, harem girl, medieval wench, and so forth. Not appropriate for school and little kids, true. Plus, who wanted to see an aging Playboy bunny with cellulite and stretch marks? Not me.

So, how about a clown? Is it me, or is there something really strange and creepy about clowns? I never liked them as a child and I sure didn't like them as an adult. I always imagined that there was some deranged serial killer lurking behind all that white pancake makeup leering at me with a mute, twisted scarlet red smile. Freaks me out!

Okay, so no clowns either. That pretty much left me with one choice. It would have to be an animal of some sort. After considerable thought, I decided upon wearing a black cat costume. It was PC, not too sexy, but kind of sexy in a slinky panther way. It was not deranged like the psycho clowns and definitely not too scary. Perfect. Black was also very slimming, which was a bonus for me. I set off to the nearest thrift store to search for some black pants and a black turtleneck sweater.

***

That afternoon at the Mommy Tree I saw Gina, Tammy, and Ana waiting for their children as usual. I walked over to them and sat down on the bench beside them.

"Hello, ladies, how are you?" I asked.

Tammy was the first to reply, of course, and she was off and running. "Oh. Okay. I worked another long shift last night and ya know what happened when I got home?" Gina, Ana and I shook our heads no; we all had half grins on our faces anxiously awaiting the new TT. I checked to see that Allen was happily playing in the dirt well out of earshot.

Tammy did not disappoint us. "Well, I walked in the door dead tired off my feet, ya know—it was a busy night with some sort of computer convention in town and those boys like to drink. They also like to tip but that's another story. Anyway, I walked in and there's Rick with his feet propped up on my couch drinkin' a beer and watchin' football. I waited to see if he would say anythin' and he didn't say nothing, so I was like, 'How about a simple hello? Don't I even get a hello anymore?' And he was like, 'Oh, hi,' just like that and he didn't even look up from his game or nothin'. So, I stepped in front of the TV to get his attention and he moves his head to look around me. Can you believe that?" Tammy shook her head and continued her rant.

"Okay, by this time, I am really pissed off and I just slam my purse on the counter and walk upstairs to my room. Then, like a dog sensing his master is upset or somethin', Rick sorta comes upstairs all sheepish and little boyish giving me his best smile. Well, you know what that little smile leads to? We had great sex. But, ya know? I still can't believe I am supportin' this bum—but hey, the sex is good so what can I say? I mean it's like my first husband all over again. Ya think I'd learn from my mistakes. With my luck, I'll get pregnant by the bastard!"

Tammy let out of deep sigh and started rummaging through her bag looking for a cigarette. She picked a cigarette out the pack and put it to her lips and lit it. Inhaling deeply, she caught Ana giving her best scowl. Tammy moaned, "Jeeesus Christ Ana, stop with the mean face already. I'll put the goddamn thing out." The cigarette was extinguished and fell to the bottomless pit of Tammy's bag.

Gina and I silently pictured Rick (whom neither of us had ever met before but had constructed as the stereotypical blue collar, caveman kind of guy) with Tammy in bed and I knew we both were thinking, *Ewww,* once again.

"Tammy, mi amiga, you need to tell that bum to jump away to the nearest bridge," Ana said trying to use her best adage for the Tammy crisis of the moment.

Tammy laughed. "Do you mean, take a flying leap off the nearest bridge? Don't think I haven't tried, Ana! I just can't help it, the sex is soooo good, ya know? After we argue and I kick him out for the, like, one hundredth time, we just end up in bed and can't help ourselves. How do I just give that up?"

Okay, at this point, *ewww* again. I had had enough and was starting to get grossed out by the whole Tammy and Rick in bed thing so I decided this was as good as any time to find out if any of these ladies had been contacted by the Queen Bee Lisa Jones.

"Oh, hey, I don't mean to change the subject" (I did) "but did any of you get called this morning to help out at the Halloween Fall Festival?" I asked.

All three ladies shook their heads no and Gina asked me for the scoop. "Well," I said, "basically I have to run a game booth for the kindergarten class during the Halloween Fall Festival. But, get this, I have to dress up."

Gina gasped. "How fun! "What are you going to dress up as?"

I looked at Gina quizzically. "'How fun?' How can you say that dressing up at *our* age is fun? Ech, I don't even want to think about it. But I *did* think about it and I am going as a black cat."

"Ooh, now that's original, Missy. I bet no one else thinks to dress up as a black cat," Tammy said very sarcastically and she started to rummage through her bag again.

I was a little defensive and annoyed. Nothing was wrong with a black cat costume. It passed all of my PC tests that I had mentioned earlier. I looked directly at Tammy and asked, "What is so wrong with dressing up as a black cat, Tammy?"

"Nothing is *wrong*, Missy. It's just not original. It's boring. But hey, if you want to be just another boring mommy at the festival then that's up to you. It's none of my business," Tammy replied, never looking up from her bag.

What the hell was her problem? I sat there fuming and tried to think of a good comeback. Nothing witty came to my mind, but something sure did to Ana's. She slyly looked at Tammy and said, "And what would you go as, Tammy? Would you dress up as an overworked, Las Vegas cocktail waitress with a lousy boyfriend who can't get enough sex? Oh wait, you dress up in *that* costume every day."

Ana smiled triumphantly. I silently cheered her. What guts! Score one for Ana!

There was a brief moment of silence. Gina and I were a little anxious to hear Tammy's reply. We could tell that Ana had said her comment in a somewhat joking manner heavily laced with the truth but how would Tammy react?

Tammy looked up from her bag. Her Caribbean ice blue eyes locked with Ana's soft, chocolate ones. Neither lady looked away. Just when I couldn't stand the tension anymore, Ana spoke again.

"Or...you could go as a chubby, underappreciated, not getting enough sex Mexican housewife and dress up like me. I don't know about you, mi amiga, but Missy's black cat is starting to sound good." Ana chuckled and wrapped her jacket around her waist a little tighter as a soft breeze began to blow.

Tammy paused a moment and then started to giggle, which promptly turned into a smoker's cough. When she finally had her phlegm under control, she said, "Whew, that was not so nice there, girl! I wasn't tryin' to jump on anyone or anythin'. I tell ya, it's Rick. He's makin' me crazy and all hormonal. Look, Missy, go as a black cat, black dog, blackbird, or whatever the hell you want! I don't care. I wasn't tryin' to be rude or nothin'. I just thought it was boring to dress up like everyone else. I just know I'd go as somethin' with a little more pizzazz that's all. Sheeesh. Ana, girl, you are somethin' else!" Tammy smiled.

I tried to image what Tammy considered "pizzazz" but the only thought that came to my mind was a topless Las Vegas showgirl. I pictured her showing up at the Halloween Fall Festival wearing nothing but a humongous feather headdress, a few silver pasties and a smile. I bet that would get ol' Queen Bee Lisa Jones a-humming. Maybe Tammy had a point. If I dressed up with a little "pizzazz" maybe the PTA wouldn't call me again. Hmmm, just a thought.

A soft, brown leaf kissed with a touch of burgundy floated down on to the top of Gina's head. "Hey, look at this leaf," she said, pulling it from her hair. "It's so pretty. I never really noticed how pretty this tree was before."

Tammy looked up at the tree and shrugged her shoulders and her acid-wash jean jacket crinkled a bit. "Hmm, me neither. Isn't it kinda weird how this tree is sittin' here in the middle of nowhere?"

"Yeah, a little weird, I guess," said Ana also looking up as a few more speckled leaves fell. She picked up a leaf and twirled it in her fingers. "I like sitting here at this tree talking with you all everyday. In a way, I kinda look forward to it."

We all nodded in agreement at her admission.

"Yeah, me too, girl, except when you are chewing me out!" Tammy said and lightly punched Ana in the arm. Ana smiled at her, put her arm around her shoulder, and rocked her small frame back and forth.

"Someone has to keep you in line, mi amiga, and that someone is me. That's the way the cookie crumbles whether you like it or not. You and I are like two peas in a pod, mi amiga, two peas in a pod." She held up two crossed fingers. "I like you."

Tammy's eyes sparkled and she said, "Good, because I like you, too, girl. You make me laugh. Ya know? I don't think I would have met you guys if it hadn't been for this tree here. On that first day, I saw you two sittin' here and I thought it would be fun to be able to join you. I didn't want to stand by myself. I don't like being alone."

Gina smiled. "Yeah, me too. I came over when I saw you three talking and I wanted to sit down. It looked like some sort of 'Mommy Tree" or something."

We looked at each other and our eyes lit up. Ana was the first to speak. "The Mommy Tree! Hey, I like that! Yeah, yeah, the Mommy Tree! That's what we should call it!"

And that was how the Mommy Tree was named.

I looked up at the magnificent tree branches of the newly named Mommy Tree with her precious leaves barely dangling on the ends. The branches held their fragile cargo of leaves just waiting for the next wind to carry them away. I thought of how gutsy Ana was. Gutsy was really the only word I could think of to describe her comments to Tammy in defense of me. Here I was, an ex-military officer, too timid and scared to stick up for myself against the brazen Tammy. Further, why couldn't I have just said no to Queen Bee Lisa Jones in the first place? Then the whole Halloween costume conversation wouldn't have happened. What was it about my personality that made me so wimpy and not able to stand up for myself and say no to others?

I was lacking self-confidence. That was it pure and simple. I would look back later and realize that the Mommy Tree was just trying to show me something that day. I needed to start being myself and to stop worrying about what others thought and said.

The school bell hummed and the little ones came pouring out of the door all lined up ready to go. Tammy, Ana, Gina, and I rose from the bench. I called Allen over to me as we all slowly started walking toward the gate. I lightly grabbed Gina's arm and held her back letting Tammy and Ana go ahead of us.

"Hey Gina, how are you feeling today?" I asked. I always asked her every day. I worried about her sometimes.

"Fine, thanks for asking," Gina said as she always did, even if that wasn't the truth. She was very determined not to let her pain show or to have to rely on anyone.

"Are you sure? When is your next treatment session?"

"Oh, this afternoon, but it's no big deal either way. We'll probably just discuss some different medicines to take." She shrugged her shoulders and I admired her courage.

"Look, if you need something, remember you can count on me." I looked directly into Gina's eyes. She smiled and gave me a hug. I hugged her back. We started walking to the gate to join the other two ladies and to greet our children.

"Hey, Missy," Gina said. "Maybe I could volunteer with you to help run the booth. Lisa didn't call but maybe it's not too late for me to help out."

I broke out into a smile. What a wonderful idea! "Sure," I said. "I could give her a call this afternoon and see what she says."

"Great," replied Gina. I watched as Ray and Ethan bounded towards us wildly waving their jack-o-lantern finger paint art projects at us. Allen ran over and hugged Ray, who proudly showed his pumpkin to his brother.

As we started to walk to my van, Tammy yelled, "See ya tomorrow at the Mommy Tree, ladies!"

Ana, Gina, and I chorused our responses, and I waved goodbye to Tammy, Ana, and their sons who were walking in the opposite direction. Gina and Ethan were just a step behind us. "Hey, Missy," Gina said as she opened her car door for Ethan. They were parked just in front of us.

"Yeeeess?" I replied in my best comic voice.

"I think I know what I am going to dress up as if we get to work together at the Halloween booth."

"If you say a stressed-out, uptight, neurotic, getting just enough sex someone like me, I'll kill you," I joked.

"No," Gina laughed. "But at least you didn't say a shy, sometimes dorky, fighting MS, getting okay sex someone like me." We both laughed.

As I started to buckle Ray and Allen into their car seats. Gina continued, "No, what I was going to say is a black cat, too. That way we could match. Would you care?"

"Oooh, how *original*! Not enough *pizzazz*," I teased in my best Tammy voice. We both laughed. "No," I continued, "I don't care. That sounds great. I'll let you know what Lisa says. Talk to you later! Meow." I slammed the minivan side door shut and waved a quick goodbye to Gina as I slid into the driver's side. Then I rolled down the driver window and yelled out to her, "Hey, let me know how things go today with your appointment, okay?"

"Okay," Gina replied and waved goodbye through her window. She drove away. I looked around before pulling out off the curb, and my eye caught the Mommy Tree in the distance. A gold and burgundy leaf slowly drifted to the ground. The tree was slowly changing, shedding her old leaves. Just like the tree, I realized I was slowly changing, too, by shedding my "old leaves" of insecurity. The martyr in me who was always complaining was drifting away in the wind. A refreshing change of attitude was just what I needed.

CHAPTER FIVE

The Halloween Fall Festival arrived sooner than I had expected. Time flew by. As it turned out, the Queen Bee Lisa Jones was more than happy to add another worker bee to her colony. Gina and I were going to run the kindergarten game booth together.

"Gina Cat" picked me up the night of the festival and we arrived at the schoolyard—about twenty minutes early I might add! We were impressed by how fine a job the PTA had done of transforming the outdoor play yard area into a haunted, spooky forest complete with paper mache trees, white sheet ghosts, and plastic pumpkins. Gina and I glanced over to the kindergarten play yard to see if the Mommy Tree had been decorated. It hadn't, but it appeared scary enough in the twilight. The tree had lost most of its leaves and her bare stick branches looked like sharp, pointy spears ready to stab someone any minute.

I steered Gina away from the tree towards the carnival area where the kindergarten booth was supposed to be located. A very frazzled Lisa spotted us and led us directly to the beanbag toss booth. Both Gina and I had to suppress our giggles when we saw Lisa's Halloween costume. No, she was not dressed as a queen bee, but close. She was dressed as a gigantic black widow spider! Her entire face was painted with black greasepaint, and she wore big bouncy balls on her head that bobbed around every time she spoke or moved, which was constantly. I guessed those were supposed to be eyes or antennae, who knows? Her garish yellow teeth flashed at us when she spoke. It was quite eerie, let me tell you. She had also cut a huge cardboard middle section and painted it midnight black with a red hourglass shape on her belly. Six pitch-black wiry, hairy legs sprouted from her middle and her arms acted as the seventh and eighth legs. She wore a black turtleneck and red and black striped stockings on her legs to complete the outfit. It was a ridiculous sight, really. For some reason, go figure, I started singing "The Itsy Bitsy Spider" in my head. When I look back now, I think what made the whole Lisa thing so funny was how *serious* Lisa was trying to be running the festival while looking so ridiculous at the same time in that costume.

Lisa instructed Gina and me on how to run the booth, as if it weren't self-explanatory enough, duh! She began, "Now, ladies, here is what you will do. First, you have to collect the tickets from the children. Just *one* ticket," Lisa stressed the word "one" like we were the kindergarteners and not the adults. "Not, two, not three, just *one* ticket from each child. After you collect the ticket you will put it in this jar." She held up a medium sized mason jar with a lid that had a slit cut on the top. Bobble, bobble went her head balls. I stifled a giggle. "Then, ladies, you will give the child *three* beanbags."

Gina interrupted, "Uh, not one, not two, just three, right?" I covered my mouth to stop from smiling. Who knew Gina could be so sarcastic? Lisa squinted her eyes at Gina. You could see that she couldn't decide if Gina was asking a serious question or making fun of her.

She took a deep breath and continued her barrage of instructions. No more singsong voice from her here. It was all business, "Yes, Gina, *three* beanbags only. No more, no less. Got it? Then, after the children throw the beanbags, if they throw at least two bags into any of the holes, then they win a prize from *this* basket." Lisa held up a big basket that had a variety of cheap, made-in-Taiwan toys. "If they only throw one beanbag in then they win a prize from *this* basket." She held up a slightly smaller basket that held stickers and small rubber balls. "If the child doesn't put any beanbags in the holes, then they will win a prize from *this* basket." She held up a small basket that held tiny packets of Halloween candies. "Every child wins a prize, got it?"

I felt like belting out in my best military voice, "*Ma'am, yes ma'am!*" But I held back. Instead I nodded at Lisa. Gina nodded, too.

"Okay then. Good. I've got to go and help the other ladies get their act together at the ring toss. Now remember ladies...only *three* beanbags." Lisa fixed her eyes on Gina, who grinned. "And only *one* ticket per child, and *everyone* wins a prize." Again, Gina and I nodded. Only a moron wouldn't get it at this point. "Okay. Good. I'll be back in an hour to check on you and bring the other volunteers."

Lisa turned around out of the booth but as she turned, two of her hairy fake legs caught on the gaping smile of the wooden beanbag board! Lisa weakly smiled and tried to pull the legs out. I think I actually heard her grunt! The problem was that her middle section was too big for her arms to reach her legs all the way. The board wobbled each time she tried to wiggle free. Wiggle, wobble, until the board started to topple over. Gina grabbed it in the nick of time to keep it from crashing to the ground. Lisa grunted and even groaned as she clawed at her hideous hairy legs. Finally, I tugged and plucked the legs out of the pumpkin's mouth. Lisa stumbled back from the force of being freed but caught herself before falling down. She muttered a weak "thank you," turned, and promptly waddled out of the booth. As soon as Gina and I were alone in the booth, we both broke out laughing hysterically.

"What in the world was that costume? I mean, it's creative and all but, oh my! It certainly has 'pizzazz'!" Gina exclaimed in between giggles.

"Oh, I know. It was so huge! What was she thinking? Did you see the bobble things on her head? Ohmygod. I will give her credit, though. She definitely put some work into that outfit."

"And what was with that speech for goodness sakes?" Gina asked. "'Not two, not three, just *one* ticket,' blah blah blah. We're not five years old! I think we can handle this. What do you think, girlfriend?"

"Oh yeah," I said. "But God forbid we give out the wrong prizes or wrong number of beanbags. Heck, she might come back and start shooting spider webs at us from out of her ass!"

We burst into another round of laughter. Gina was laughing so hard that tears ran down her face and smeared her black eye pencil cat whiskers. We finally got a hold of ourselves, fixed our faces, and buckled down to some serious carnival business.

All was going well at the jack-o-lantern booth. I watched as small kids tried so desperately to toss their beanbags into the holes. I loved how their little innocent faces would beam with excitement as they selected their prizes. I also started to notice a pattern in the kids' costumes after awhile. All the little boys were dressed as superheroes like Spiderman, Batman, and Superman, or else a monster. All the little girls were dressed as Disney princesses: Cinderella, Belle, or Snow White. It was very cute and I was actually enjoying myself quite a bit.

By this time, Gina and I had our routine down. In a strange Tonto voice, I chanted the following in my head: *One ticket per child. Three bean bags each child. Two equals big basket of cheap Taiwan crap. One equals balls and stickers. None equals candy. Big spider woman Lisa shoot ass web if don't get right.*

We were about twenty minutes into the carnival when I spotted my husband and sons approaching us. Ray was desperately searching for the jack-o-lantern booth looking for me and I watched his face light up as he spotted it. He started pointing at me and tugging on Eric's pant legs. I smiled as Ray—dressed as Spiderman, of course—and Allen, dressed as The Hulk, ran over to me.

"Hi, guys," I said as I ruffled their hair. I gave them both a big hug but I'm not sure either of them felt it. Both boys' costumes were thickly padded to resemble real superhero "muscles." It was so cute and manly. "Did you guys buy some tickets so you can play?" I asked looking directly at Eric.

"Of course, Missy," Eric replied while handing out two tickets to Ray and Allen. I made quick introductions between Eric and Gina. Then the boys gave Gina their tickets, which she promptly put in the jar. Gina gave three beanbags each to Ray and Allen.

On his first try, Ray threw his bag directly into the grinning mouth. He missed the target on his second bag. On his last bag, he threw it into the pumpkin's left eye. I handed Ray the big basket filled with the made-in-Taiwan crap and he picked out a tiny green, plastic soldier tied to a parachute.

It was Allen's turn. He missed on his first throw. He threw it into the pumpkin's nose on the second try, but he missed on his third bag. I handed Allen the smaller basket with the stickers and rubber balls and watched as his face fell through the floor. He looked up at me with pleading eyes.

"Why can't I have a paratrooper too like Ray, Mommy? Didn't I do good?" Allen asked.

My heart stopped for a moment. I panicked a little thinking, *Uh oh. Here comes a tantrum in the making.* But that really wasn't the case at all. Allen wasn't demanding or whining or doing anything annoying like some kids would. He had asked such a pure, innocent question. I guess that was why it hurt me so much when I explained the "rules" to him and tried to assure him that he had done a good job, too.

"Okay, Mommy." Allen said and he gently picked out a blue rubber ball. He looked sadly down, clutching the ball in his tiny hand. I noticed a small wet spot, obviously from a tear, on Allen's bulging green Hulk "muscle" chest. Gina noticed it too. She looked around the booth's entrance checking to make sure that the Lisa/Spider and her possibly web-shooting ass wasn't nearby. When she was satisfied that the coast was clear, she quietly handed Allen another beanbag. Allen nailed his beanbag right into the pumpkin's mouth. I hugged him and handed him a green paratrooper. Allen grinned and muttered a polite "thank you" after some prodding from Eric. I mouthed a silent "thank you" to Gina, too.

A surly, chubby Sleeping Beauty showed up and shoved Allen out of the way, waving her green ticket at me. "It's my turn. I want to play," she whined. I gave Gina her ticket and rolled my eyes at her when the little girl wasn't looking. Gina gave Sleeping Beauty three beanbags. Whack, whack, CRASH! She had missed all the holes but had ended up knocking down the board with her furious throws. Gina tried to step away from the falling board but lost her balance and fell. I reached out and tried to grab her arm, but my actions were too little too late. After she fell, Gina lay on the ground and was slow in getting up while Sleeping Beauty briskly demanded her prize.

No apologies! I angrily threw a few pieces of candy at her. She stuffed her mouth with chocolate and merrily skipped away. Eric gently lifted the board and freed Gina's foot, then reached his hand out to her and helped her up.

"Thanks," she said. "I can be so clumsy sometimes." Embarrassment was splashed across her face.

"It wasn't your fault, honey. That girl was a brat! And where in the world are her parents? I think I might just have to hunt down the Wicked Witch and have that Sleeping Beauty put back to sleep!" I spat, still angry at the rude child.

"Yeah, she was kind of a brat, huh?" We all laughed. My boys were anxious and they wanted to try their luck at a few different games. Eric kissed me on the cheek, said his goodbyes, and left.

After a few more children had played and won, Gina and I heard a very familiar phlegmy cough approaching our booth. It could only be Tammy. She stepped into our booth and coughed once more. Tammy took one look at us, shook her head and bellowed, "Oh naaaw, no no. Well, well, well. What do we have here?"

Gina and I silently locked arms as a united front and braced ourselves for the oncoming Tammy assault. We both grinned from ear to ear.

"Jesus. H. Christ, girls. As if one boring cat wasn't enough, now I've got to put up with two? Major disappointment, girls. Big time let down. But, oh well. Whatever." She paused and nudged Jeremy closer to us. "So what's up, pussycats?"

Gina playfully pawed at Tammy with her hand like she was going to scratch her, then let out a tiny hiss. Jeremy, who was dressed as a white ninja, handed Gina his ticket, and we watched in amazement as Jeremy nailed all three of his beanbags squarely and with exact precision into the center triangle nose of the board.

"Not bad, little guy," I said handing him the larger basket. I raised my eyebrows at Tammy and nodded in approval. I had been watching children play this game for the last forty-five minutes or so and Jeremy was the best player I had seen so far.

Tammy's older son, Jason, was standing far back from the booth and nervously looked around. He was dressed all in black with a big, hooded cape that shielded his face. All I could see from under the hood was shaggy brown hair framing his face and blue eyes. He carried a menacing looking silver sickle—he was supposed to be dressed as the Grim Reaper.

Jason spoke up, "Come on, Mom." (It sounded like Maaahm.) "Let's go. This is the baby booth and I don't want to be caught dead here." He fidgeted in his costume and motioned for Tammy and Jeremy to hurry up.

"What in the hell is your hurry, Jason? I promised Jeremy that he could play a few games. Just stop it, will ya?" Tammy snapped back at him. She handed Jeremy another ticket.

"Mom (Maaahm), let's go!" Jason whined. "This is embarrassing."

"Oh, knock it off. Everything is embarrassin' to you. No one can even tell it's you under that get-up, so just stop it. Go wait over there if you want to." She pointed to a nearby trashcan, and Jason slunk away.

Bam, bam, bam. Jeremy nailed the nose again. Tammy smiled proudly. "He's gonna get a baseball scholarship someday. I can feel it, or at least wish it."

Gina and I nodded in agreement. I really thought he might. He was that good.

"Have you guys seen Ana yet?" Tammy asked while Jeremy nailed another three beanbags.

"No," I replied, handing Jeremy another toy. "She was supposed to come tonight but she hasn't been to our booth yet. We only have about five or ten more minutes until we're done here."

"Oh, okay," Tammy said. I turned my back to her for a moment and reached down to fill the small basket with some more candy. As I was down there filling my basket with Tootsie Pops, I heard a deep, male voice enter the booth.

"Ah, there you are, babe. I've been lookin' all over for ya." I could hear the smack of his lips kissing Tammy.

"Where have ya been, Rick? I told ya I was gonna be with the boys playin' games and that the festival started at six. I've been waiting for you for, like, an hour." Tammy snapped at him like a pit bull ready for battle.

"Oh, excuuuuse me, babe. I didn't realize your ball and chain also had a watch." Rick's words dripped with sarcasm.

I kept leaning down so I wouldn't interfere. A second later, Gina's head popped next to mine. She silently mouthed the word, "Eek" to me and grimaced. She, too, had ducked to escape the impending confrontation between Tammy and Rick.

"Shut up, Rick. Just shut up," Tammy hissed. She pushed Jeremy out of the booth. "Go wait with your brother for a minute, Jeremy. I want to talk to Rick alone." Jeremy trotted off to stand next to the Grim Reaper, who turned his back to him.

Tammy turned to Rick. "Look, I worked a double shift this morning so that I could get this time off tonight. This festival is important to Jeremy, so I'm here. Ya know, first it's dealin' with shit at work, then it's Jason givin' me shit about not wantin' to be here, and now it's *you* givin' me shit. I've had just about enough shit for one day to fill a wheelbarrow! So just tell me without any of your lies, where in the hell have you been all this time?"

Rick looked down and exhaled a deep breath. "Okay, babe, sorry for all the shit." Curious, I glanced up only to see that he had leaned in to kiss her again and he wobbled a bit, unsteady on his feet. Tammy's face puckered and she shoved him away.

"Goddamn it, Rick, have you been drinkin'? Have you been hangin' out a BJ's again when ya should have been here?"

Rick looked at Tammy as guilt swept across his eyes. "Well yeah, babe. That's what I was gonna say. I told you I was gonna stop at BJ's for a quick happy hour drink and then I was comin' here. Did ya forget?"

Tammy's face turned a pale shade of rose and she hissed, "Did I forget? Did I *forget*? I didn't forget nothin' because you didn't tell me that, asshole! What is the matter with you, Rick? What in the hell are you doin' stoppin' by the bar before comin' to a school festival? Did ya get that, Rick? This is a *school,* for Christ's sake! The place where there are kids and teachers around? Oh, shit, I just hope we don't run into Jeremy's teacher with you sloppy drunk and all."

Rick changed into a stiff, awkward stance with his arms folded. He lowered his voice to a deep growl, "I am not 'sloppy drunk,' Tammy. I am not an idiot. I had a few beers, that's it. If you are so embarrassed to be seen with me then I'll just go home."

"Oh, you mean to *my* home? Ya know, the home where I am paying all the bills? Shit, when are you goin' grow up, get a job, and start actin' like a man?"

A mother with her two girls both dressed as Cinderella started to enter the booth as Tammy was speaking, but she quickly shuffled the girls away after hearing the word *shit* and Tammy's angry tone, shooting Tammy a dirty look.

"Goddamn it, Tammy, I am a 'grown-up'!" Rick hissed back, pointing his finger in Tammy's face. "I'm twenty-two years old and have been on my own since I was eighteen, so don't start in with all your motherly crap now!"

Gina and I looked at each other. Our eyes widened in shock. Hold the phone, here. Had Rick just said he was twenty-two? That meant that he was only one year older than Tammy's oldest son, Johnny "The Doobie." Oh my, my, my! The plot thickened.

After this new tidbit, I had to sneak another peek at what Tammy and Rick were doing. As I glanced up, I saw that Rick softened a bit when he saw the stricken, hurt look on Tammy's face, and he reached out for Tammy's hand. "Look, babe, I know you work hard for us and I do love ya and all. I didn't mean to upset ya by going to BJ's. Hey, I didn't tell ya yet, but my buddy Jack has a lead on a construction job for us at one of the casinos for next week. He knows the foreman and he can maybe squeeze us both in. I'll finally get a job break in this town. Things will change, babe, I promise."

Tammy inhaled a deeply and let her breath out slowly just like she had done with me during our argument. "Okay, fine. Whatever." Gina and I heard a long, wet kiss and we both grimaced.

After what seemed like an eternity, I felt Tammy's hand on my back and she said, "Okay, Tweedledee and Tweedledum. Ya can both come up now. Show's over. I want y'all to meet Rick."

Gina and I slowly rose to our feet and dusted off the dirt that had stuck to our black stretch pants from kneeling on the floor. As I straightened up, I glanced over at Gina, who was looking at Rick. She was just standing there staring. I could see her mouth was slowly gaping open and shut like a fish. I gave Gina a strange look and then I looked from her to Rick. Whoa, Nelly! I suddenly understood Gina's temporary fish mouth and developed one of my own! Standing before us was a modern-day Greek god! Rick was absolutely gorgeous. He was young, lean, tanned, and completely handsome. He reminded me of Tom Cruise, Mel Gibson, and Brad Pitt rolled into one perfect male body and face.

Rick carelessly flicked a piece of his black-as-soot hair away from his creamy jade eyes as he held out his hand in greeting to Gina and me. Gina feebly took his hand and I swear I could see her melting right there on the spot, like butter in the microwave. Rick shook my hand next and my knees actually trembled. We both managed to stutter a few greetings, and Rick smiled his stunning, dazzling, Crest Whitening Strips smile back at us. All the while, Tammy stood to the side smiling her "I told ya so" smile at us while nodding her head up and down in triumph.

Tammy walked over and stood between Gina and me facing Rick. She put her arms around our shoulders and whispered to us, "What did I tell ya, ladies? Is he a catch or what?" Taking into account that Rick was drunk at a school function, inconsiderate, and unemployed, I'm not sure I would have chosen the word *catch* to describe him. But I knew what Tammy was referring to and it did not include any of the above listed traits. With Tammy, it was all about sex, sex, and more sex. So yeah, considering she had snagged herself the next male supermodel, he would be a "catch" in her book. Gina and I nodded to her question but I could see that Gina, too, had followed my thought process on the subject.

Tammy continued with her praise of her man, "Let me tell ya, girls, if you think he looks good now, you should see him naked and in my bed!" She let out a raunchy whoop and slapped us both on the back, almost knocking Gina down again. Rick, slightly embarrassed now, reached out to help Gina with her balance. Her butter was melting again.

Rick, after that, was desperate to get the heck out of the booth. He shot Tammy a pleading look like a dog begging for a scrap of food at the dinner table. Tammy caught the look and let go of our shoulders as she nodded to him. Rick said a quick goodbye to us. I watched him leave, slightly weaving a bit. He grabbed the side of the booth's wall to help straighten out, almost taking the flimsy cardboard down with him.

Tammy kissed her hand and blew it at us. "See ya at the Mommy Tree, girls. I've gotta go keep my man happy! Bye!" She twirled and left the booth. I watched as she hooked her arm in Rick's and steered him towards her two sons.

Gina and I looked at each other and, once again, burst out laughing. Gina was the first to speak, "Did he just say he was twenty-two? So he is only..."

"Yep, one year older than her son, Johnny 'The Doobie'," I interrupted.

"Oh my! He is cute, but awfully young. And how did Tammy...?"

"I know, I know," I interrupted again. "How did Tammy snag him? I don't know. I mean, he's a bum with no job and she is supporting him. He, in turn, gives her good sex. Perfect arrangement for them, I guess."

"Yeah, you're probably right. Whew. I just don't know if I could handle being with a twenty-two-year-old at my age. I mean, I go to bed at nine o'clock!" We both laughed.

I caught sight of two black balls bobbing in the distance out of the corner of my eye. I nudged her and pointed in Lisa's direction. "Why do I suddenly feel like Little Miss Muffet?" Gina giggled.

Lisa's black face paint was streaked with sweat marks. One of her bobbles drooped and was just barely hanging on by a limp piece of fuzzy tape. She was missing one hairy leg and her other legs were grotesquely twisted. I noticed an ugly rip in her red and black stockings, and her cardboard middle was dented and smeared. The Lisa spider looked like she had just been stepped on by a giant shoe!

Lisa sighed heavily and leaned on the fragile cardboard walls of the booth. They wobbled slightly under her weight. "Aaaah. Ladies. Help is on the way. Kim and Sally should be here soon. How did things go?"

Gina and I both said, "Great, just fine." Blah, blah, blah.

"Good. Look, the PTA really does appreciate your help tonight." Lisa paused and took a deep breath. "What I really mean to say, is that *I* really appreciate your help tonight. Thank you both very much."

I answered, "You're welcome, Lisa," and smiled at her. "Hey, you know? I should really be thanking you. You did a great job with this fair tonight and everyone is saying it has been such a great time."

Lisa's tired face beamed slightly and her drooping shoulders straightened a bit. "You think so?" she asked.

"Of course," I reassured her. "This has been wonderful for the kids." I could feel Lisa's inner perkiness revving up again.

Gina, also sensing Lisa's need for approval, jumped in with her praises. "Yeah, Lisa. Everyone stopping by has been saying what a great festival this has been this year. Good job!"

Slowly, Lisa lifted herself away from the booth walls. Her yellow teeth flashed at us again as she broke into a huge smile. She straightened up and readjusted the drooping bobble on her head. "Thank you, ladies. I think I needed to hear that."

There was a slight awkward pause as we all stood there looking at one another. Lisa spoke first. "Okay. Here come Kim and Sally. You two are officially dismissed and are off duty." She gave us a mock salute. I mock saluted her back and then Gina and I gathered up our purses and walked away.

"Whew, I am glad we are done, girlfriend. I could really go for something to eat and drink right about now," Gina exclaimed.

"I promised to meet Eric and the boys at the food tent. You can join us if you like. Are you meeting Gary and Ethan somewhere, too?" I asked.

"Yeah, I am supposed to meet them by the front entrance. I'll go find them and then let's all meet at the food tent, in say, fifteen minutes?"

"Sounds good," I replied. "I'll save you a place and a corn dog."

We hugged and went our separate ways. As I slowly meandered towards the big, white food tent in the middle of the school's outside basketball blacktop court, my stomach grumbled from the delicious aroma of popcorn and corn dogs. My pace quickened a bit.

When I finally reached the tent, I was momentarily stunned by the complete and total scene of chaos looming before me! There were people everywhere! Some were standing in a line that snaked around the tent waiting patiently for their turn at the food. Other people were walking aimlessly around the tent looking for an empty table while precariously juggling two or three cardboard cartons that were dripping Coke and dropping fries as they walked by. Little superheroes darted in and out from under the tables like dogs chasing a rabbit. They were playing tag as their parents frantically called their names out in vain. A blue, sparkly fairy princess waved her magic wand at me and yelled "Abracadabra, I just turned you into a frog!"

"Ribbit, ribbit," I replied back to the little fairy princess. She waved her wand once more at me and disappeared into the massive waves of people. I slowly and gently bumped my way toward the center of the tent where the tables were located, scanning the room desperately looking for my familiar Spider-man, Hulk and "hunk." Finally I heard my name being shouted above the roar of the crowd.

"Missy, Missy. Over here, amiga!" It was Ana. She was standing on the table bench seat waving her arms back and forth, trying to gain my attention. I waved back and once again gently bumped my way over to her table.

"Hey, Ana. How are you?" I gave her a hug.

"Good, good. This is a crazy-loco place, no? Where is your family?"

"I don't know!" I replied in exasperation. "I was supposed to meet them here in the tent but I had no idea it was going to be like this! There's no way I'll be able to find them here. What's worse is that I am supposed to save a seat for Gina, Gary, and Ethan, too! And to top it off, I'm *starving* but there is no way I'm going to wait in that line. Oh well." I sighed.

Ana smiled at me. "No worries, amiga. You can sit here with me and my family, okay? You might be able to see your family and Gina's, too, if you stay in one place. You said you were hungry, amiga? No problem. We got lots of food."

She turned and nudged a very handsome, dark haired Hispanic gentleman dressed in an expensive Armani suit. He nodded and scootched over, nudging "Batman" Eli to move down, too. I thanked her and took the sliver of a bench next to Ana, who wordlessly handed me a basket of french fries and a corn dog. I hesitated. I did not feel comfortable taking her food.

"No, no, Missy. You take it," Ana insisted. "You'll never get through that line. I bought extras. I always buy at least one extra of something. No problem. Let me tell you, nobody goes hungry at *my* table, amiga." She winked and placed the basket of food in front of me.

It flashed in my mind just then how Ana had told us about how she was often hungry as a child due to her poverty. I realized she was serious about giving me the food. I was a little embarrassed about having used the word *starving* in front of her before. I offered to pay for the food but Ana just smiled and shook her head no. I thanked her as graciously as I could and picked up the corn dog.

"Missy, did you meet my husband, Xavier?" Ana asked. I had a mouth full of corn dog so I had to shake my head no instead of answering her. Ana once again nudged the attractive Hispanic man sitting next to her. He turned to me and smiled.

He really was very good looking with slicked back jet-black hair. Every hair was perfectly trimmed. His chocolate eyes sparkled and were framed by long, inky black lashes, and his smile was bright, genuine and warm. My overall impression was that this man had class. It was the kind of class that often comes from having a little bit of dough in your pockets and a successful career. Xavier leaned over and reached his arm around Ana's back. I immediately noticed a silver and gold Rolex watch on his wrist and wondered if it was real. He extended a very well-manicured hand.

"Hello. I'm Xavier, Ana's husband."

"Hello. I'm Missy. Pleased to meet you."

Xavier shook my hand firmly, but not too firmly, since I still had my fingers intact. Why was it that most men who shake hands always try to impress you with their manly strength and almost break your hand in the process? Go figure.

"The pleasure is mine," Xavier smoothly replied. He let go of my hand and lovingly rested his hand on the small of Ana's back. "I've heard a lot things about you from Ana. I'm glad we have finally had the chance to meet."

"Good things, I hope!" I laughed nervously at my own attempt at humor.

"Of course, of course," he replied. Although Xavier was Hispanic, I did not notice a trace of an accent like I sometimes could with Ana when she spoke.

"What do you do, Xavier, if you don't mind my asking?" I asked since I was curious to know where the dough came from.

"I practice entertainment law. Maybe you have seen our commercials on TV? I work at the firm of Morales and Morrison. I'm the Morales."

It all clicked now. Morales and Morrison was the top law firm for entertainment contracts. Some of the top performers in Las Vegas were represented by Morales and Morrison. So *that* was where the dough came from. Xavier was definitely starting to become my idea of the perfect "catch." Charming, well educated, wealthy...

"Very good. How interesting," I said.

"It can be," he smiled. Eli tugged on his daddy's suit sleeve. "Excuse me for a second, Missy." I nodded at him and he turned to Eli, who needed help pouring ketchup on his fries.

I nudged Ana, winked at her, and smiled. I leaned over and whispered, "He's quite a catch, Ana! You go, girl!"

Ana beamed at me and started to pull on her shirt. "Oh, he's too good for me, I know that, amiga. I'm very lucky to have him."

I took her hand away from her shirt. "You're not the lucky one, my dear. He is! You can see that he loves you very much. He's lucky to have such a sexy hot tamale mama!"

Ana blushed, giggled and nudged me back. "Speaking of sexy hot tamale mamas," she said, "has anyone seen Tammy tonight?"

I filled her in on the whole Rick episode and she burst out laughing.

"No no no! Rick is only twenty-two? Why, he's just a baby! No wonder she is having so much problems with him. Aye, yie yie. What are we going to do with her, hmmm?"

I laughed, too.

Out of the corner of my eye, I spotted Gina, Ethan, and a man that must have been her husband, Gary, wading through the swarm of people. Both Gina and Gary both glazed expressions of disbelief on their faces. Ethan, however, was grinning ear-to-ear, enjoying the excitement of the crowd.

I took a moment to observe Gary. He was a man of average build with light blond, wispy hair and bangs that fell just below his eyebrows. He had cornflower blue eyes, a thin nose, and proportionally shaped lips. He was dressed in the typical college graduate student uniform of blue jeans and a T-shirt with the UNLV logo sprawled across the front in bright red letters—complete with Birkenstock sandals worn with white tube socks. Okay, besides the tube socks and sandals bit, I thought that overall Gary was an attractive man.

Ethan grabbed Gary's arm and dragged him towards the food line. Gary was in a tug-of-war between Gina, who was pulling him towards the center tables where I had been standing, and Ethan, who was pulling in the opposite direction towards the food line. Gina lost the battle as Ethan twirled Gary towards him. Gary turned back to Gina and yelled something to her that I couldn't hear. Gina shrugged her shoulders and started to drift towards the center of the tent, obviously searching for me.

I, like Ana before me, stood up on the table bench and yelled Gina's name. Gina stopped and cocked her head to one side. She looked like a dog that had just heard a dog whistle but couldn't quite place where the sound was coming from. I cupped my hands around my mouth and yelled her name with all the force I could. That did it. Gina looked directly at me and I saw the cloud of confusion leave her face. She slowly began to walk towards me as a little demon Gold Power Ranger jumped out from under one of the tables and ran smack into Gina. He backed up and dashed back under another table. She stumbled briefly but regained her balance. At last, she made it to our table.

"Oh my goodness! Would you look at this place? This is a nightmare!" Gina gave me a hug. She didn't see Ana sitting next to me.

Ana heard Gina's voice, turned around and exclaimed, "Well, look who the Missy cat dragged in." She started to chuckle at her own joke since Gina and I were still in our cat costumes. Gina smiled and gave Ana a hug. Ana made the same introductions to her family that she had made with me, and I saw that Gina was as impressed with Xavier as I had been. Since there was no more room at Ana's table, I stood up so that Gina could sit down. Reluctantly, she sat where I had been sitting previously.

"Where's Eric, Missy?" Gina asked.

"I have no idea, girlfriend. I couldn't find him in this mess. I'm going to have to go and try to find them again though." Gina nodded and I stood up again, thanked Ana, and said goodbye to Xavier.

"Okay, I'm off. Wish me luck!" I started to go but Gina held me back.

"Wait, Missy. I wanted you to meet Gary."

I looked at the food line and saw that Gary and Ethan were at the very end. It was going to be a while before they made it to the table. "Let's do this, Gina. Why don't I go introduce myself to Gary in line? I really have to meet up with Eric and the boys. Is that okay?"

Gina nodded again. "Sure. I'll go take you over there." We both said our goodbyes to Ana and off we went. I grabbed Gina's arm so that I wouldn't lose her and we rode the surging wave of people over to where Gary and Ethan were standing. Gary leaned over and gave Gina a quick kiss on the cheek.

"Hi, honey. How are you doing?" he asked.

"Good, I'm fine," Gina emphasized while Gary still held protectively onto her arm. I saw that he was worried about Gina and how her stamina was holding up after working our shift and in dealing with the crowd.

Gina continued, "Gary, I want you to meet my friend, Missy."

I extended my hand. "Hi, Gary. Pleased to meet you." It was déjà vu all over again. After a few rounds of polite conversation, I was really starting to get anxious about finding Eric and the boys. "Hey, Gina, would you mind if I excused myself? I've really got to go and find the rest of my family."

"Sure, Missy, no problem. I hope you find them soon. Do you need help?" Gina asked sincerely.

"Oh no, no, I can find them. I have a feeling they are in the back of the tent somewhere so I'm just going to make my way over there. It was really nice to meet you, Gary. Eric and I will have to have you both over sometime for dinner. I know the boys will enjoy playing with each other and I look forward to getting to know you both better!"

Gary smiled. "Sounds like a plan, Missy. You cook the food and we'll bring the wine." He paused. "Well, that is, if you drink wine."

"Does a bee buzz?" I replied with a quick "ha ha ha." I was attempting to be funny but in actuality I sounded quite nerdy. Gary gave me a quizzical look but then he actually laughed. Gary was a kind man, after all.

"Ooooh-kay, Missy. Good then. Gina and I enjoy a nice Merlot every now and then, so I have just the perfect bottle in mind. Just let us know when you want to get together."

After what seemed to me about four hours of aimless wandering around the food tent, I finally spotted Eric and the boys crunched together trying to share a small picnic bench seat with three other people. Eric waved me over and I sat down with a loud sigh of relief. I was exhausted! Eric put his arms around my shoulder and I gratefully rested my head on his arm.

Allen immediately jumped off of the bench seat and thrust a small plastic bag of prizes at me. "Look, Mommy, look at all the stuff I won!" He was so excited and proud to show me all of the goodies he had earned. I nodded my head and smiled a little cheesy grin at him. Then I gave him what I call my best "happy mommy" face. You know? The one where you smile, nod your head, all the while saying "yes, yes," even though you are not *really* listening. I could still fool Allen with this technique. I really didn't want to disappoint him and make him think that I didn't care about his toys even though at that moment I was too tired to care. Does it make me a bad mother to admit that sometimes I am selfish and not always in tune to my children's every desire or need? No, I don't think so. I think it is just the truth sometimes.

The evening was getting late by this time. My daily routine and schedule were way off and I was feeling edgy from my lack of control. We had all eaten enough cotton candy, soft pretzels, soda, and other standard carnival food items to last us a lifetime. I knew that I was going to have to take one of my acid reducer pills the minute I got home or this carnival food would be with me all night long. Eric and I gathered up the boys and left the carnival for home.

***

In the minivan on the way home, I looked behind me at my two boys in the backseat. Both Spiderman and The Hulk were worn out little superheroes in deep sugar, junk food and carnival fun induced sleep comas. I smiled at the two of them peacefully sleeping then winked at Eric, who was driving, and held my finger to my lips. Eric quickly glanced behind him and saw the boys sleeping as well. Allen's right hand was curled up in a tight fist. Peeking out of the bottom of his palm was the green paratrooper he had won from my kindergarten game booth. I smiled again.

"You know, they really had a good time tonight," Eric said to me.

"I know they did and I'm glad. That festival was a lot of fun. It was a little crazy, but fun. I know Allen was so excited to win that paratrooper. Look at him holding it right now."

Eric glanced once more into the backseat and smiled when he saw Allen with his prize. "He is so funny. Just a little toy like that makes him happy."

"Hey, did I tell you that I met Tammy's boyfriend, Rick, tonight?" I said, brimming with excitement.

After a beat of silence, Eric raised his eyebrows at me. "Well? What's he like? What's the scoop?"

I loved sharing a bit of good gossip with Eric. "You are not going to believe this but Rick is only twenty-two years old! Tammy is going out with a twenty-two-year-old stud boy! And, yes, he is a stud, my dear. No offense to you, but that boy could be the next male supermodel of the world."

"That doesn't surprise me considering everything you've told me about Tammy. She sounds like a pretty hot chick herself," Eric replied with a slight twinkle in his eye that I didn't see right away. Naturally, my jealous streak exploded before I could catch on that Eric was only trying to pull my chain. Clink, it was pulled all right.

I whipped around and faced him as much as I could but the seat belt caught me in the throat. I gurgled and then managed to sputter, "Hot chick? Tammy? *My* Tammy? I mean, she is good looking in a very hard-core biker chick kind of way. She is good looking if you like fake blond, fake boobs and even fake *eyes*." I paused a beat. My mind was whirling in confusion. "Do you really think Tammy is what you would consider a 'hot chick'?" My brow furrowed. My palms were sweaty. I couldn't believe that my husband of all people could possibly succumb to Tammy's "pizaaz." What was it about this woman that made men fall all over her? The insecurity monster inside of me screamed in agony.

Eric smiled, reached over to take my damp hand, and laid it on his lap. He chuckled softly at my obvious jealousy. "Missy, I'm sure Tammy is sexy. What guy wouldn't like that kind of woman?" His eyes were twinkling again but the green eye monster in me was blurring my vision and I still didn't see his joking manner.

My eyebrows shot up in surprise. Eric was right, of course. Tammy was sexy. What was bothering me was that deep down I knew I wasn't as sexy as her. Who has time to be sexy when they are cleaning toilets and wiping snotty noses all day? I turned and faced the car window, pulling my hand away from Eric's lap. Eric laughed and grabbed it again. I turned away from the window and faced Eric once more. His eyes were gentle and warm.

"Missy, you know I am only teasing you, right? Yeah, Tammy is probably okay looking but I'm sure she is nothing compared to you. You are the woman I adore and married. You are the total package. Tammy is just about sex. There are lots of women out there like her but only one you, Missy." He smiled at me. Okay, my green eye monster retreated slightly. I hated myself for being so insecure.

"Thanks, Eric. I love you. I'm sorry for being so jealous. It's just hard sometimes, you know? I'm in that in between age where I feel too old to run around in tight skirts and high heels like the younger college girls, but still too young to be wearing support hose! I know I am supposed to be a mature woman at this age but frankly I am still searching for who I really am! I don't feel young and pretty anymore but I don't feel mature and wiser either. This aging thing is so confusing."

A tear trickled down my cheek. Eric reached over with his free hand and brushed it away.

"Oh, just forget it. I'm just having PMS right now." I tried to joke the issue away. But Eric knew me better than that.

"No, you're not having PMS right now. I know when you are having PMS and this is nothing compared to *that*!" Eric replied and we both laughed. "It's okay to feel a little insecure at times, Missy. It happens to all of us. As far as wearing tight skirts and heels, hell, I won't complain if you do! You've got the best legs in Vegas." I smiled at the compliment. "I didn't mean to upset you," he continued. "I didn't realize this was such a big issue for you. You'll find yourself in time. I'm sure lots of other ladies feel this way. You should talk to your girlfriends and I bet you'd be surprised at what they say."

I sighed. "You're right. I should probably talk to Gina about it. I think she out of anyone would understand."

Eric pulled the van into our driveway. We got out and each lifted a sleeping boy into our arms. Ray and Allen stirred a bit as we went into the house and took off their tiny shoes, undressed each boy and put them into their superhero pajamas. We tucked them into their beds and shut off the light. As soon as I quietly closed the door to their bedroom, Eric scooped me up into a huge hug, surprising me, and started to kiss my neck. I pulled away a bit and giggled, but not too loudly since I didn't want to wake the boys.

"Come here, sexy cat mama," Eric said playfully and pulled me close again. I forgot that I was still wearing my cat costume.

"You know," I replied in between kisses, "I was just about to go put on a tight skirt and some high heels. Wanna help me with my support hose?" I used my sexiest drawl.

Eric laughed. He picked me up caveman style, threw me over his shoulder, and walked us to our bedroom. He gently kicked the door shut so that we wouldn't wake the boys. That night, I showed Eric that Tammy wasn't the only "hot chick" on the block. Yep, this ol' lady still had the touch. Giggle, giggle, smirk, smirk.

CHAPTER SIX

  It was hard to believe how quickly Thanksgiving snuck up on me, "like a thief in the night," as Ana would say. One minute I was trick-or-treating with the kids and stuffing my face with chocolate and other assorted candies. And just for the record, I just have to say that I love the smell of Halloween candy all mixed together in our big clear plastic Tupperware bowl. They should bottle that candy smell and sell it as perfume. Can you just imagine the perfume counter at Macy's selling the brand new fragrance "Eau de Tricks n' Treats"? I predict that it would sell out in a minute. Ah, the fresh smell of mixed candy. Bliss, just pure bliss.

  So, after stuffing our faces with candy, my family and I were now looking forward to stuffing our faces with turkey and, well, stuffing. It was Wednesday, Ray's last day of school before the big four-day Thanksgiving break holiday. Allen and I waited patiently at the Mommy Tree bench that afternoon. I felt a cool breeze whip around my ears and blow my hair and turned away from the wind and zipped up Allen's windbreaker. I noticed that it was quiet in the schoolyard. No "zombie" parents yet. We were pretty much alone. I watched, mesmerized, as the last few leaves from the Mommy Tree's proud branches swirled in a circle from the wind at the foot of her massive trunk. My mind wandered as I made mental preparations about the dinner menu for my Thanksgiving party.

This year, I was going to have the whole Mommy Tree gang and their families over to my house. As it turned out, no one really had any family plans for this Thanksgiving, so we all decided to meet at my house for dinner.

I was so lost in my planning preparations that I jumped a bit when I felt a soft tap on my shoulder. Ana was standing right next to me. "Hello, Missy. Someone step on your grave? You jumped like a cat on a hot tin roof." Her eyes twinkled with amusement and her face was bright and cheery. I loved the way she talked in clichés. It made me smile.

"Hi Ana. I'm sorry I jumped like that. I was just kinda lost in thought planning the food menu for tomorrow's dinner. I'll be hitting the grocery store this afternoon after school gets out, which is not a trip I am looking forward to, I might add! I just wanted to make sure I remembered everything," I replied. The wind whistled by my ears once more. "Whoo, it is definitely cool out here today. That wind is freezing!" I folded my arms across my chest to try and keep warm.

Ana smiled. "You got that right." She blew her breath on her hands to try and keep them warm. "And, no, Missy, amiga, I don't envy you going to the store today. It will be a nightmare for sure. You need any help?"

"No, no, I'll be fine. Maybe a little stressed out, but fine nonetheless," I replied with a giggle.

I glanced over Ana's shoulder and saw Gina slowly getting out of her minivan in the distance. She struggled with balancing her cane on one arm and using her other arm to close the heavy side door to the van. Her legs wobbled and she almost fell when the weight of the sliding door pulled her off balance. Gina grabbed the handle on the door with both hands to keep from falling completely down, and her cane landed with a hollow thud as it hit the ground. Gina used both of her arms to pull herself back upright, and glanced around to see if anyone had seen her stumble. I quickly averted my gaze so that she did not see me watching her but I could still see her out of the corner of my eye.

Satisfied that no one had seen her almost fall, Gina took a deep breath, smoothed down her tan corduroy jacket, and bent down to pick up her wooden cane. Then she started the long trek across the grassy distance to the Mommy Tree.

Gina waved at me when she saw me. I waved back. When we were close enough to see each other, my eyes betrayed me. At one look, Gina knew that I had seen her incident. I smiled at her but she quickly looked away.

"Hello, ladies. How's it going?" Gina said casually. I also noted she was a slightly out of breath from the walk.

"Good, amiga. How are you?" Ana asked.

"Oh, okay, you know, the usual. I've got my good days and my bad days just like everyone else. Are we still on for Thanksgiving tomorrow?" Gina directed the question to me while adeptly changing the subject.

"Of course," I answered. "You know me, I've been planning this party right down to the last, tiniest details. The hardest part has been trying to decide how to set the table and where to put everyone. My house is small, but there should be enough room for everyone. You are all still coming, right?"

Ana and Gina both nodded their heads.

Tammy walked up and plopped her arms around Gina and Ana's shoulders, poking her head in the middle of the two ladies. They looked like a three-headed monster standing that way. "What's with the head bobbin', girls?" Tammy asked.

"Oh, we were just saying that Ana and I are still going to Missy's for Thanksgiving," Gina replied moving slightly so that Tammy's arms dropped off of her shoulders. Tammy stepped in between Gina and Ana.

"Cool. So, are ya completely stressed out yet, Missy?" she asked.

"Yep," I replied and rolled my eyes. Tammy laughed and shook her head. The metallic school bell chimed and the kids poured out of their classroom doors. The first thing I noticed was that they were wearing yellow construction paper headbands with large, brown turkeys glued to the front. The kids' turkeys bobbed and bounced with each step they took. It was a sight to see, let me tell you. I stifled a laugh as I watched the gaggle of turkeys approach the front gate waiting for dismissal. Ray was dismissed first and he ran over to me clutching his headband with his right hand so that it didn't fall off. I gave him a big hug. Allen was jumping up trying to take the headband, but I stopped him.

The Mommy Tree gang all with our kids in tow started walking towards our cars. Gina turned to me and asked, "So, what time should we be there, and what can I bring?"

"Oh, about noonish. We'll eat early and let the guys watch football. We ladies can do something else like—" I replied, but Ray had interrupted me.

"Hey, Mommy, Mommy, Mommy," he said frantically trying to get my attention. "Mommy, Mommy." I ignored him at first and continued to try to talk to Gina about the Thanksgiving details. Ray tugged my pant legs. "Mommy, Maaaaawwwwmmmmy."

"Excuse me a second." I stopped and whipped around to look at Ray. "Whaaat?" I whined, annoyed that he had said "Mommy" at least one hundred times.

"Mommy, Mommy, did you know that I have four whole days off of school?" Ray asked. His voice oozed excitement.

I stared blankly at my son. *That* was the big thing he had to say, which had warranted interrupting my conversation with an adult? I suddenly felt like one of those cartoon characters that eats a hot tamale or something. You know, their head turns red and their eyes bulge out and steams comes out of both ears? Well, that was me at that moment. I suppose I was angry because every time I tried to have a decent conversation with an adult, either Ray or Allen interrupted me. It was especially bad when I was on the telephone. What is it about little kids that see their parents on the phone and immediately start whining, fussing, or fighting with each other? I think I can count on one hand the times where I didn't have to pause halfway through my call and yell at my boys, "I'm on the phone! Knock it off!"

Ray was very excited about his holiday and oblivious to my anger. I took a deep breath and let it out slowly. A chilly wind blew once again through my hair, cooling my thoughts down. I bent down to Ray's face level and said, "Ray." My teeth were slightly clenched, but I was still civil. "Ray," I repeated, "when Mommy is talking to another mommy, it is rude to interrupt. I know that it was important for you to tell me about your holiday, but Mommy's conversation was important, too. You need to learn to wait your turn."

Ray's face fell all the way to his toes. Tears welled up in his big brown eyes. "Sorry, Mommy," he mumbled.

"Mommy?" Oh boy, oh boy. It was Allen this time. I turned to him.

"Allen, the same thing goes for you, too," I snapped. "I was talking to Ray just now and you interrupted me. You need to wait your turn."

Allen knitted his brows together. "But, Mommy…"

"No!" I screeched at him. Both Ray and Allen looked at me with their eyes widening in surprise. Gina and Ethan had turned to me at this point as well. Gina smiled sympathetically at me. She sensed that most of my anger was from the stress of the Thanksgiving dinner party and not really from the kids' interruptions.

I took another deep breath. Think happy thoughts, Peter Pan. Big breath, blow out. Out with the bad air, in with the good. "Ooooh-kaaay. What do you want, Allen?"

He held up a crinkly brown leaf. It was a beautiful, perfect leaf from the Mommy Tree. Allen's tiny hand reached up to my waist to show me the leaf. "See, Mommy? I wanted to show you my leaf. Don'tcha like it?" His face beamed with pride. He was shielded by the excitement of his find and hadn't really noticed my irritation.

Calmly, I took the leaf from Allen and looked at it closely. There were no worm holes, missing spots, or stains that are so common with the last batch of fall leaves. No obvious signs of nature's abuse. I held the brittle, coarse leaf in my hand like it was the most fragile piece of glass. At any minute, the pressure from my fingers could crumble it into a thousand pieces, but for some reason, I instinctively protected it. I was mesmerized by its simplistic beauty and weakness.

Wham! The Mommy Tree had struck me hard with her leaf. I realized at that moment that my children were my leaves, just as precious and fragile. I could crumble them with the pressure from my fingers or even the harsh words of my mouth. One day my tiny "leaves" would "fall off," "blow away," and start their own lives. I just hoped that they, like Allen's flawless leaf, wouldn't have too many worm holes, torn spots, or stains as they got older. It was clear at that moment that it was my job to protect them. I said a little prayer of thanks to God and to His amazing Mommy Tree and grabbed Allen in a huge bear hug.

"I love you, button," I whispered in Allen's ear. Allen grinned with glee. I grabbed Ray, who was still looking down. "I love you too, sugar bean." Ray looked up and smiled his toothless grin at me.

We started walking again towards the car. Gina looked at me with her eyes crinkling at the corners. Her mouth had formed a closed half smile. She came over and patted me on the back. "Hang in there, Mama. We've all been there, that's for sure," she whispered.

I smiled back at her and we all piled into our respective minivans. As I pulled away from the curb, I waved to Gina and gave a playful honk of my horn. She waved back. I was off to fight the masses at the nearest discount bargain grocery store. It was going to be a battle for the last box of Stove Top stuffing and turkey gravy. Oh boy, lucky me.

***

On the morning of Thanksgiving, I tore through my house like a cleaning robot gone haywire. No dust bunny was spared in this cleaning frenzy of mine! Eric and the boys just stayed the heck out of my way. They were no dummies. They know that when I get started on a "company cleaning" kick, then all heck breaks loose and no one is safe. I mean, why is it that whenever company is coming over I feel this compulsion to clean everything right down to the tiniest nooks and crannies as opposed to just my normal weekly cleaning, which, by the way, does a good job, too? I know I want my house to be spic and span perfect so that the company doesn't think we live like pigs. It's almost like a "cheesy grin" for the house. The house looks perfect when you first step in, but don't look too closely or you will see the closet bulging from all the toys stuffed in there at the last minute and the dirty breakfast dishes thrown into the stove out of view.

I think I became this obsessive cleaning freak (OCF) after completing the Officer Candidate School program. Literally, there were some days where all we did was *clean.* We polished brass doorknobs, cleaned bathroom tiles with our toothbrushes, scrubbed floors, etc. You name it, and we cleaned it at OCS. After having the need for cleanliness drilled into my head about a gazillion times I guess it stuck.

So here I was transformed into a raging OCF, when I looked at the time and noticed that I hadn't put the turkey on to cook yet. Aggghh! I promptly dropped my Swiffer Wet Jet and washed my hands in the kitchen sink. Then I rubbed the ample bird's body with butter, sprinkled some spices on it, and placed it into the oven. Phew.

With that done, I jumped into the shower and cleaned myself up. Only two hours to go until my company would arrive. I watched as Eric and the boys plopped themselves on the couch in the living room. The muffled sounds of a football game droned on in the background. I shook my head in amazement at how relaxed they were. I still had to set the table, make the salad, open the Stove Top Stuffing box (ha! got the last one!), peel the potatoes, get the corn ready, make the gravy, bake the rolls, cook the green bean casserole—my list went on and on. No time for me to watch the old pigskin game! My inner martyr bawled with frustration.

The doorbell rang at precisely noon and I yelled for Eric to get the door. As he opened the door, I heard Ray squeal with glee at seeing his friend, Ethan. I heard a whoop of excitement and caught the flash of three boys running to Ray's room.

I wiped my greasy hands on my apron as Gina came into the kitchen juggling a bottle of red wine and a basket of freshly baked rolls. We hugged and exchanged hellos. I immediately liked how she had chosen a very festive outfit for the occasion, a fall vest stitched with gold, brown, and burgundy leaves on the front over a green turtleneck top. The whole look was finished off with a tan corduroy long skirt and brown leather boots. I thought the outfit suited her, and the green turtleneck accentuated her green eyes beautifully.

I thanked her for the wine and rolls and placed them on the crowded counter. "You look great, Gina, really great. I love the vest!"

"Thanks, you don't look so bad yourself! Those denim pants are very slimming on you."

"Thank you. I call these pants my 'fat pants' because they stretch, and after all the food I'm going to eat today, I going to need some stretching room."

Gina laughed. "Yeah, ain't that the truth."

I poked my head into the living room and noticed that Eric and Gary had introduced themselves. Gary waved cheerfully at me before both men immediately engrossed themselves in the football game.

I popped back in the kitchen. Gina said, "Alrighty, girlfriend, what can I do to help?"

"Oh, thanks, Gina. Would you mind setting out these chips and dip for the guys out there? I just haven't had a chance to do that yet."

"Of course, no problem. So, Missy, you going nuts yet?" Gina dumped a bag of chips into the bowl.

"Nuts, yeah, put some nuts out there, too," I replied, obviously not listening to her as I looked in my cupboard for my gravy bowl. Gina chuckled and rubbed my shoulder with her free hand as she carried the chips out to the men.

The doorbell rang again and I heard Gina call out that she would get it. She came back to the kitchen with Ana and Xavier trailing behind. Xavier held out another bottle of red wine for me. I noted the year and appreciated his fine choice. I also noticed that he was, once again, impeccably dressed, this time in black slacks and a light gray cashmere sweater. He smelled slightly of freshly squeezed lemons. No doubt he was wearing some sort of expensive designer cologne.

Ana handed me a sweet smelling apple pie. She, too, looked lovely in a turquoise blue suede pantsuit. Silver hoop earrings hung from each earlobe. Her face was bright and her makeup was subtle, yet effective in highlighting her warm brown eyes.

I said a very hearty thanks for the goodies and put the wine next to Gina's bottle and the pie on the stove top. Xavier started fidgeting nervously and anxiously glanced in the direction of the football game. Gina came back from the living room and poured a bag of pretzels into a bowl. She popped one into her mouth and held out the bowl to Ana and me. Ana grabbed a handful. I declined.

Xavier jumped in, "Hey, ladies, what would you like me to do to help? They say I'm a whiz in the kitchen." He gave us a playful wink.

A penalty whistle sounded from the football game and we could clearly hear Gary moan in disapproval at the referee's call. Xavier whipped his head around and rocked back slightly on his heels to try and see the game through the kitchen entryway.

Gina, Ana, and I smiled at each other at Xavier's obvious good manners. We all knew that while his manners were in the right place, his heart sure wasn't.

Ana jumped in, "Xavier, you can do all us ladies a favor by staying out of out of our road. Too many cooks in the kitchen spoil the pot, no? Besides, between the three of us, I think we've got can do this dinner thing. Now, shoo, you…shoo." She waved her hands at him and gently started to push him out of the kitchen.

Xavier held up his hands in mock surrender, "Okay, okay. If you insist…"

"We insist," Ana, Gina, and I chimed together in unison as we broke into laughter.

Gina looped her arm around Xavier's and picked up the bowl of pretzels. "Come on, Xavier, I'll go introduce you to the husbands." As Gina and Xavier walked out of the kitchen together, Gina winked at us over her shoulder and whispered, "Sweet guy, Ana!" Ana beamed and shyly looked down.

After they left, Ana leaned over my shoulder to see the green bean casserole that I was preparing. "Smells good, amiga, real good. I can't wait for dinner. Thanksgiving has to be my favorite holiday. I can't get enough of all of this yummy food!"

"Don't forget yummy and extremely fattening! My diet will be shot to heck after today."

"You? Diet? You don't need to diet, amiga. You are thin. Now me? That's another story. I need to lose at least ten pounds. Maybe more, no? I'm tired of looking like a blubber whale."

"Ana!" I exclaimed. "You are not a 'blubber whale.' How can you even say that? You look great so don't even worry about a diet."

"You know what is so funny about my being fat now? I used to be so skinny as a tiny girl. I was so skinny my mama used to say that I was going to blow away in the wind.

I was skinny and then I got pregnant with Eli. I just ate and ate and ate. I was huge! I still haven't been able to lose the weight even now. I'm trying, though. I've been trying for a long time."

Ana pushed back a loose strand of her hair that had fallen out of her blue leather headband. She took a big sigh and continued, "You know, I think I've tried every diet out there. Atkins, Sugar Busters, the South Beach Diet, Dr. Phil, Oprah Winfrey, you name it, I tried it." As Ana listed each diet she held up a finger. "The only diet that will work, and I know it, is the 'Stop Eating So Much Crap Diet.' But you know, I said to myself early on in life that I would always give myself something if I want it. If I want cake, I'm going to eat cake and that's that. So, I guess I'll just stay fat. Hey, you need any help in here with the food, Missy?"

I paused and patted Ana's arm in a reassuring, understanding sort of way. "Sure, how about helping me out with the salad?"

Ana reached for my crystal salad bowl and deftly began tearing the crisp romaine lettuce into smaller pieces. Gina came back into the kitchen.

"Hey, Missy, the men are asking for some beer. You got any?"

"Yep, check the fridge."

Gina pulled out three bottles of Miller Light and walked back into the living room. While she was gone, the doorbell rang again, and Gina called out that she would get it again. A few moments later, Gina and Tammy came back into the kitchen. Tammy gave everyone a big hug. She smelled like cheap, flowery perfume and stale cigarettes. Her jean skirt was faded and too short, and her top was cut so low that it didn't leave much to the imagination. Her hair was pulled back into a messy ponytail and her eyes looked tired, puffy, and slightly bloodshot. When she hugged me, I could smell alcohol on her breath. Tammy pulled another bottle of red wine out of a brown paper bag. She laid the bottle next to the others on the counter.

"What is with all the red wine, ladies? Am I that much of a wino?" I jokingly asked.

All three of my friends replied in unison, "Yep." We all giggled.

I noticed that Tammy had come into the kitchen alone. Rick was still standing in the entryway trying to figure out where to go. Jeremy had run off to find the other boys and Jason was trying to blend into the wall. I was just about to go say hello when I saw Eric get up from the couch and introduce himself. After awkward handshakes, Rick and Jason followed Eric back into the family room where the rest of the men were gathered around the boob tube.

"You think Rick is okay in there with the guys, Tammy? I mean, he doesn't really know anyone," I said.

Tammy shrugged, taking off her jean jacket and draping it on top of a chair. "Who cares?" she harshly replied. I caught Ana's eye; we both sensed Tammy's tension regarding Rick.

After a brief silence, Tammy was the first to speak. "Say, speaking of wine, let's have some. Let's get this party started. Gotta opener, Missy?" She put her bottle on the counter, grabbed Xavier's bottle, and started to untie the plastic wrap from the cork.

Ana raised her eyebrows. "It's the middle of the day, Tammy!"

Tammy scoffed at her, "Oh for Christ's sake, Ana, it's already noon! Even Little Miss Manners herself would approve.

Plus, like Jimmy Buffett says, 'It's five o'clock somewhere,' right?"

I told Tammy to take the wine glasses from my dining room table that I had set for dinner, smirking slightly when I saw that she had returned with the bigger goblets for water and not the smaller glasses for wine. I don't know if she grabbed the goblets out of ignorance or because that was maybe her normal wine glass size. Either way, I wasn't about to argue with her; after all, a goblet of wine was starting to sound pretty good after the hectic morning I had had.

Tammy grabbed the wine opener that I slid to her and expertly popped the cork with four swift turns. She was obviously a wine opening pro. "There ain't no cork I can't pop," she joked while the three of us laughed at the crude humor. "I sometimes hafta fill in for one of the bartenders down at Caesar's when we're runnin' short."

So, that explained the expertise, I thought.

Tammy sniffed the cork and sighed. "Ah, nothin' better than the smell of a good merlot." She turned the bottle and read the label. "Excellent year for this merlot. Should be tasty!" She smacked her lips and started to pour our goblets full. Then she picked up her goblet and swung it around, making the wine swirl in a purple, hazy circle. She held the glass up to the light and peered at it closely. "Mmmm, good clarity." Tammy took a big whiff of the wine from her glass. "Smells a little oakey with a bit of strawberry mixed in." She held the glass to her lips. "Well, as Ana here would say, 'down the hatch.'" Tammy clinked each of our glasses as we raised them in a toast. Ana, Gina, and I took a polite sip of the liquid and watched as Tammy took a large gulp of her wine, draining half of the goblet. She set her glass down with a sigh. "Ahhh, much better!"

I was slightly dumbstruck by Tammy's knowledge of wine. She seemed to know what she was doing up until the point where she guzzled the wine down like a sorority girl on spring break. Funny, though, because I would have bet that Tammy was more of a "wine in the box" kind of girl and not a connoisseur of fine wine.

I had put the finishing touches on my green bean casserole and I noticed that Ana had already made the salad and was putting it away in the fridge. I finally had a break until it was time to fool with the turkey and make the stuffing and mashed potatoes. I twirled once around to check and see if anything else needed to be done.

"Take a load off there, amiga," Ana said as she slid a chair over in my direction. I reached for my wine goblet on the counter and sat down next to her.

"Don't mind if I do, sister. Whew. I'm glad Thanksgiving only comes once a year."

"Thanksgiving only comes once a year, but don't forget the big Christmas dinner, Easter dinner, Fourth of July parties, and birthdays," Ana said ticking each holiday off with her fingers.

"Stop, just stop!" I interrupted, putting my hands in the air in a mock surrender. "Hey, Ana, this wine is good!"

"Thank you, Missy. I thought of you when I bought it. I'm glad you like it," Ana replied.

"Well, I like it, too," Tammy said and reached for the bottle. "Like it so much don't mind if I have another glass." She refilled her goblet to the almost overflowing point. "You know," Tammy said, "I always thought we were supposed to drink white wine with turkey, right?"

I replied, "Right."

"So, tell me again why we have three bottles of red wine sittin' on the counter and not one bottle of white wine in sight? Sheesh, Missy, I thought you were runnin' a class act dinner here!" Tammy joked.

Sheepishly, I answered, "Well, I do sorta have a bottle of chardonnay cooling in the fridge. I wanted to chill the white wine before serving it; that's why it's not out."

Tammy raised her glass in a mock toast. "I knew you wouldn't let us down, Miss La Di Da." She winked and took another gulp of her wine.

A chorus of male groans filled the air as the whistles from the football game blew in the next room. "Hey, babe, how about gettin' us all another beer," one lone male voice called out from the living room.

There was silence in the kitchen. We ladies looked at each other. Tammy, Gina, Ana, and I knew that the lone male voice belonged to none other than Tammy's boyfriend, Rick. Poor man. The men had probably played some childish game like Rock, Paper, Scissors to pick their sacrificial beer lamb.

Tammy scrunched up her face, shook her head in disbelief, and leaned back in her chair lifting it off the floor slightly. She hollered back, "Hey, *babe,* why don't you kiss my *ass* and get it yourself!" Gina, Ana and I erupted into giggles and I almost choked on the sip of wine I had just taken. We could hear the other three men roar with laughter at Tammy's comeback. Tammy leaned forward in her chair and thumped the chair back onto the floor. "Well, ladies, let the fun begin." She took another large gulp from her glass. A few seconds later, Rick flew into the kitchen. He was obviously mad and a little embarrassed.

"Tammy, we need to talk...*now.*"

"Not now, Rick, I'm helping Missy with dinner." Tammy waved her hand across the kitchen table. She stood and picked up the bottle of wine, pouring more into each of our glasses. "See?" she said and sat back down. Rick watched the four of us sitting at my kitchen table not doing anything but drinking wine. Gina, Ana, and I were desperately trying not to laugh. I had covered my mouth with my hand and Ana was coughing slightly. Gina's eyes were watering; she had taken her glasses off and was wiping them with the back of her shirt. Rick appeared dumbstruck for a moment. His mouth gaped open and then shut again. The poor beer lamb was trying to figure out the joke, which made the situation even funnier to us.

Suddenly, Tammy stood up, walked to the fridge, and grabbed four beers. She quickly popped the tops and handed them to Rick. "Oh relax, babe. It's Thanksgiving, for Christ's sake. But, hey, don't say I don't ever do nothin' for ya." She leaned over and gave him a peck on the cheek, leaving a smear of red lip prints. Rick wiped the kiss mark away and stalked out of the kitchen, clinking his beers together.

"You're welcome!" Tammy sarcastically yelled after him. "Jerk," she muttered to herself.

Back in the living room, we could hear the men razzing Rick, who said in a very loud voice, "Well, you know, once I told her what was what she saw it clear all right." Beer bottles clinked together in a toast.

Ana's husband Xavier mocked, "Oh man, I know, I know! I think we all know the deal, right guys?"

Meanwhile, back in the kitchen, another bottle of wine was opened. Glasses were once again filled. Tammy was the first to speak up. "I'm sorry about the little scene there, girls. Rick is not used to bein' at a real Thanksgiving dinner party.

He doesn't really know how to act at one. Thanksgiving to him always meant a drunk father picking a fight with his mom and the whole mess endin' up with the cops at the house. He kinda had a rough life growin' up so we'll have to cut him some slack. Besides, Rick has been a little edgy recently especially since that construction job he was hopin' for didn't work out. It seems like all we do nowadays is bicker and fight."

"He still doesn't have a job, Tammy?" Gina asked.

"Nope, and it doesn't look like he's gonna have one any time soon." Tammy took another gulp of her wine. "I just don't understand how he keeps blowin' every opportunity he gets. You wanna know why he didn't get the construction job?"

Our heads nodded around the table.

"Well, he showed up late and hungover to the job site and the foreman showed him the door even before he got a chance to say anythin'. It's gettin' hard for me, ya know? I can't keep supportin' him and my three kids and workin' like a dog every day down at the casino. I'm gettin' too old for this crap. I just don't know what I'm gonna do. I don't like being alone but I don't need all his crap right now either. I just don't know what to do anymore." Tammy hung her head.

I reached over and put my arm around her shoulder. "Hey, hey. It's okay. I understand what you're going through and I know things are tough right now."

Tammy whipped her head up. "Do you? Do any of you 'Miss Perfects' with your perfect husbands and lives really understand?" Tammy saw the stricken looks on our faces and said, "Aw hell, girls, I'm sorry. That was really rude of me and I didn't mean it."

However convincing the apology was, I and everyone else at the table knew she had really meant it. A new guest named "Uncomfortable Silence" was sitting at the table with us now.

Gina cleared her throat and picked up the bottle of wine. "All right then. Let me just say one thing. This 'Miss Perfect' needs another glass of wine because this morning when Ethan was not listening to me when I told him to pick up his toys, all Gary did was sit on the couch not saying a word. He didn't stick up for me at all or try and discipline Ethan one bit. In fact, he did just the opposite and told me that Ethan could pick up the toys later. Ethan happily skipped away and my authority as a mother was completely undermined once again. I thought I was going to explode." She refilled her glass.

Ana took the bottle from Gina and said, "Oookay, well this 'Miss Perfect' needs a refill because in the car on the way over here, Xavier and I got in a huge fight because of my outfit. He told me I looked chubby in it. Why he waited to tell me in the car instead of at home where I could maybe change or something, I don't know? I mean, what did he want me to do? Whip another outfit out of my purse? And the 'chubby' comment? You don't want to know what I said to him about that!" Ana clunked the bottle down on the table.

It was my turn. "And this 'Miss Perfect' needs more wine because I was so stressed out over this dinner that when I was cleaning the house, I actually tried to suck up Eric and the kids with the vacuum." The three ladies looked at me in disbelief. I continued, "Well, no, I didn't really try to suck them up for real, but believe me I wanted to. They were all just sitting there doing nothing while I worked my butt off. So, fill 'er up!"

I grabbed the bottle and made a dramatic display of filling my glass, emptying the bottle. I then proceeded to open another one. Ana and Gina erupted into giggles. Tammy's mouth curved upwards slightly. Without a word, Tammy raised her glass in a toast to us. Ana, Gina, and I nodded at her silent toast and all took a sip of our wine.

One chair was empty again. "Uncomfortable Silence" had just left the room.

We sat drinking wine and our conversation kept flowing, in more friendly waters now, and all was forgiven. Before anyone knew it, it was time to eat. I hustled around the kitchen silently congratulating myself on the perfect timing of the turkey and sides being finished at the same time. I laid out everything in my best Martha Stewart buffet manner with my special serving plates and other assorted doodads.

After everything was laid out, I took a very brief moment to bask in the "afterglow" of preparing this wonderful meal. I gazed lovingly at my beautiful table as I lit the two golden yellow candles set in the middle. I really do take pride in my ability to set a beautiful table, but I surely can't take all the credit. I owe this skill largely to my mother.

As a little girl, I distinctly remember how my mother would always set the most gorgeous tables for special holidays. I remember watching her begin the whole process by carefully polishing her mahogany Ethan Allen dining room table with lemon scented furniture polish. To this day, the smell of Pledge floods my senses with warm memories of my mother's table-setting ritual. Next, she would select one of her finest linen tablecloths, usually snow white, and iron out any wrinkles. She would then lay the cloth over the top with a soft, gentle touch. Depending on the holiday, she would use her most special china. I'll use Christmas as an example because her Christmas tables were always my favorite ones. For Christmas, she would usually use her best white bone china trimmed with a silver ring around the edges. She would then set out her Waterford Crystal water and wine glasses with the etched pattern that always reminded me of tiny snowflakes clustered in the center of each glass. Of course, the best silverware would be used with emerald green-stitched satin napkins that contrasted perfectly with the crisp white tablecloth.

Finally, my mother would create my favorite thing of all, the center decorations. At Christmas time, my mother would lay down a red satin square cloth. On top of that, she would fill a sleigh-shaped silver bowl with real pine boughs and holly sprigs carefully encircling a fat, ruby red candle. On the side of the silver bowl, she would use her silver candlesticks, each holding another tall red candle.

I know I am not doing her ability justice here with just my words. I'll just say this, her tables were always simple, elegant creations oozing with her innate sense of class. That pretty much sums up the whole thing. I just hope she would have been proud to see my Thanksgiving table that year. It's was too bad that she and my dad lived too far away and I couldn't share this holiday with them like I would have liked to.

Although I'm not as adept at the table setting ritual as my mother, I have to admit that my Thanksgiving table looked pretty good. I had used a buttercream yellow linen tablecloth and my worn, but favorite, white basketweave pattern everyday china dishes. Although not Waterford, my Mikasa Outlet Store wine and water glasses are trimmed in gold, giving them a touch of class. Just don't look too closely or you will see where the gold has worn off in some places. The paper the movers used to wrap the glasses in during my million moves with the military somehow rubbed off the gold. Go figure.

Anyway, my dishwasher safe silverware flanked the side of each plate. Real silver was not a luxury I could afford at that time. For napkins, I used a Wal-Mart bought Thanksgiving cloth pattern whose colors matched perfectly with my tablecloth. As a center piece, I used my matching Boy Pilgrim and Girl Pilgrim candlestick holders with the yellow candles sticking out of the tops of the pilgrim's hats. They sound tacky, but believe me they have an antique look to them that makes them somehow appropriate. I scattered a few burgundy and gold colored leaves I had picked up from the Mommy Tree for an added finishing touch. I thought it was appropriate to add a part of the Mommy Tree on this special day. It was due to her that all of us had met in the first place.

For the kiddie table, which was really just Eric's old poker table from college, I threw on a plastic yellow table cloth and used paper plates decorated with large turkeys dressed as pilgrims in the center with matching cups. I thought it looked cute and festive.

As I finished lighting the candles, I heard the click and saw the flash bulb of a camera go off. I winced slightly as Gina said, "You know me, gotta take a picture for the scrapbook!" *Oh boy*, I sarcastically thought to myself. Oh well, to each his own.

I called everyone to dinner and for a brief minute I thought I was in the middle of a cattle stampede. I stood in the kitchen and watched as men, children, and ladies whooshed by me, grabbed their plates from the table, and filled them with grub. The theme from the TV show *Bonanza* whirled in my head. I swear I could hear the snap and crackle of whips and "yaw yaws" from cowboys rustling up the herd.

Everyone settled down to the table with their plates brimming over with food, and then Eric stood up and lifted his glass for a toast. "I just wanted to say thanks to everyone for coming over here today to celebrate Thanksgiving with me and my family. It's really great that all of us could get together like this and share this day. I also wanted to thank Missy for all her hard work in the kitchen and to thank all the ladies for helping out with the dinner." Everyone nodded their heads in agreement.

Tammy lifted her wine glass a little higher than the rest of us and it wobbled slightly. A drop of red wine splashed over the brim of the glass onto my butter cream tablecloth. Tammy grabbed the back of her chair and shakily stood up. She waved her glass around and slurred, "Hear, hear, let's here it for the bird and the broads." She grabbed the back of her chair once more and slowly eased herself down into her seat.

A few chuckles erupted around the table, from the men of course. Jason, in typical sixteen-year-old fashion, slumped lower in his chair and hung his head down in embarrassment over his mom's behavior.

"Stick 'no class' in front of 'broad' and you've got Tammy," Rick muttered under his breath but loudly enough for all of us to hear, although we all pretended not to.

Add that chair again; "Uncomfortable Silence" had joined us now for dinner.

Tammy blushed slightly. "Don't start with me, Rick. Not here and not now. This is a family event but you wouldn't understand that now would you?" She reached for her glass of wine. Instead of picking it up straight, however, she ended up knocking the whole glass over! Wine dribbled silently down my tablecloth and pooled in a purplish blob on my carpet.

"Shit!" Tammy shouted. She grabbed onto the table and tried to stand up from her chair. Her chair toppled over as she clumsily started mopping up the dripping wine with her napkin. "Shit, shit, *shit*!" she screamed. By this point, all eyes and little ears from the kiddie table had turned toward the table. I heard, "Oooooohh, she said the S-word," and several giggles coming from their direction.

Rick shook his head. "Unbelievable," he muttered. "You can dress her up but you just can't take her out." Tammy's blue eyes flashed at him but she said nothing.

Now, I was already on top of this spilled wine thing—as much as I wanted to stay and see the unfolding drama, cleaning came first! The tablecloth was probably ruined, but I could still save the carpet. I ran back into the kitchen as fast as I could and I grabbed a handful of paper towels.

I was back in the dining room in a flash. "Hey, didn't someone say that 'a party isn't a party until someone spills some wine?'" I said in a lame attempt to diffuse the situation. "Come on, let's all sit down and finish dinner before the turkey gets cold

"Uncomfortable Silence" shifted in his chair. I frantically looked at Eric and silently pleaded with my eyes for him to do something so that my party wasn't ruined.

He got my message. He cleared his throat and said, "Okay…you know, this is Thanksgiving. Why don't we go around the table and name one thing that we are thankful for this year?" Xavier and Greg nodded their heads and Ana and Gina both chimed in, "Yeah, yeah, good idea."

"Okay then, I guess I'll start," said Eric. "I'm thankful for my children, for Missy, and for all of you for coming over tonight."

I beamed at Eric. What a lifesaver! "Whose next?" he said.

Xavier stood up and toasted with his proper wine glass, not the water goblet, "I, too, am thankful for Ana, Eli, and to you and Missy for sharing your home with us today. I am thankful to share this day with you all as well."

Ana's face lit up like someone had turned a light bulb on inside of her. She gently took Xavier's hand as he sat down.

Gary, not to be outdone, stood up with his wine glass. "Yes, I am thankful for my lovely wife, my wonderful son, and all of our kind friends sitting here today." He sat down as Gina's eyes sparkled, her cheeks flushed pink with pride.

Rick leaned back in his chair until the front legs were slightly off the floor. His eyes scanned the table until they rested squarely on Tammy. "Want to know what I'm thankful for? Well, I'll tell you people what I'm thankful for. I'm thankful for Jim Beam whiskey." Ana snickered softly until she realized that Rick was not making a joke. He wiped a piece of his coal black hair from away from his youthful face and continued, "I thank Jim Beam for making whiskey because that is the only thing that helps me put up with all of Tammy's constant nagging."

Using a high pitched voice clearly meant to imitate Tammy, he continued, "Rick, why don't you have a job yet? Rick, clean up this house. Rick, make the kids dinner. Rick, do this. Rick, do that." Rick stopped and held up his hand, cupping his fingers making it look like a mouth. The mouth/hand moved as Rick said, "Nag, nag, nag." Tammy's face fell like a withered rose. I could see that Tammy was biting her tongue in order to not say anything to make this scene even worse. She was putting on her best manners but I could see that it was getting hard for her to control anger.

Rick abruptly rose from his chair and said, "Well, Tammy, I think it's time that I told you I'm moving out tomorrow morning. I was gonna wait to tell you later, but what the hell, now is as good a time as any. I just can't take any more of this shit." More giggles from the kiddie table. Rick paused and said cheerfully, "I think I need another beer. Anyone else?"

Dumbstruck, we all shook our heads no.

Rick started to walk to the kitchen but Tammy shot up out her chair, knocking it over, and grabbed Rick's arm. She swung him around so that they were staring at each other face to face. It was like two boxers who were staring each other down before the big fight.

Tammy shrieked, "You've got some nerve leaving me, you bastard, after everything I've done for you! I should have left your sorry, no job, no brains ass a long time ago. You... you...*loser*! I'm glad you're leaving! Take your shit and don't let the door hit your ass on the way out!"

"Ooooooh, she said 'ass.' That means butt!" Allen blurted out. The other children all giggled again. Allen got up from his chair and started to wiggle his little butt back and fort all the while chanting, "This is my ahhaass, this is my buhhutt, this is my ahhaass."

"Oh. My. God!" I exclaimed, mortified by what I saw. It was if someone had put superglue in my chair, I couldn't move. I just couldn't stop Allen's wacky "butt dance." The rest of my adult guests, except Tammy and Rick, muffled their giggles in their napkins.

Eric started to rise from his chair to stop his child but Gina quietly signaled for him to stay seated. Smiling, she got up from her chair and gently directed Allen out of the room. She came back and escorted the rest of little ones, who were all laughing hysterically now, to the kitchen. Ana followed Gina's suit and picked up the kiddie table and gingerly carried it and its contents to the kitchen.

When all the little ones and Jason had cleared out and Gina and Ana had returned, I looked over at Rick to see what he was doing. The color had drained from his face. Pure anger radiated from his eyes. He took a deep breath and yelled, "You're calling *me* a loser, Tammy? Take a long look in the mirror at *yourself*, sweetie. I'm not the one with three kids shaking my ass in a bar every night tryin' get bigger tips. You're pathetic. Absolutely pathetic. I can't believe I ever got involved with a pathetic loser like you."

Tammy looked like she had been slapped. She blinked quickly a few times. She closed her eyes for a second and wobbled back on her heels. "What did you just say to me?"

"You heard me."

Well, let me tell you. I could have almost died right then and there. I didn't know what to say. Where was Little Miss Manners when you needed her? *Dear Miss Manners, my drunken friend and her live-in almost teenage drunk boyfriend are having a screaming match in the middle of my Thanksgiving dinner. Any advice? Signed, Hostess without the Mostest.*

Eric finally intervened. He rose from his chair and stood off to the sides of both Tammy and Eric. "Hey, hey, hey you two. Why don't you just calm down, take a deep breath for a minute, and finish your dinner? Missy has gone to a lot of work to make this a nice meal for everyone and I would hate to see her hard work go to waste. We're all friends here, so please...sit down." Although his words were phrased as a question and as a gently pleading, Eric's tone conveyed just the opposite. It was an order, not a request. Both Tammy and Rick got the message that Eric was not going to let them ruin his wife's Thanksgiving party. Reluctantly, Tammy picked up her chair and sat down. Rick excused himself to go to the bathroom. He was obviously embarrassed and wanted to flee the room as quickly as possible.

There we sat. Everyone ate in virtual silence. Tammy picked at her food, barely taking a bite, and either Rick was taking the longest bathroom break in history or he had snuck out and was not coming back. My money was on the latter. Gina and Xavier became the chatter bees and attempted to make small talk, to no avail.

A referee whistle from the football game sounded from the TV in the family room. Eric, Xavier and Gary glanced at each other. After a few moments, Eric rose from his chair, "Um, hey, I'm going in the kitchen to get some more rolls. Anyone want any?" He glanced at Xavier and nodded slightly at him.

Xavier rose from his chair catching on to Eric's true intention with his roll ruse. "Uh, yeeees, Eric. Why don't you let me help you with that?"

"And, don't forget me! Someone has to get the butter." Gary chipped in as he almost knocked his chair over getting up. Gina stared at Gary like he had lost his mind. The three men left for the kitchen. They, like Rick, did not come back to the dining room.

Gina was the first to comment on their long absence. "Missy, I think your house has a man-sucking black hole in it. No matter what room the men go to, they don't seem to come back."

Ana chuckled. "Yeah, so I've noticed. Say, Missy, where can I get one of those for my house?"

I looked around the table at the ladies and the male empty chairs. "Ladies, that 'man sucking black hole' has a name. It's called the TV, and I think the men are powerless under the influence of the Dallas Cowboys. I'll bet you a million dollars that is where they are right this minute." I added, "Including Rick, Tammy."

Tammy looked up from her plate and smiled weakly at us. I continued, "Okay. Ladies. What should we do? Do we force them back into the dining room to finish dinner with us or do we let them watch the game?"

Tammy snorted and waved her hand at the family room. "Hell, let 'em watch the game. Who can blame them for leavin'?"

Gina grabbed Gary's plate while Ana took Xavier's. I picked up Eric's plate and looked at Tammy to see if she wanted me to take Rick's plate. She nodded at me. Then Ana, Gina and I went to the family room and handed the men their dinners. Rick was indeed there. We made a quick stop in the kitchen to check on the kiddie table and then we went back to the dining room.

I had just sat down to finish my dinner when Tammy snidely said, "I sure gotta give it to you, Missy, this has been one helluva dinner party."

Confused, I replied, "What do you mean by that?"

"'What do you mean by that?'" Tammy mimicked me. "What do you think I mean by that? You're a smart girl, figure it out."

Feeling a little angry, I said, "Wait, wait, waaaait. Are you implying that your relationship with Rick falling apart was somehow *my* fault because I threw this party? If so, then that is absolutely the craziest thing I have ever heard!"

Tammy replied, "Then I guess you can add 'crazy' to 'pathetic loser.'" She slammed her napkin down on the table and broke out in sobs. I threw my napkin up in the air in frustration. I just couldn't take any more drama! Gina and Ana rose from their chairs. They put their arms around Tammy and knelt down beside her.

In between sobs, Tammy said, "Ohmygod. I am so (sob) sorry (sob), Missy. My life is such a (sob) mess!"

I knelt beside Tammy and put my arms around her, too. "It's okay Tammy. Look, I'm sorry that this whole Rick thing had to blow up at my house. I know this is hard for you right now. But believe me, you are going to be better off without him in the long run. He was too young and too immature for you. What he did to you tonight shows how childish he really is. I mean, who really starts a fight and breaks up with someone during Thanksgiving dinner anyway?"

Gina interrupted, "Yeeeah, plus he's too stupid to see that he is losing the best thing that has ever happened to him."

I rubbed Tammy's back as tears still fell silently down her face, "Tammy, I know Rick said hurtful things to you in front of us and that was embarrassing for you. It would have been embarrassing for any of us. But remember, we are your friends. We don't believe anything that loser said. You are not a pathetic loser. You are one of the strongest, bravest women I know. You have single-handedly raised three fine boys. Don't let that jerk get the best of you."

Tammy wailed, "I thought I loved that 'jerk,' Missy. I really did."

Wisely, Ana softly asked, "Loved him or lusted after him? Can you really say to that you and Rick had a love relationship, or was it just good sex? Amiga, you need someone who is going to support your dreams, be your friend, give you a happy home for you and your children. You need someone to respect you. You don't need no immature boy who has *nada* to offer you and who is pulling you down with him. You are better off without him. Adios, or as the Terminator would say 'Hasta la vista, baby!'"

Tammy looked up at Ana. You could see the wheels in her mind turning, processing what Ana had just said. Then she winked at Ana and wiped a tear away. She blew her nose into her napkin. I cringed thinking about her snot in my cloth napkin, but I said nothing. Tammy drew a deep breath, straightened her shoulders, and proudly declared, "Okay, so who died and turned you into Dr. Phil, Ana?"

We all chuckled.

Tammy seriously continued, "But, ya know, you're right. I know you are right. I've known it for a long time too, I just didn't want to say it. By sayin' it, I am admittin' to being alone again and that is gonna be hard. But when Rick and I get home tonight, I'm gonna to seriously and calmly ask him to pack his things if he hasn't already. I don't need him in my life. Part of me wants him in my life, but the smart part of me needs him to go. He's no good for me. There. I've said it. He's just no good for me."

Tammy paused for a moment, letting her own words sink into her soul. Anguish was written on her face. She was torn between companionship and loneliness. It was a tough choice that only she could make.

When she was ready with the decision made, she continued, "I mean this thing with Rick has been comin' to a head for a while now. Like I said earlier tonight, all Rick and I have been doin' recently is fightin' and screwin'. It's like all our fightin' made the screwin' better in some weird way. Outside of that, Rick and I don't have nothin' in common. He can't relate to my children or to me on any real level, and I can't relate to him except in the bedroom. Know what I mean?"

Oh, we all knew what she meant. It meant that the old Tammy, with all her crass stories and raw talk, the Tammy that we had come to know and love, was coming back to us. She was going to be all right. That was one thing I had learned about Tammy. She was a fighter who didn't stay on the ropes for long.

Ana sweetly added, "I think you mean that you are finally on the road to recovery. It might be hard for you for a while, amiga, but it's going to be all right. I promise you. You are not alone anymore. You'll always have us no matter what. Okay, so we can't do *everything* Rick did for you" (we giggled) "but we can be your friends and your support line. We're not going to let you down. *Comprende?* Okay?"

Tammy nodded.

"Okay, I think what you need right now to cheer you up is some of that apple pie that I baked this morning. Anyone else up for any?" The three of us groaned, "Yes!" I rose from the kneeling position I was in, knees cracking, and began gathering plates from the table. Gina gave Tammy one last shoulder squeeze and helped me with clearing the table. Ana left the dining room and went to the kitchen to excuse the children from the kiddie table. Tammy drained the last bit of wine from her glass and met us in the kitchen.

Things pretty much settled down after that. After only a few crumbs remained of Ana's pie, everyone, except Ana and I, who began washing the huge pile of dishes, settled down comfortably in my family room to watch the rest of the game. Everyone eventually succumbed to a "turkey coma" and the rest of the evening passed rather pleasantly.

The day finally drew to a close. Ana and Xavier were the first to leave with Gina and Gary following close behind, Gary carrying a sleeping Ethan over his shoulder. Finally, Rick and Tammy decided to leave. With barely a thank you, Rick quickly scooted out the front door with Jason and Jeremy slinking behind him. I gave Tammy an extra long hug and whispered, "It is going to be all right, Tammy. Hang in there and call me if you want to talk, okay?"

Tears welled up in Tammy's eyes and she bobbed her head up and down. With clear determination, she forced her tears to stop. She reached out and hugged Eric. Then she stepped back, took a deep breath, turned to me, and said, "Thanks, Missy, for dinner and everything."

She stepped outside onto our front porch and began walking to her car. Suddenly, she turned around and said, "And just for the record, I think this was one of the nicest Thanksgivings I have ever had, even with the whole Rick thing. It's the first time I can remember bein' thankful for anythin' besides havin' my kids." Tammy paused. "Ya know? I'm thankful for that crazy tree at the school. That tree gives me somethin' to look forward to everyday. I love seein' you, Ana, and Gina at that tree and hearin' all your news and stuff. You three give someone like me hope that I can someday have a normal life, too." Tammy chuckled to herself. "I'm thankful that you, Ana, and Gina are my friends." She nodded her head at me and abruptly turned towards her car before I could reply.

My heart ached a little as I watched her get into her run-down car. The driver's side door squeaked shut and Tammy pulled out of our driveway. Although I knew that Tammy's whole world was falling apart, I also knew that she was going to be okay. It was just hard to watch someone that I cared about hurting so much when there was little I could do to help.

Eric came up behind me and put his hand on my shoulder. I waved goodbye to Tammy as her car drove away. After her car turned the corner, Eric and I silently went back inside into the warmth of our happy home. I knew that I had a lot more to be thankful for than I had even realized before.

***

Rick moved out of Tammy's house the day after Thanksgiving. Tammy, at least on the surface, appeared to be coping well. *Life goes on*, as Ana would say, and we all just went right along with it.

CHAPTER SEVEN

The Christmas holiday season snuck up quickly on me that year. Christmas was a crazy time for me, what with trying to balance the holiday shopping, the parties and all the other festivities of the season. Okay, I'll admit it. I went a little nuts. Not psycho crazy or anything, just a little unglued. My brain actually hurt when I flipped the calendar to December and I started worrying about all the things I needed to do that month.

To cope with the stress of the holiday season, I furiously started making what I call THE LISTS. I make lists for everything from groceries to gifts to what's on TV that week. I'm embarrassed to admit, however, that that year was different. The stress of the season finally got to me. That year, I snapped over the silliest of things. I snapped over a school photocopy machine.

My infamous "blow up," as Eric lovingly calls it, all began with a simple telephone call from my favorite PTA lady, Lisa Jones. I was just minding my own business making a list of how many socks and pairs of underwear Ray had when Lisa called me out of the blue. Her familiar sing song filled my ears. "Miiissseee?"

"Yesseeeee?" I replied mimicking her singsong, but not in a mean way.

"Hi, this is Lisa Jones from the PTA. Remember meeee?"

Duh! Like I could ever forget the spider-from-hell costume.

"Of course," I replied, "How are you?"

"Great, just great. How are you?"

"Surviving the Christmas chaos and trying to not turn into a Grinch."

I heard fake laughter. "Oh, I know. I know." A pause. "Look, Missy, the reason I am calling is that the PTA is having their annual holiday party for the kids in the cafeteria at the school and I was wondering if I could count on you for some help this year."

It was my turn for a pause. Of course I wanted to help make the party fun for the kids, but it wasn't not as if I didn't have enough to do already. I had lists to make, for goodness sakes! Lots and lots of lists! And there was no way I was dressing up as an elf or Mrs. Clause! This woman had her pride, after all.

"Well, Lisa, I would love to help out but I am just so busy right now trying to prepare for Christmas. I don't think I have any time to come into the school."

"Oh, come on, Missy. We really need your help and it is to help the *kids* afterall."

And she did it. She had pulled out the big guilt guns and threw helping the kids at me. There was only one thing to say, "Sure. I'd love to help." I bit my thumb in frustration.

"I knew we could count on youuuuu, Missy!" Lisa gleefully exclaimed. "The party is all taken care of but we need someone to help make copies of the information flyers for the party that the teachers need to send home with the students. Would you be able to do that for me?"

Make copies? That's it? No dress up, no millions of cookies to bake, no popcorn to pop? I was elated! My spirit soared. Making copies was easy. All I had to do was just stand there and let the copy machine do all the work.

I eagerly answered, "No problem. Just let me know when and where and I'll be there." Lisa gave me the particulars. I was to meet her at the school the next morning in the utility room. I hung up with her and promptly put "Making copies for PTA" at the top of my list of things to do.

***

The next morning, I woke up bright and early ready for my big copy-making debut. I put on my most comfortable pair of tennis shoes and jeans and hustled the kids into the car. At the school, I parked and kissed Ray goodbye and waved to Gina at the Mommy Tree. She was going to make sure he got to class safely. Gina waved back and shouted, "Have fun," to me as Allen and I hustled to the front office.

I was actually a little excited and butterflies were playing tennis in my stomach. I don't know why, but every time I walk around the halls of a school I get nervous. Maybe there is a magical shrinking machine fixed in the front door of every school that promptly reduces the self-esteem of every adult that walks through it, making us feel like children again. Of course, teachers and staff are immune to the machine because they probably have some sort of anti-shrinking device hidden in those laminated name badges they wear around their necks. Or maybe the anti-shrinking device is hidden by all the millions of keys each teacher wears on his or her stretchy wire key rings attached to the wrist. Jingle, jingle, jingle.

It's like I am transported to an alien space craft and I have to find my way out to get back to Mother Earth. Like on a spaceship, I have always wondered why the hallways always have weird names like pods, quads, or sectors. Go figure.

At the front office I was tersely told by an older lady office worker to sign in at the "Mother" computer. A few moments later, "Mother" whizzed and her printer spit out a sticker with my name on it. Terse office lady then barked at me to report directly to the red quad, utility staff room, sector 5, room 12. I had to stop myself from giving her the Spock from Star Trek hand wave. I opted for a simple thank you instead and left the office.

As Allen and I weaved our way down the hall, I became distracted by a wall display of gingerbread men tacked on top of a very colorful red and white striped gingerbread house in the middle of the kindergarten green quad, sector 3. I stopped and stared briefly at the mangled expressions on the faces of some of the construction paper dolls and smiled. Most of the gingerbread men had crooked mouths and their eyes were various colors of beads stuck on with white glue, which had seeped out of the sides and crusted. Some of the dolls had wisps of yellow and brown yarn hair stuck on every which way. Each doll was charming in its own way despite some obvious imperfections. They reminded me slightly of wacky voo doo dolls.

I continued to admire the crude artwork as my eyes scanned for Ray's doll. In the middle amongst a group of other gingerbread men, I finally saw it: I instinctively knew it was his before checking for his name. Ray's doll was very meticulously decorated. Both blue eye beads matched and were positioned precisely in the middle of the face. No crusty glue seeped out of the beads. His doll's mouth was carefully drawn in a straight red line unlike some of the other dolls that had curvy, carefree mouths. The yarn hair was not just sticking out; instead, each string had a very distinct place. Ray's dolls clothes were carefully drawn on and were bright and cheery in color. Just like Ray, I thought, his doll was orderly, colorful, and just plain beautiful. Tears briefly welled in my eyes as I imagined his excited face and tiny hands holding fat crayons and glue making his precious doll.

Then, my heart stopped. A gasp caught in my throat. Something had caught my eye and I was deeply disturbed. In the bottom corner of the gingerbread house almost hidden by another paper doll taped over it was one lone gingerbread man. This gingerbread man had no bead eyes, no yarn hair, and no clothes. Deep, dark purple crayon was scribbled violently over this doll and it had no other features except one raw, ugly red crayon streak that served as its mouth. Fresh tears welled in my eyes. It didn't take a psychologist so see that that the child of this gingerbread doll was clearly in pain. I didn't want to imagine the horrors of this child's world, but this doll silently screamed them out to me. This child was only a kindergartener, a five-year-old, and already he was deeply hurting.

Not only was I disturbed by the pain this particular doll represented, I was upset that this poor doll had been shoved away to the very bottom of the house. The purple gingerbread man had been purposely put where no one would see it and the ugliness it represented. I reasoned, of course, that the teacher probably didn't want to bring attention to this child and that appropriate counseling was most likely being held, but for some reason I wanted that doll to be front and center of the house with all the other dolls surrounding it and putting their construction paper hands on it in support. That doll was the kind of thing that people needed to see to be reminded of the enormous responsibility that we have as parents and the tremendous damage we can do to our children.

I took a deep breath, let it out, and bent down to hug Allen tightly for a few minutes until he started to squirm and protest. I put the sad doll in the corner of my gingerbread house memories. I just couldn't bear to think about it anymore, but I would certainly never forget it.

When we finally reached our destination, I walked into the utility room and my nose was bombarded with the burning rubber smell of the copy machines at work. Allen plugged his nose and whined, "Ewwww," and I almost did the same thing. I spotted Lisa and walked over to her. "Good morning," I yelled above the whir of two copy machines furiously spitting out papers.

She looked up from her pile of papers and smiled. "Good moooorrrniiiinng. I'm sooo glad you made it. You'll have to wait a minute for an open machine but I have the fliers right here. Thaaaank you soooo much, Missy, I really appreciate your help! You do know how to work the copy machine, right?"

I looked at her in disbelief. Of course I knew how to use a copy machine, duh! Like who didn't? It doesn't take a genius to put the paper on the glass, push a few buttons, stand back, and watch paper come out. I don't think you need to have a Copy Machine Master's Degree to make copies.

I simply nodded my head. Lisa smiled and handed me the basic information flier, told me to make 320 copies, and nodded toward a copy machine with a big 2 stuck on the lid. "That's the machine you have to use, number two," Lisa said.

Allen giggled when he heard the words "number two," a.k.a. "a poopie." Lisa glared at him and continued, "I've already plugged in my code so you can use number two next." Another giggle from Allen. "Don't use the other machines because you won't have my code and it is *very important* to put a code in. Oh, and just leave my copies and the copies you make when they are done on the table over there. I'll pick them up later, Okay?"

I mouthed "okay" to her since the whirring noise was still very loud.

Lisa smiled, waved goodbye, and turned to leave. Then she stopped and looked back. "Ohhhh, one *very* important thing. Do not try to fix the machine yourself if it gets jammed. Mr. Geary, the principal, does not like the parents to try and fix the machines themselves. If number two gets jammed, just go tell Ms. Kotchkins in the front office and she'll come fix it for you. You probably met Ms. Kotchkins when you checked in. She is such a sweetie!"

Wait, did she just say that the cranky office lady in charge of the "Mother" computer was a sweetie? Maybe I had been transported to another planet after all! I smiled again at Lisa and waived goodbye to her. Allen and I were alone in the utility room waiting for number 2 to stop its first printing job.

Finally, Lisa's copy job was finished and it was my turn to go. I took her copies out of the output tray and placed them on the designated table. I walked back over to number 2. She, as I had for some reason begun to think of her, hummed peacefully and I gingerly lifted her lid to put the flier on the glass. I shut the lid, punched in the number of copies, pressed the green start button, and Allen and I sat back to watch the copies come out.

All was going well. The copies were piling up neatly in the output tray. After a while, Allen and I started playing "Rock, Paper, Scissors" to pass the time. And then, suddenly, all hell broke loose. Number 2 made a horrible screeching sound and stopped making copies! Allen and I looked at each other.

Allen was the first to speak. "What was that, Mommy?"

I walked over to number 2 and looked at the computer screen on the top. "I don't know, honey," I answered Allen. The computer screen beeped at me. Beep, beep, beep. The screen read, "Paper Jam in Tray 1." Beep, beep, beep.

Okay, I thought to myself. *No big deal, just a little paper jam. I'll just go to the office lady, Ms. Kotskiss. Or was it Ms. Kotskins? No, no, no, that's not right. Lisa said her name was Ms. Krotchkins. That's right, Ms. Crotchety Krotchkins.* I smiled at my own humor, grabbed Allen's hand, and off we went down the colorful quad halls back to the Mothership office.

There was another lady working the counter at the office when we arrived. I very sweetly asked for "Ms. Krotchkins" and noticed the funny look I got from the lady behind the counter. She told me to wait one minute and disappeared into the bowels of the office. A few moments later, the cranky office lady from before walked out. She took off her glasses, which were tied to a metal chain around her neck, and stared at me with cold gray eyes. She finally said, "Yes, what is it?"

I smiled my brightest smile hoping to crack this lady's icy personality and asked, "Are you Ms. Krotchkins?"

The cranky office lady furrowed her gray brows and her plump face turned red. She glared at me. "I am Ms. *Kotchkins,* yes." She emphasized her last name as Kaaawtchkins. With horror, I realized my stupid mistake. I had inadvertently called her by a very much less flattering form of her last name. Crotch. Kins. Crotch. Get it? Oh my God.

I noticed the lady who had retrieved Ms. Kotchkins was trying not to laugh in the background. Her shoulders were shaking and she was wiping her eyes. Well, if Ms. Kotchkins treated her office mates the same way she treated me then at least I had made that other lady's day with my verbal slip. I could just imagine the giggles around the water cooler later!

Some of my embarrassment faded a bit thinking this happy thought. I apologized, of course, to Ms. Kotchkins for the mispronunciation of her name and told her about the copier jam. Ms. Kotchkins glared a few more seconds at me and ordered me back to the utility room. She said she would be there in a minute. I thanked her and quickly left the office, thankful to get out of there with my head still attached to my neck.

So there Allen and I sat in the utility room. We sat and sat and sat. No Ms. Kaaawtchins in site. Number 2 still beeped away, beep, beep, beep. Finally, after about thirty minutes of waiting, I had an epiphany. Why couldn't I just fix the copy machine myself? I mean, after all, I had been an officer in the military. A college graduate. A working professional at one time. A woman who had made two human beings with just her body! Of course, I could fix something as simple as a mere paper jam! Ha!

With my new sense of power and purpose, I rose from the floor where Allen and I had parked ourselves and strode over to number 2. Beep, beep, beep. I scanned the computer screen and pressed the help button. The beeping stopped! I was elated. Allen clapped. The computer screen told me to open Side Tray 3, Side Tray 4, and Front Tray 5 to look for the paper jam in Tray 1. Okay. I took a deep breath. I scanned the machine looking for any labels that would identify Side Tray 3, etc. I found none. I leaned down and felt along the edges of number 2. I still couldn't find the trays. After a few moments of frustration, I decided to do the next best thing and just open every tray that I saw. A few minutes later, number 2 lay bare-naked open with all her trays exposed to the world.

I cautiously peeked through number 2's frame and tried to locate the jammed piece of paper to no avail. I knew then that I had to get up close and personal with Number 2.

Like a surgeon about to do open heart surgery, I approached number 2's trays with caution and precision. I tenderly pried open the tray doors and stuck my head inside, seeing what I believed was Side Tray 3. There I was, nosing about when I saw the scrunched up paper stuck in the cog of Side Tray 1. Carefully, I stuck my hand inside number 2 and tried to grasp the paper that was stuck in a rubber roller. The stuck paper looked like a crinkle crisp frozen french fry, and I warily tried to grab the end and pull it free. However, I quickly withdrew my hand after it was seared by the hot rubber roller and watched as the paper rolled under the roller even farther out of reach!

As I recoiled from the hot roller, my arm smacked into the tray door and I heard a tiny metallic pin fall to the floor. The tray door now hung limply to the side. *Damn*, I thought to myself. *Damn, damn, damn.* Since I wasn't willing to risk burning myself again, I sat back on my haunches and tried to think of a way out of this mess.

Allen came over and sat down next to me. He looked inside at the entrails of number 2 and said, "Wow, Mommy, I think you killed number 2." Giggle, giggle.

I glanced over at him. "Yep, I think you're right, sweetie. Number 2 is dead."

"Boy," Allen replied. "That meanie lady is sure going to be mad at you now."

Panic raced through my mind when I thought about Ms. Kaawtchkins' reaction to this mess. Immediately, I thought I could just cover the whole thing up. She already knew about the paper jam so technically I was still okay. She didn't have to know about my fixing attempt. Swiftly, I slammed all of the open trays shut, all except for Side Tray 3, which still hung limply on its hinges like a broken arm on a rag doll. *Damn, damn, damn,* I thought again. I had broken Side Tray 3 and there was no way to hide it. Ol' Crotchkins was sure going to kill me now.

I decided there was only one right thing to do. I'm a parent after all and I have an example to lead. So, I took Allen's hand and marched straight to the Mothership office and 'fessed up completely to Ms. Kotchkins.

Let's just say, Ol' Ms. Kaawtchkins did not take my confession too well.

After a few moments of intense glaring and huffing, she finally walked back with me to the utility room to survey the damage for herself. You would have thought I was showing her the body of a dead murder victim with blood all over my hands the way she reacted to seeing the broken tray door. Her face went pale, her hands started to shake. She turned and stared at me in disbelief.

"You...you...you" and "principal" was all she could stutter. She ran out of the room, almost knocking Allen down. I could hear her shoes clicking down the hall. She yelled back, "You...you stay there!" Oooookay. Allen and I sat down on the ground once more to wait for my impending sentence of doom.

About five minutes later, Ms. Kotchkins came back with a very skinny, wiry man in a well-tailored suit trailing behind her. Both of their expressions were angry, and as Allen and I stood up, I put Allen behind my back to protect him. The man, I could tell, was probably very attractive when he was not wearing such a mean expression on his face. Both Ms. Kotchkins and the man went over to number 2. The man stroked number 2 fondly, almost like a lover, and murmured, "It's okay, it's going to be all right, girl." My Creep-o-Meter skyrocketed after hearing that!

The man looked directly at me and said, "Did you do this?"

I swear his tone reduced me from a thirty-year-old to a five-year-old in 2.2 seconds. Meekly, I muttered, "Yes."

The man inhaled deeply, rubbed his temples and continued to interrogate me. "Why? why, why, why did you try and fix the machine when clearly there is a sign that says not to? *Why?*"

Now, this sign business was news to me. "There's a sign?" I stupidly asked.

The man and Ms. Kotchkins exchanged knowing glances and the man said in a very condescending tone, "Yes. Why yes, there is a sign. A *big, yellow* sign on that wall right there that says very clearly that all parents are not to fix the machines by themselves. Instead, they are to go and let Ms. Kotchkins know about the problem. Do you see that, *big, yellow* sign?" As he said "big, yellow sign" he made a box with his fingers.

"No, I did not see the big, yellow sign," I replied. It was a true statement, I hadn't seen the sign until just then. However, this man and his attitude were starting to annoy me. I continued, "Look, I don't know who you are but I don't appreciate how I am being treated over this. I thought it was an easy jam that I could just fix myself."

"Well, you thought wrong and now this machine will be out of order for at least a week until we can get a repair man in here," the man stiffly replied.

"I'm sorry that I inadvertently broke the machine but I am not sorry for trying to fix it in the first place. I have been waiting here for over a half of an hour for someone to help me. Look, just who do you think you are anyway, treating me like this?" I asked the man directly.

"Who am I?" the man laughed slightly as Ms. Kotchkins stifled a giggle. "Who am I? Why, I am Mr. Alvin Geary. You may have heard of me. I'm the principal of this school."

Stunned, I blinked at the principal. This condescending, blown up buffoon was my son's top education official? I mentally began calculating the costs of a private school that I was immediately transferring Ray to after today. I couldn't believe that this tyrant and his bozo staff member were in charge of my son's education!

My feelings of intimidation ebbed away and were replaced by anger. Did this idiot man treat a child who confessed to doing something wrong in this same belittling manner? Something inside of me went a little wacky just then. All the stress of the holiday season bubbled up inside of me ready to explode. Some wires deep in my brain were crossed, and I felt very, very, legitimately angry.

With a deep breath, I began my infamous tirade, "Mr. Geary, with all due respect," I began, "I am absolutely offended by the way you are treating me over this mistake. How dare you mock me with your condescending attitude? I'll have you know that I did go to Ms. Kotchkins" (I said her name correctly this time and with enunciation) "and that she ignored my request for help. My time is precious and I did not want to wait all day for her to show up."

Oh boy, oh boy! I was on a roll and I didn't stop there. "And another thing, I didn't have to come back and tell anyone that I broke this machine. I could have just left and no one would have known that I did it. Instead, I actually confessed my mistake, and the reward I get for my honesty is you two making fun of me! What kind of example are you two setting, especially in front of my child? Look, I am just a parent volunteer. Without us parent volunteers helping out in the classrooms or wherever, this school would have problems. I'm here for the children, not for you. I am not paid for my time, so that means I certainly do not have to stand here anymore and be treated like this by you or any other member of your staff!"

My voice rose up a notch and my cheeks burned. I took a deep breath and said icily, "I thought it was a simple fix. Turns out it is not. Oh well. Too bad. Deal with it!"

I gathered my purse and took Allen's hand. Before leaving, I turned one last time and pointed my shaking finger at Mr. Geary, "And you, Mr. Geary, ought to be ashamed of yourself. I expected more from you of all people."

Surprisingly, Mr. Geary flushed in embarrassment. Maybe there was hope for him after all.

I then turned and pointed at Ms. Kotchkins, "And you, Ms. Kaaawtchkins, can take your mean, lousy attitude and go stick that up your big, yellow sign!"

Ms. Kotchkins gasped in shock. Allen giggled. By now, even my lips were shaking I was so nervous, and my adrenaline had pumped into high gear. I had never spoken to anyone, let alone school officials, like that before in my life!

After that, Allen and I promptly left the room. I actually ran with Allen down the hall as fast as I could to get away from Mr. Geary and the Old Crotch, as I have since nicknamed her. My heart was racing as I hit the front doors of the school. The warm sunshine felt good and I inhaled deeply. Whew, I had escaped from the Mothership of the Mean Pod People and was safely back on Earth. I quickly buckled Allen into his car seat, fighting back tears. My emotions were getting the best of me. I stepped on the gas and sped off for home.

***

I saw Gina first that afternoon at the Mommy Tree. She could see that I was still upset. "What's the matter, Missy? Are you okay?"

I nodded weakly. More tears formed but I squeezed my eyes shut hard so that they would not fall. Gina put her arms around my shoulder and we sat down on the edge of the Mommy Tree's bench.

"What happened, Missy?" Gina questioned again. By this time, Ana and Tammy had arrived and they could see how upset I was.

"Hey, girl, what's up?" Tammy asked, and I could see the concern on Ana's face.

I shrugged my shoulders, took a deep breath, and told them the whole copy machine story. Tammy started laughing, especially at the "Ms. Krotchkins" part—for some reason I knew she would get a kick out of that!

"What's the big deal?" Tammy asked when I had finished. "So, you told off the principal! I think that's awesome, girlfriend! Good for you for standing up for yourself. That ass had it comin'. That's the kind of thing I would expect you to do, Miss Military! But what I don't get is why this is botherin' you so much. You're acting weird. Snap out of it, sister!"

I looked blankly at Tammy and her eyes searched mine. It took a minute for what she had just said to sink in. She was right. They all couldn't understand why I was so upset because the only person they saw was the tough exterior I put on as a cover up for the real me inside.

I was a fraud. Yep, I was a bona-fide one-hundred-percent faker. I was a shy, insecure mess, but they didn't know that because I had kept that hidden deep down in a dark part of my soul for so long that at times I had even fooled myself into believing the lie. These three ladies who had become a cherished part of my life had no clue to who the real me was, and I was afraid to let them in on my secret. Would they still like me if they saw what was underneath my "tough girl" mask? In that short span of seconds, I decided that it was time to let the cat out of the bag, as Ana would say. These ladies were too important to me and it was time I faced myself and accepted who I really was once and for all. I hoped they would still like me after my confession. I felt scared and empty.

I took a deep breath and blew it out. I let the tears that had been forming fall freely down my cheeks. "No, Tammy," I said quietly. "I am not strong at all. In fact, I am the weakest person you probably know. Standing up for myself today was one of the hardest things I've had to do."

The three of them looked at me in surprise. I continued, "Yes, I've had military training but that doesn't make me military strong. I have been such a fool for so long pretending to be something I'm not! I've been putting on my own brave front for the world and I've been afraid to let people see the real, insecure me. I think today has finally made me see that it's time for me to just open up and stop worrying about what people think."

I stood and started pacing back and forth. The dam was open and there was no way to stop my verbal flood now. "I'm so tired of always pretending to be in control!" The tears were pouring down my face now. "I am so tired of being that person that everyone turns to in a crisis. Why do I always have to clean up everyone else's messes? *Why?* Because I am ol' reliable Missy, that's why!"

My voice rose semi-close to hysterical and Tammy tried to stop my pacing. I shrugged her off and continued my second tirade of the day. "I'm tired of being the strong, boring one. You know? I'm the one who is so predictable that I've become a cookie cutter plastic person! I'm just plain tired of not being true to the real me! There is a real me who has feelings that get hurt and who is scared most of the time. The real me who is just fumbling through life with her hair on fire just trying to do the best I can!" I paused and took a deep breath. "I am not in control and I am not strong. There, I said it."

I sighed and sat down on the bench. My shoulders slumped forward and I felt a sense of release and exhaustion at the same time.

Gina came over and sat next to me. She handed me a Kleenex and I took it thankfully and wiped my tears and blew my nose. Gina softly said, "It's okay, Missy. We all understand what you are saying. So you put a brave face on for the world to hide your insecurities? So what? We all do that! Every one of us hides our vulnerabilities to protect ourselves from getting hurt. Okay…so you are not the 'tough girl' we all thought. Big deal! None of us act like who we really are all the time. We like you. Brave front or not, it's no big deal to us."

Tammy interrupted, "Okay, okay, she gets the point, Gina." She softened it with a wink, and Gina smiled. "No, seriously, Missy, Gina's right. Who the hell cares if you aren't the gung ho military lady who has got it all together like you've been pretending to be? I don't, and in fact this makes me like you better. You're finally learning to open up and act like a real person instead of some fake robot with no feelings. It was kinda annoying how you are always so in control of everything like your life and feelings and stuff. Well, you get the point. I'm glad this has happened. Hallelujah, sister! Welcome to the real world!"

I wasn't sure if I was supposed to be offended by Tammy's comments or take them as a compliment. Knowing Tammy, the new and improved "weak me" took them as a compliment.

Ana sat down on the bench next to me and gave me a warm smile. She took my face in her hands. "It's okay to realize that you don't have to act so perfect all the time, but don't fool yourself into thinking that you are not strong inside. There is a fine line there, no? See it?"

I nodded that I did, although it was hard to do because Ana still had my face in her hands. She let go and pulled me to her for a big bear hug. I was worried I was going to get snot on her shirt from all my crying.

The school bell rang so we didn't have time to talk about it anymore. I looked around to see if anyone else had noticed my self-realization epiphany. Oddly, as the year progressed, I noticed that hardly any other parents were coming to the schoolyard. Most waited in their cars until the gate swung open and the children came out. It was weird but true.

I looked up at the Mommy Tree's branches and saw them swaying slightly in the breeze. The bald branches had crooked little fingers sticking out on the ends, and they were gently waving at me. I stretched out my arm and with my hand I slowly, very slowly, wiggled my fingers one after the other from pinky to thumb. I was no longer empty. I felt full.

Gina walked with me back to our cars. Ana and Tammy trailed behind. Gina said, "So, if you're not the 'strong one' anymore then what am I going to do now? I mean, didn't you know that you've been my strength since mine is obviously failing?" She waved her cane at me and smiled weakly.

Her smile suddenly turned into a thin, serious line. She stopped and turned her full attention to me. "I need you, Missy. I need you to be strong for me now more than you know. It's okay to sometimes let your emotions get away from you because you're human and we all do that. But don't ever think that you are weak and foolish, because you are not."

She grabbed my arm. "Stay strong for me, Missy. Please," she repeated. "I need you right now more than you know." It was a plea not a statement and it scared me to death.

I searched Gina's face. Her eyes were dark, hiding something. I didn't know what was going on but my gut feeling was that it was something bad. I smiled at Gina, took her hand, and squeezed it. She squeezed back and smiled at me, but her eyes were still dark.

It wasn't until I got home much later that I realized I still had the school's visitor badge stuck to my sweater and that I had not officially checked out.

***

Lisa called later that week to tell me that another mom had finished the job for me. She thanked me anyway for trying my best, blah blah blah. After the Mommy Tree confession, I realized that I could allow myself to fail, to cry, and to finally stop caring about what other people thought of me. So, I wasn't as tough or as perfect as I had pretended to be, but I was also no wimp either. I could fail and my friends didn't care. For the first time in a long time, I felt happy. I know *happy* is a simple word but it perfectly captured how I felt. Happy. I felt happy.

Sure, on the other hand I felt guilty for letting Lisa down and for yelling at the principal. But what could I say? Oh well. Too bad. Deal with it. I felt happy.

CHAPTER EIGHT

Despite all my worrying, Christmas came and went without too much of a hitch. My lists were completed and it was time for me to focus on the brand new year ahead. That January, the ladies and I not only celebrated the birth of the New Year but also the birth of our spicy, sweet Latina friend, Ana.

The "Ladies-Night-Out-Birthday-Party-for-Ana" thing started out as Tammy's idea, and in retrospect that alone should have clued us in to the kind of night we were going to have. Oh yes, it was certainly a night that none of us ladies would ever forget.

Tammy planned a fun night out at one of Las Vegas' trendy hip nightclubs located inside an equally famous hotel in the heart of the Las Vegas strip. The plan was for Gina, Ana and me to check into the hotel and wait for Tammy's day shift to end. Why a hotel? Well, a hotel guaranteed that that no one had to drive home after having a few cocktails, a detail that only Tammy was really worried about, and so that we moms could have one free night to ourselves.

Tammy had told us that her oldest son, Johnny "The Doobie" would be watching her kids for her. Tammy and Rick were still broken up and it didn't look like they were going to be getting back together anytime soon. The rest of us were lucky to have our husbands to watch our children for the night.

The night started out normally enough. We checked into the hotel as planned. We were all very excited. I mean, this was our one free night out with no kids, no husbands, and no dirty dishes to clean. We could sleep in until noon the next day with no little people with grumbling bellies waking us up at the crack of dawn. We were going to wear real clothes, nice clothes like skirts, blouses, and high heels with (gasp!) nylons to someplace else besides church. We were going to drink cocktails and read magazines by the pool all afternoon without having to worry about the kids drowning! For one night only, we were trading in our worn out sweatpants and bleach stained t-shirts for nail polish and nylons. We were going to let our hair down and Sin City had just better watch out!

After checking into the hotel room and putting our stuff down, Ana closed the curtains to the room and lay down on the queen size bed that she was going to share with Tammy. Immediately, the room became quiet, peaceful and so, so dark. Gina and I followed Ana's lead and fell onto our own queen size bed with a dull thump.

"Whew," Ana sighed. "I don't think I want to move. Wait, just listen for a minute..."

Gina and I strained our ears trying to hear what Ana was referring to. I was the first to speak, "What? What are you listening for?"

Ana sat up in bed and looked at me. "That. Right there. You hear it?"

Again, Gina and I tried to hear what Ana was hearing but we didn't even know what we were supposed to be listening for. All I heard was the muted slam of a door in the hallway. After a few moments, I asked Ana again, "What?"

Ana smiled. "That, mi amiga. That right there. That is the beautiful sound of absolute nothing. That is the peaceful sound of silence. If I do nothing else tonight, just having a few minutes of silence and peace and having nothing to do but lie here on this bed is the perfect birthday present. Ahhhh." She lay back down on the bed and closed her eyes. "You know what?" she said, breaking the silence, "I don't remember the last time I took a siesta, you know, a nap in the afternoon. I haven't done this since I was a little girl. Well, amigas, today is my day and I am going to take a little siesta right now. You ladies don't mind, no?"

Gina rolled her head over and looked at me. We both smiled. Visions of cocktails by the pool, aka "Tammy's Master Plan," passed briefly through our thoughts; but then the reality of the dark, quiet room engulfed our souls completely. "Good night," Gina and I said in unison and each grabbed our pillows. Oh, a siesta. A nap. The two most beautiful words in the world to a mother of toddlers and kindergarteners. We all found ourselves fast asleep within a few minutes. Some party girls we were turning out to be.

I woke up to the sound of someone banging on our door. At first, I thought it was Ray playing carpenter with his toys, but then I remembered that I was in a darkened hotel room. Gina sat up and sleepily rubbed her eyes. The banging continued, and then we heard shouting that was unmistakably Tammy in the hallway.

"Hellooooo, is anyone goin' to open this goddamn door? I gotta pee real bad. I know y'all are in there." Bang. Bang. Bang.

Gina and I both shook our heads and chuckled, I rose from the bed and noticed that Ana was still snoozing through all the noise. When I unlocked the door Tammy flew in the room like a whirlwind. Her cannon ball style black purse swung wildly and almost hit me in the face. "Where's the bathroom? I gotta pee somethin' fierce!" Tammy exclaimed.

She stopped for a minute and looked around at the darkened room and saw Ana asleep on the bed. "What? Did she pass out or somethin' already? I knew I'd miss all the fun. God, I hate my job. Ohhh, wait, tell me later, I gotta go."

She rushed into the bathroom and slammed the door. Through the bathroom door, she continued, "So? Tell me all the nitty gritty details. What happened?"

I responded, "Oh, well, we really haven't been up to much of anything. We were all just taking a nap, you know. Ana's asleep. She didn't pass out."

The toilet flushed and I could hear Tammy washing her hands. She came out of the bathroom with a puzzled look on her face.

"Taking a nap? You ladies have been taking a nap? What happened to goin' to the pool and havin' some drinks, ya know? This is your whole 'day off from the kids' thing, and you're tellin' me that you napped all day?"

I nodded. "Yes."

"Jesus, Mary, and Joseph! Thank God I showed up when I did to get this party started! Unbelieeevable. I leave you three alone for a few hours and all you do is sleep. I see I gotta do all the work around here."

Tammy shook her head and started rummaging through her purse. To my surprise, she pulled out a corkscrew and a bottle of wine from her purse! She popped the cork and filled four of the hotel's glasses.

I eyed my glass nervously, imagining a million strep bacteria swimming happily in my wine. I had seen a news expose show in which a team of investigative reporters found, like, a gazillion strep bacteria and other germs in hotel glasses alone. You don't even want to know what they found on the beds. Ew, ew, double ew. My can of Lysol was packed in my bag, ready to be used.

"Well, should we wake up Sleeping Beauty or what?" Tammy asked. Without waiting for a reply from us, she leaned over Ana and gently shook her. "Wake up, sleepyhead, or we're gonna party without ya!"

Ana opened one eye slowly and then shut it again. "Go 'way," she said groggily. "Siesta."

Tammy smiled and shook her harder. Ana pushed Tammy aside. Tammy rushed over and flung open the curtains. Gina and I instinctively winced, expecting sunshine to flood the room, but instead we were greeted by darkness and the bright neon lights of the strip. It was nighttime and the Las Vegas lights were sparkling. Tammy picked up a glass of wine and held it over Ana's head.

"Hey, birthday girl, ya got ten seconds to get up and join this party before ya get a little shower surprise," she said, grinning wickedly. Gina and I watched in fascination wondering if Tammy would actually dump the wine on Ana. All I could think was what a mess that would make, and that Ana and Tammy would have to sleep in the mess later. Luckily for all of us, Ana sat up.

"Don't you even dare joke like that, Tammy!" Ana grabbed the glass from Tammy's hand. Tammy smiled and hugged her.

"Happy birthday, amiga!" Tammy exclaimed and raised her glass in a toast. Gina and I followed suit. We all took a drink and I secretly prayed that the alcohol in the wine had killed any strep bacteria in my glass.

Tammy abruptly jumped off the bed. "Well, ladies, I gotta take a shower and get out of this uniform. Try to keep yourselves busy. No more sleepin'! There's more wine in my purse if you need it. I'll be back in a jiffy." She went into the bathroom and closed the door.

I started laughing. I whispered to Gina and Anna, "There's more wine in her purse? Ohmygod, how does she keep so much stuff in there?"

Gina laughed, too. We finished our little glasses in a few sips and I refilled each glass. Then we each took turns getting dressed and using the desk mirror to fix ourselves up.

Tammy eventually came out of the bathroom and the three of us stared at her outfit in surprise. I don't even know how to describe it. It was two parts punk rocker, two parts valley girl, and five thousand parts whore. I couldn't help but stare at her exposed flesh peeking out between strategically ripped holes in her denim skirt and black fishnet stockings. Her severely teased hair was held in place by at least a can of hairspray, and it gave her the look of an untamed lion. Her makeup was plastered on; I could see a brown line marking the edge of her face where it ended. Then it hit me who Tammy looked like to me. She looked like one of the zombie extras from the Michael Jackson "Thriller" video! I stifled a giggle and took a sip of wine.

Gina's mouth dropped open, but she was the first one to finally speak. "Uh, Tammy, honey, is that what you are wearing tonight?"

Tammy looked at her with surprise. "Yeehes. Duh? Isn't this a great outfit?" She twirled around and I caught of flash of a neon pink thong nestled between her butt cheeks as her skirt flipped up in the wind. Ohmygod.

I could see Gina struggling with her response. I knew she didn't want to hurt Tammy's feelings, but she also didn't want to lie. Gina slowly said, "Yes, that is certainly some outfit there, girl, but don't you think you should maybe tone it down a little?" She noticed a flash of hurt in Tammy's eyes so she quickly added, "Uh, I mean, you look great, it's just that I don't think any of us really brought anything quite like that to wear tonight." Gina gestured to her own plain black dress.

The hurt vanished from Tammy's eyes and was replaced by amusement.

"Hell, that's no problem. I brought plenty of outfits. You could always borrow somethin' of mine to jazz yourself up a bit."

Gina's eyes widened in surprise. I could see the wheels in her head turning trying to figure out the polite way to get out of this one! Tammy opened another bottle of wine from her purse and took a big swig from the bottle. I couldn't think of a thing in Tammy's wardrobe that would compliment my own black miniskirt and red blouse!

We gave up on trying to change Tammy's mind. It was time to get this night going! Each lady took one last look in the mirror and primped, and then we left for the club.

We waited patiently in the club line, which stretched halfway around the casino. Tammy secretly passed each of us her flask filled with whiskey. The whiskey was horrible tasting, but I drank it anyway. My throat burned with every sip. Secretly, I felt a small thrill sneaking the drink in line because it was against the rules! Dah dah! I, "Missy-who-never-breaks-any-rules," was actually defying the rules of a casino establishment. Oh the thrill! I was enjoying myself! Whoo hoo! What a rebel I thought I was. The four of us were giggling and passing the flask back and forth. Finally, we made it to the front of the line and we were in!

Blaring music and flashing neon lights assaulted my senses the minute we entered the club. Stale booze, cigarette smoke, and a hint of moldy vomit wafted into my nostrils. All I could see were clumps of people everywhere. Some were standing at tall tables while others were walking around, drinks in hand, in straight lines like a stream of ants carrying leaves back to the nest. I was gently pushed by Tammy from behind to go forward into the bowels of the club. I clutched on to Ana so that I wouldn't lose her and I felt Gina grab my other arm. Her cane dangled loosely from her free arm. Together, the three of us stepped into the mob of people.

We walked endlessly around the club. Tammy finally spotted an empty table near the exit door. "Shit," she exclaimed. "We're too far back. No one will see us from here. Let's find something else closer to the dance floor action and the bar."

"There is nothing else, Tammy, and I am not circling around this club anymore. My feet are killing me in these heels!" Ana promptly sat down and took off her shoes. She started rubbing her feet.

Tammy looked mortified, "What in the hell are you doin', Ana? You can't rub you feet in here!"

Nonplussed, Ana replied, "Why not? There's a rule about not rubbing your feet? My feet hurt and I'm rubbing them! Oh well. Too bad. Deal with it." She winked at me and continued massaging her aching toes. Tammy rolled her eyes and sighed.

We sat down at the table and attempted several times to catch the attention of the one lone waitress working our area. No luck. She was either blind or purposely ignoring us. A few minutes later and a few tables down, a group of good-looking college aged boys sat down. Our waitress immediately went over to them. She flashed a flirty smile and took their order. Well, there went the blind theory. Go figure. Finally after Tammy whistled and shouted at her, the waitress took our drink order. She frowned at us and left.

I sat at the table and took in my surroundings. All I could see were hordes of people everywhere, and they were all young. Young, young, and young. Most of the girls were scantily dressed, showing off their perfectly toned youthful bodies. Many had their bare midriffs showing and lower back tattoos on display. I watched as lust-filled boys clumsily attempted to talk to them. Some were successful in gaining a dance or a drink while others were ruthlessly turned away. Sure, I had been to the clubs when I was in college, but for some reason I didn't remember the club scene being like this one. There was an air of seediness in this club that I didn't remember being in the clubs of my youth. Was it the club scene that had changed, or was it just me that had changed? I felt very uncomfortable and overdressed in my plain black skirt, red shirt, pearls and high heel shoes. At that moment, I realized something. I was a mom! *A mom in a bar*! Aaagh!

Our nasty waitress finally appeared with our drinks, and none too soon for me. The four of us raised glasses in a birthday salute to Ana. It was too loud in the club for any of us to talk to one another, so we sat there silently until Tammy shouted, "Hey, ladies! Let's go dance!"

I cupped my hand over my ear because I was sitting the farthest away from Tammy and couldn't hear her that well. All I could hear was the pounding of the base from the speakers in the club. Boom, boom, boom.

Ana shouted, "What?" Boom, boom, boom.

"*Go dance!*" Tammy screamed. Boom, boom, boom.

Gina and Ana both shook their heads no and I shook mine no, too. Tammy frowned at us and finished her drink in one gulp.

We sat there. We started to get bored and I was feeling a little dizzy from my drinks. Tammy desperately scanned the crowd, sizing up her best option for the night. She licked her lips and winked at one of the college boys sitting at the table a few feet from ours. The guy laughed and turned to his friends. Tammy shrugged her shoulders and sought out her next prey. Ana nervously played with her wedding band, Gina tapped her cane on the floor in time to the music, and I just sat there fiddling with the straw in my gin and tonic, bored out of my mind. Boom, boom, boom.

Just when I didn't think things could get any worse, the Super Creep found me. Now, if you've ever been to a club then you know who I am talking about. The Super Creep is the guy that every lady dreads. He's the one who never takes the polite hint that you are just not interested. He sits too close, dances too close, and is just a plain pain in the ass loser who is usually too drunk to know that he's being obnoxious. The Super Creep is usually smack dab in the midst of his midlife crisis and can credit two or three divorces to his name. The Super Creep always has the cheesiest pick-up lines that he thinks will actually work and is not afraid to use them! He likes to wear thick gold chains and cheap suits. Need I say more? There's always one in every club, and no matter what club I am in I am always the Super Creep magnet. That night was no exception.

I spotted him before he spotted me so I tried to hide behind Gina's shoulder. "Gina, shield me! It's the Super Creep! No matter where I am or what I am doing some Super Creep always finds me! Help!"

Gina leaned to the right to try and cover me but it didn't matter. The Super Creep saw me and it was all over. There was no stopping him as he made a beeline stumbling over to our table. Ana groaned and looked away.

"Good evening, ladiesssh," the Super Creep slurred as he fingered a thick gold chain hanging limply on his hairy chest. "How are you beauties doin' tonight?" He asked all of us the question but his watery eyes were aimed at me. He leaned on our table and flashed his best cheesy grin then winked at me. I cringed. "Can I buy you all a round of drinksss?"

I could smell his foul booze breath. Gina, Ana, and I immediately jumped to our polite "no, oh no thank yous," but I winced as Tammy accepted his drink offer and motioned for him to sit down in the empty chair next to hers. The Super Creep plopped down on the chair and put his arm around the back of Tammy's chair. Tammy beamed.

The nasty waitress finally took our drink order again and I felt the Super Creep staring at me. I gave him a cool, polite smile and looked away fast. I was hoping he would get the hint and go away. He didn't. He took out a tube of Chapstick and rolled the ball of the tube over his lips, slowly and methodically in a pathetic attempt to be sexy. Ew. Gina caught the Chapstick show and giggled at my discomfort.

Tammy, oblivious to the Super Creep's attempt to flirt with me, actually moved her chair closer to his! She asked him, "So, what's your name, stranger?" and cocked her head to the side, sweeping her fingers through her tangled hair. Her finger got caught in a clump of hairspray and she awkwardly tugged it out. Her elbow almost hit the Super Creep in the face.

The Super Creep's eyes didn't leave my face. "My name is Dick. Dick Decker." He emphasized the "Dick" part and sneered. Gina and Ana both snickered into their napkins. I tried not to laugh either because I didn't want to be rude. Tammy was the only one who seemed impressed.

"What? What did you say?" Tammy asked. It was still hard to hear over the boom of the music but I had a strange feeling she just wanted him to repeat his name again.

"*Dick...Dick Decker!*" the Super Creep yelled.

"Dick Decker, huh? I *like* that name. I like it a lot," Tammy purred.

Yep, I was right. She just wanted to hear his name again, only louder. Ewwwww!

Dick tore his eyes away from me and smiled at Tammy. I could see the light bulb light up in his mind. Ol' Dick Decker was thinking maybe he might get lucky tonight!

"You like my name, sweetheart? That's good, real good. Bet I can guess your name. It's got to be 'Angel' because something as good lookin' as you must have been sent from heaven." He was directly looking into Tammy's eyes now. There was Corny Pick-Up Line #1 and counting.

Tammy batted her lashes at him and replied, "You can call me 'Angel.' I like that name but just remember I can be a devil, too, if you know what I mean!"

She put her hand on his polyester covered thigh and started to rub it up and down. Dick guffawed and ran his fingers through his greasy, thinning hair. His other hand fingered his chest chain again.

I leaned over to Gina and whispered, "I feel like I am stuck in the middle of some B-grade porno flick!" Gina burst out laughing and accidently spilled her drink on her top. She tried to wipe up the spill with the flimsy bar napkins on the table but that didn't work too well.

Dick jumped to his feet and almost knocked over the flimsy table. He leaned all the way over the table with his napkin in hand. "Here, honey, let me help you with that." He clumsily tried wipe at the spot with his napkin but was obviously only trying to cop a quick feel of Gina's breast.

Gina grabbed his napkin from his hands and curtly replied, "No thank you. I can do it myself...*Dick.*"

Dick sat down and said, "Oh, sorry, sweetie. I was just tryin' help." He held up his hand in mock surrender but lewdly winked. Gina glared at him.

We sat in silence. The music was still thumping away. Ana, Gina, and I were trying to ignore Dick's lecherous looks while Tammy pined away for any scrap of attention he would throw her way. A slow song started to play and all I could make out from the song were the words "Ooh, ooh, baby, do me harder like that time before." Ohmygod. I was getting too old for this scene!

The young hipsters rushed to the dance floor eager to bump and grind away with each other. Dick stared at the dance floor, entranced by the tribal, primitive scene before his eyes. A bead of sweat broke out on his brow. He coughed into a dirty handkerchief and tore his gaze away from the writhing bodies. That's when he remembered me. Oh boy.

"Uh, hey honey, let's say you and me go dancin' a bit." Dick coughed into his dirty napkin again and wiped the sweat about to drip into his eyes. I ignored him and turned in my chair so that my back was slightly to him.

"Uh, uh, I *said*, hey, *honey*...you *wanna dance?*" Dick practically screamed to the back of my head while he was leaning over Tammy. There was no way to avoid him now without looking rude, and as much as he was being annoying, rude is one thing I am not.

"I don't think so, Dick. I've got a headache," I replied as believably as possible. Wait, did people even use that as an excuse anymore? I wouldn't know since the last time I had been asked to dance by a drunken total stranger was at my cousin Sue's wedding back in like...what? *1992!* What did those hip girls out on the dance floor say nowadays when they didn't want to dance with the Super Creep? Who knows? Not me. I was just a *mom* at a bar in the middle of the Las Vegas strip. Ohmygod. I wanted to go home.

Dick appeared disappointed by my rejection for exactly one second before he turned to Gina next. One, one thousand...

"How about you, sweetie? Wanna dance?"

"Nope. Can't. Sorry." Gina held up her cane and shrugged her shoulders. Dick shrugged his shoulders back. One, one thousand...

Dick turned to Ana and looked her up and down. He opened his mouth like he was about to ask her to dance but then quickly shut it. Abruptly, he turned to Tammy instead who eagerly jumped up and grabbed his arm. The two of them went out on the dance floor and jiggled with the best of them.

I was furious that the Super Creep hadn't even bothered to ask Ana dance even though she would have turned him down. Not only was he a Super Creep but a bona fide bastard, too!

Ana smiled weakly at Gina and me. I could see the hurt of rejection in her eyes. She took her drink and gulped it down in one sip. Then she stood up, "Well, amigas, I say I've had enough fun for one evening. I think I will just go back to the room." She started to gather her purse but Gina grabbed her arm and stopped her.

"Wait, Ana, wait a minute. Don't let that loser upset you! Stay for a bit. Besides, we can't leave Tammy while she is still dancing."

Ana thought about it for a minute and sat down. "Okay, but I'm only staying until she comes off the dance floor. That's it." Gina and I nodded in agreement.

We sat in silence again. I was desperately trying to think of the right things to say to soothe Ana's bruised ego. Nothing came to mind so I lamely didn't say anything at all.

Tammy finally came off the dance floor after what seemed like an eternity to the rest of us. She and Dick were both sweating like pigs. Tammy's makeup was practically dripping off her face, and Dick's face was flushed and blotchy. Dark, wet spots stained his shirt under his armpits. He took his dirty handkerchief from his back pocket and wiped his perspiring brow. Tammy wrapped her arm around Dick's and wouldn't let go. Ana stood up and grabbed her purse again. "I'm going, Tammy. Are you coming?"

I saw panic flash in Tammy's eyes. I could almost hear the thoughts in her head: *Should I stay with my friends or grab the one guy who is paying attention to me tonight. Stay with friends? Stay with guy? Friends? Guy?*

She whined with desperation, "Why? Are you sure you wanna go now, Ana? How about another drink?"

"No. Now."

"Now?"

"*Now.*"

Dick shuffled his feet and tried his best lazy smile at Tammy again. He said, "Why do you hafta go, Angel? Why don't you let your friends go and you stay here with ol' Dick?"

Gina, Ana, and I stared at Tammy. The moment of truth had come. It was the age-old dilemma that many a single lady had faced in her life. Did you ditch your friends or stay with the man? My answer was always, without question, stay with your friends. Remember "Loyal Missy"? This, however, was different because this was Tammy we were dealing with. Who knew what she was going to do.

A moment passed. Then a minute. Tammy's eyes pleaded with Ana. Tammy wanted to stay. It was obvious to everyone. I guess that is why we were all shocked when Tammy turned to Dick and said, "I'll have to take a rain check, Dick. We'll have to do it again some other time. It's my friend's birthday and I'm going back to the room with them. Sorry."

Dick looked stunned and then he became angry. Very angry. He shouted, "Are you tellin' me that you are leavin' me because this fat broad and her bitchy friends say so? What kind of crap is this? I didn't spend all night buyin' ya drinks to go home alone, you bitch!"

Oh. My. God! The Super Creep was metamorphosing into the Super Duper *Duper* Creep! I'd only seen this once before and it was not a pretty sight. It was time to leave and fast. Ana, Gina, and I grabbed our purses and I pulled at Tammy's arm to go.

She shrugged my arm off and squinted her eyes at the Super Creep. "Listen up, Dick. I may be a bitch, but that is a helluva lot better than being an asshole like you. Nobody talks to me or my friends like that!" And then, strangely, Tammy leaned up seductively, pressed her breasts against his chest, and whispered something in his ear that I couldn't quite hear. She stood back and slowly ran her tongue over her lips. The color drained from Dick's face and he swallowed hard. Then Tammy turned on her heels, picked up her big black bag, and hooked arms with mine. The four of us headed out of the club leaving a stunned Dick behind.

We burst out laughing the minute we hit the elevators. When we reached the room I plopped onto the bed. I took off my pumps and started to rub my aching feet. Ana headed to the bathroom and locked herself in. Tammy and Gina sat down on the chairs. Tammy whispered, "Hey, did anyone think to get a cake?"

I went to the closet and pulled down a small white cake from the shelf, congratulating myself for my clever hiding place. Tammy went to her bag and to our amusement pulled out a lighter and birthday candles. We placed the candles on the cake and lit them up. Gina, Tammy, and I began to sing "Happy Birthday," hoping Ana would come out of the bathroom. We sang it once, twice and after the third time I knocked on the bathroom door. "Hey, Ana, come on out. We're trying to sing you 'Happy Birthday.'"

No reply from Ana so I knocked again, "Hey, Ana, are you okay? Come on out, birthday girl!"

Slowly the bathroom door creaked open and Ana's tearstained face appeared. Her eyes were swollen and her mascara was smudged under them.

"No, Missy, I am not okay. This has been the worst birthday of my life," Ana sniffed.

Tammy gently pushed me aside. "Hey, you're not supposed to be crying on your birthday! What's up, girlfriend? Come on out and talk to us."

Slowly, Ana came out of the bathroom and Tammy gave her a big hug. The two ladies looked at each other in the long dresser mirror. Ana said, "Look at us, amiga. It's Beauty and the Beast."

Tammy whipped around and gently shook Ana by the shoulders. "Don't you dare call yourself a beast, Ana. You are beautiful!"

Tears welled up in Ana's eyes. She softly said, "No, I am not. Just look at me. I am a big, fat, old blob. Hell, I can't even get the Super Creep to ask me to dance! How sad is that? Look at my outfit! I look like a giant blueberry! There's enough material here for a circus tent." She pulled her shirt out for emphasis and tears rolled down her cheeks.

I didn't notice it before, but I did see how Ana kind of looked like a blueberry. She was wearing a blue one-piece velvet jumpsuit that had a metallic purple tinge to it. It didn't help that her hair was damp from sweat and was hanging limply around her tear-swollen face.

Tammy shook Ana's shoulders again and sternly said, "Don't you cry on me. You listen to me and you listen good. You are not a big, fat, old blob. You are a beautiful woman and don't you ever put yourself down! Look at yourself!" Tammy swung Ana around to face the mirror. "Look! Right there. You want to know what I see when I look at you? I see a smart, kind, strong lady who has the whole world by the ass! You've had to scratch your way out of a hard life and you won! You're a great mother and a wonderful wife and just an awesome woman."

Ana hung her head down while the tears continued to fall silently. Tammy put her finger under Ana's chin and raised it up so she was looking in the mirror again. Tammy continued softly, "I see you, not your body. I see you and you are gorgeous."

Ana smiled at Tammy and then, something changed in her. Her face went from sad to mad in about thirty seconds flat. You could almost see Ana's thoughts turning around and around in her head like a hamster on a spinning wheel. She angrily wiped her tears and said, "You know what, amigas? Tammy is right! Right, right, damn right!"

Ana pounded her leg with her fist with every "right." She continued, "I am so sick of trying to be skinny all the time, no? I am so sick and tired of trying to be something that I am not and never will be! I will never be a model or someone on TV or someone in the movies, and I am soooo sick of trying to look like those fake, plastic people!"

Ana's accent thickened as she continued, "You know something else? In my country you were skinny because you were poor and didn't always get to eat. But here in America, the rich are the skinny people! I think there is something no good with that! That's just so loco crazy to me! I can finally afford to eat as much as I want, and damn it, I'm going to eat!"

Tammy, Gina, and I were shocked as Ana jumped up and started pacing the room. She stopped, muttered a few things in Spanish under her breath, shook her head, and then quietly said in English, "Okay, amigas, I may not be skinny but I am a good person and I am proud of that. Xavier and I have had to work hard to be where we are at today. We have a nice home, Xavier makes good money, and most importantly to me, we have three meals a day. There were many times I did not have anything to eat for dinner when I was a little girl. There was just no food. Food is important to me. I promised myself as a little girl that I would always have food no matter what. Okay, I know it is not good for my body to eat too much food, but you know what, amigas? I worked hard for that food and now I'm going to enjoy it!

Ana stopped her pacing and she faced the mirror. "Yes, mirror, I may be fat to you and to everyone else, but to me, I am gorgeous and I am finally happy with myself!"

Gina, Tammy, and I stood up and smothered Ana with a group hug in front of the mirror. There were a few "whoo hoos" and "go, girls" being said by all as Kleenex was passed around.

And then the infamous IT happened. I don't know why I said what I did but I said IT and I couldn't take IT back. I opened my mouth and said, "Ana, it was not Beauty and the Beast in the mirror anyway honey. It was more like Lady and the Tramp."

There. I said IT. I don't know why I said IT. Maybe it was the booze, maybe not. All I know is that I instantly regretting saying IT the minute IT came out of my mouth. My hand flew to cover my mouth. Gina and Ana both burst out laughing, but Tammy looked stricken and slowly turned away from Ana and faced me.

"What did you just say?"

"Oh, Tammy! I'm so sorry! I didn't mean to say that. It just came out. I don't know what's the matter with me. I'm so sorry! I didn't mean it."

Tammy stared at me. "Then why would you say it if you didn't mean it?" I could see the anger and hurt simmering behind her eyes.

I stammered, "Uh, I don't know why! It just sorta came out. I'm really, really, really sorry, Tammy!"

Then Tammy turned to look at Gina and Ana. "Oh you two think that it was funny? Is that how you think of me?" She was getting angrier and more hurt by the minute. "All of you can just go to hell if that's what you think! Who needs friends like you! I am not some two bit whore, ya know, even if that is what you think of me." Her eyes clouded over with tears.

Ana went over and gave Tammy a hug. Tammy tried to pull away from Ana's embrace but Ana pulled her back. "Oh,

Tammy. Don't cry, amiga. We know that you are not a whore and you know that Missy was only trying to be funny. I was being such a downer and she was just trying to make it light again. No harm, no foul, right?"

Tammy looked at me. I was putting on my best humble cheesy grin. Tammy squinted her eyes and then surprisingly came over and gave me a hug, too. "Okay, okay. So it was a joke. Not a *funny* joke, but still a joke. I guess I have to learn to laugh at myself. Whatever."

I hugged her back. Gina picked up Ana's birthday cake and brought it over to us. The candles had almost melted down completely and their flames flickered feebly. Ana closed her eyes and made a wish, and with one swift blow the candles went out. We cheered, clapped, and got down to some serious cake eating. Ana took two pieces and grinned at us.

Gina wiped a piece of frosting from her mouth with the back of her hand. She said, "I don't know about all of you, but I think I need some more food! For some reason, I'm still hungry!"

Tammy swung over to the side of the bed and picked up the food flyers from the table. "Pizza anyone?" she asked.

We immediately nodded yes and Tammy placed our order. I stood up and peeled my nylons off. Gina, Ana, and I decided that our sweatpants and T-shirts were starting to look good again so we changed and made ourselves more comfortable. By this time, the pizza arrived and we hungrily dove in.

We were sitting on the floor in a circle with the pizza and a bottle of champagne in front of us. In between bites, Ana piped up. "Okay, I've just got to know. What in the world did you see in Dick Decker, Tammy? I mean, come on, you've got to see that he is a creep. What's the deal, amiga?"

"Wait, make that a Super Duper Creep," Gina butted in.

Tammy shrugged her shoulders and nonchalantly replied, "Uh, I don't know. He was nice to me. He made me feel special, I guess." She continued eating her pizza.

Ana, Gina, and I looked at each other. It was sad to think that Tammy needed a Super Creep like Dick Decker to make her feel special.

I softly said, "Tammy, you can do so much better than someone like Dick Decker."

Tammy stopped eating. "Oh yeah, you are so right, Missy," she said sarcastically. "A thirty-something divorced Mom with two kids and one grown kid still at home who works as a waitress in a casino bar can have her pick of men!" Her tone became serious. "Just what would any of you three know about the dating scene, anyway? At least Dick was buying *me* the drinks this time and not the other way around like I always had to do with Rick. So, yeah, he may not have been a great catch in your books, but he was a great catch for me."

"Tammy, you don't give yourself no credit. I think you need to stop hanging out in bars and start meeting some decent men somewhere else," Ana said.

Tammy took a gulp of champagne and replied, "Just where do you think I am gonna meet any 'decent men', Ana? I work in a bar, for Christ's sake, and I can't remember the last time I went to church, so that let's that option out. I don't play golf and all my friends are married with married friends. All the cousins and brothers are taken too. So, what's a girl to do if you can't go to a bar?"

We all let Tammy's words sink in for a minute. Where *did* you go to meet "decent men" if you were not a churchgoing, golfing, professional woman with single friends? But wait!

This was the Age of Technology! Plenty of people were using technology to find dates.

"What about Internet dating options?" I said excitedly. "I also remember reading about speed dating nights where you meet all kinds of men for about ten minutes and then rotate! What a great idea!"

"Yup, it is a great idea. Been there. Done that. I met Rick at one of those. Remember him? I'm not doin' that again."

Gina piped in, "Just because you met one bad apple at Speed Dating Night doesn't mean that you won't meet someone else who is good. You should give it another try!"

Tammy stood up to go to the bathroom. "Look, ladies, I appreciate what you are tryin' to do but it's no good. I'm okay bein' single and alone. I mean, I'm not really alone anyway because I have you three, right?" She smiled and turned away. The bathroom door thunked shut.

Gina, Ana, and I looked at each other, our eyes registering the same thoughts. None of us wanted to be Tammy at that moment. After the night I had in the bar, I realized that I was getting too old for the college dating scene. I imagined I was Tammy and felt a sense of hopelessness. Tammy's words "I'm okay bein' single and alone" haunted me because I knew them not to be true for myself. Was Tammy really okay being single and alone? I thought not or she wouldn't be desperately seeking the attention of men the likes of Dick Decker and Rick Stampler. Right then, I realized I just wanted to go home and hug my husband and little boys.

Tammy came out of the bathroom wearing a large robe and sat back down in the circle. "Aw, no, what's with all the mopey faces? Is this a party or what?"

Gina meekly raised her hand. "I opt for 'or what.' I'm getting too pooped to party!" She shakily rose from her crossed leg position and headed next to the bathroom with her toothbrush in her hand.

"Okay," Tammy said. "That's one down. Who's up for more champagne?" Ana and I shook our heads and rose to make our way to our beds. Gina came out bathroom and Ana was next. Tammy finally got up from the floor and sat down on her bed.

It was my turn in the bathroom and off I went. A few minutes later, I emerged and saw that Gina and Ana were already asleep. Their chests were moving in a rhythmic pattern. I saw that Tammy was lying down in her big robe and it appeared that she was asleep, too. I quietly tiptoed over and shut off the hall light.

Darkness enveloped the room and my head felt weary from the late hour and the booze. I lay down on the bed and shut my eyes.

I was almost asleep when I was suddenly jerked awake by a bump in the room. I snapped my head up expecting to see a masked intruder, but instead I saw that Tammy was taking off her big robe and was fully dressed underneath. She grabbed her purse and her small suitcase. She didn't see me so I slowly lowered my head back onto the pillow.

Wham! It hit me that she was sneaking out to meet Dick Decker! That must have been what she had whispered to him about before we left the club. We hadn't asked her at the time about what she said to Dick because I think deep down we all knew. She had put on a "brave front" for us but had told Dick something different. I felt slightly fooled and acid churned in my stomach as I thought of her being so lonely that she wanted to be with that creep. Tears sprang to my eyes and I felt like a tornado was spinning out of control in my body.

"Tammy," I softly said when I heard the hotel door latch spring open.

Tammy paused but did not answer me. I whispered, "Tammy, don't go. Please don't go. Stay here with us. I mean, we could talk some more if you want to. You don't have to go."

There was another pause but then I heard the door firmly shut and the lock clicked into place. Tammy was gone. "Be careful, Tammy," I whispered to the dark. I lowered my head and felt such a deep sadness for her. Part of me hoped that Tammy would come waltzing back in the door and would realize her mistake but all of me knew that was not going to happen. I flipped over onto my back and stared blindly at the ceiling.

A few seconds later, I felt Gina's hand gently squeeze mine in the dark. She was awake and must have heard me pleading with Tammy. We lay there in silence. We had no words for each other now. Gina's hand squeeze had said them all. My eyes eventually grew weary waiting up for Tammy and I drifted off to a restless sleep.

***

Tammy was not in the room when I woke up the next morning. Ana did not ask too many questions about Tammy's disappearance, and I really did not have many answers. I think she figured out where Tammy had probably gone. The three of us decided to skip breakfast; we wanted to check out and go home sooner rather than later.

As I was packing my things, I noticed three Hershey Kisses lined up on the table. Tammy must have placed them there for us before she had left last night. It was her simple way of apologizing to us for leaving. I picked up my chocolate piece and my heart ached for a minute. Gina and Ana came over and they silently picked up their pieces, too. The three of us hugged each other and exchanged knowing glances. We were all going home to our families and we were each so thankful for them. We quickly finished packing our things and checked out of the hotel. "Ladies Night" was officially over, and we couldn't wait to go home.

I never did talk to Tammy about what happened after she left the hotel room that night. There wasn't much to say. The four of us pretended her sneaking out hadn't happened and we moved on just as before. Tammy knew, though, that we knew that her single act of bravado was just that...an act. Tammy wasn't the only one putting on a brave front for the world. All I could say was, "Be careful, Tammy. Be careful."

CHAPTER NINE

There's a feeling that comes with spring, a feeling of excitement and of new beginnings. A feeling of change. Change that would touch my friends and me in very different ways.

Ana, Gina, and I were waiting by the Mommy Tree for our children that fateful spring day. I looked up at the Mommy Tree and saw her little buds starting to pop out. The buds were fuzzy and reminded me of the hair on little chicks. The Mommy Tree was changing just like we all had changed a bit this year. We were starting to blossom and bloom in our own unique ways. Whereas the sun and warm weather was the catalyst for the Mommy Tree's new growth, ours was our friendship with each other.

I looked away from the Mommy Tree when I heard Tammy's car door slam in the distance. She was walking quickly towards us and had a slip of paper in her hand. "Hey, ladies," Tammy yelled across the schoolyard. She flapped the piece of paper at us and breathlessly sat down on the Mommy Tree's bench.

"What do you have there?" Gina asked as she tried to peer at the piece of paper.

"This?" Tammy said as she held up the paper. "Oh, this, my dear friends, is my ticket to freedom! You are not goin' to believe this but I have decided to back to school. I'm startin' classes at the community college in a few weeks."

Ana, Gina, and I rushed over and gave her a big hug. Tammy stepped back and beamed at us. "I know. I know it sounds crazy but I've been doin' some thinkin' recently. I took a good look at my life and I didn't like I what I saw. I don't know, it seems like ever since Ana's birthday, I just didn't feel comfortable in my own skin anymore, ya know? I think I saw myself in all of your eyes and I didn't like what I saw starin' back. So, I decided to make a change and go back to school for my associate's degree."

Gina smiled at Tammy. "That sounds wonderful, Tammy. I am so proud of you. This is such a big step! What will you be studying?"

"Nursing. I think I would like to work in a hospital with children or somethin' like that."

I stepped forward, "That sounds like a great idea, Tammy. You would be an excellent nurse. You have a strong nature."

"I ditto that, amiga! Plus, think of all those single doctors you may meet!" Ana piped in.

Tammy held her piece of paper in her hand and shook her head from side to side. "I still can't believe I actually signed up." Her expression suddenly changed. "Oh no! How am I goin' tell the boys? This means extra helpin' around the house and stuff for them. Maybe this wasn't such a good idea after all. How am I goin' work at my job, go to classes, and take care of the boys, too?"

Ana reached over and took Tammy's hand. "No problem. I can help with baby-sitting or around your house. Plus, Jason is old enough to take on some more responsibility. Johnny is a man now and he can share some of the responsibilities of the house. I say you go for it, girl, no matter what."

I chimed in. "Yeah, no matter what, you have to do this for you and for your future. Don't start second guessing yourself now, Tammy. We are all here to help."

Tammy scanned our faces and saw all of our support. She smiled and quietly folded the slip of paper and put it in her bra. "There, that's for safe keepin'," she said. "Lord knows I'll never see it again if I put it in my purse."

We laughed and heard the school bell chime. Ana, Tammy, and I quickly rose to our feet and started walking towards the gate. Allen was already at there waiting anxiously for his brother to come and line up.

After walking a bit, I noticed that Gina was not with us and I glanced back over my shoulder to where she was still sitting. She was fumbling with her cane and slowly trying to rise up from the bench. I ran back and gently grabbed her arm and helped her to her feet.

Gina gave me a meek smile. "Thanks," she said, "But I can take it from here."

Our eyes locked for a second and a chill went up my spine. I knew in that split second that something was very wrong. Just like Tammy and me, and even Ana to an extent, Gina was putting on her own brave front for the world. In that second, however, Gina's eyes betrayed her and I felt her terrible secret.

"Gina?" I softly asked and took her arm gently.

She waved my hand away, "Not now, Missy. The boys are coming." I watched as she put on her mask and smiled deeply for Ethan. How many times had she put on that same mask for me and I hadn't seen it? What kind of self-centered friend was I that I couldn't feel her pain, too? My stomach churned and my legs felt weak.

The boys bounded up to us, breathless. Ethan flung his backpack at Gina and ran towards the car. Ray followed him as his backpack slid off of his shoulders. Allen trailed not too far behind but was yelling, "Wait for me! Wait for me!"

Ana and Tammy walked with Gina and I for a bit. Tammy gave me a puzzled look. She could sense something was wrong but didn't know what to ask. Ana made light talk until we all reached our separate cars. I waved goodbye to Ana and Tammy and started to buckle Ray and Allen into their car seats.

Gina had parked in front of me, and she walked to my open van door. "Missy?" she asked.

I turned around and faced her. "Gina, I…I…" I stammered. My face blushed with embarrassment.

"It's okay, Missy. Don't worry. Look, why don't you come over for a bit so we can talk. I think it's time that you should know a few things about what's going on with me right now."

I gave her a worried look. "Are you sure you're comfortable talking about this? I didn't mean to force it out of you but somehow I just knew something wasn't right. I'm so sorry to step on your privacy and I completely understand if this is none of my business."

Gina took my hand, "Actually, I'm glad you know. I could really use a friend right now. I just didn't know how to tell everyone some things without them feeling sorry for me. Come on over, we can talk more without the 'little ears' in the car seats hearing us." She smiled at me and I gave her a hug.

I followed Gina to her house, my stomach in knots the entire time. I knew that she was going to tell me some bad news about her health and I just didn't know if I would say or do the right things. How do you handle the fact that your friend whom you love is dying? I prayed that God would give me the strength and right words to say as I pulled up in her drive way.

When we got inside Gina's house, Ray, Allen, and Ethan ran up to Ethan's room to play. I followed Gina into the kitchen where she was preparing a pot of tea. An awkward silence filled the room and I shifted in my seat. The tea was poured and I sat back to wait for the words I didn't want to hear.

Gina took a deep breath and let it out. "Okey dokey... here it goes. As you know, I have MS and it is a progressive disease, meaning I will never get better, only worse. For the past few weeks, I haven't been feeling too great. For starters, my eyesight is starting to fail me. I'm starting to sometimes see in double vision and I'm having trouble reading and driving at times. I'm also starting to lose more of my motor control capabilities, like you saw today with me having trouble getting up and down." Gina paused and looked me straight in the eyes. "I'm dying, Missy. I always knew that but for some reason it seems like my body is speeding up the process all of a sudden. I'm really scared. There, I think that is the first time I've really admitted it to anyone else, but I am *really* scared."

My eyes welled up with tears and I reached out for her hand. I softly asked, "What about the doctors, Gina? What do they say about all this? Is there something they can do to help?"

"Well, I was just getting to that," she calmly replied. "Gary and I have been seeing many doctors and they are all saying the same thing. It looks like I may need to start a different hormone therapy to try and help my nervous system send signals to my brain. Problem is, the hormone therapy is very expensive, and with Gary being in school, we just don't have the money to do the therapy in a private institution here. There is a medical school, however, in Chicago that is willing to give me the hormone treatments as a test subject free of cost. It also means that I will have to move to Chicago."

"Oh, Gina," I said, "I'm so glad that there is a possible treatment for you!"

Gina smiled weakly. "It's just a treatment option that may inhibit some of the disease, but you have to remember that it is not a cure. I'm eventually going to die from MS, but I'm doing my damnedest to make that a long time from now!!"

"When will you move?" I asked. I had a million questions and my mind buzzed.

"We'll move as soon as Ethan finishes the school year. In the mean time, Gary's parents will be coming out to stay with us to help. I don't know what will be worse…the move to Chicago or surviving my in-laws for the next three months!" Gina laughed, trying to make light of the situation.

I smiled and took a sip of my tea, letting everything sink in for a moment. "So, does Ethan know yet about the move?"

"No. Gary and I will tell him soon. We didn't want to upset him too much with all this right now. It will be better when his grandparents come for support."

"Do you have a place to live? What will Gary do for a job? What about school for Ethan? What are you going to do?" I blurted out like a bumbling idiot. So much for control under pressure.

Gina laughed. "Missy, Missy. Please. Gary and I have thought all of this through and there are no other options for me. Gary is going to stop school for a while and go back to work in sales. He can get a job. That's the least of our worries. As far as a house, we'll find something. Don't worry about us. We'll be fine."

"I know, Gina. I know you'll be fine. I'm sorry for my outburst. I just don't know how you can sit there and be so calm about all this." I got up from my chair and paced around the kitchen. "Is there anything I can I do to help?"

Gina paused. Then her face lit up like she had just had an epiphany. "You can help by doing what you've been doing all along. Just be my friend and pray for me. I never really realized until this year how important a strong friendship could be in shaping my life. Ya know, all along I've been putting on this brave front just like you did, pretending that I had everything under control and that I didn't need anyone to help me. I used to hate it when people tried to help me after they saw I was using a cane. I wanted to show everyone that I could do it alone. I wanted to prove that I was *normal* somehow even though I know I will never be normal in a physical sense again. I told myself the lie of not needing anyone for help for so long that I, like you, began to believe it.

"But you know what? I have finally accepted that I can't do things as well as everyone else. I have MS and it sucks big time, but I just have to deal with it the best I can. This year you, Ana, and Tammy have really shown me that it's okay to be vulnerable and that the best way to deal with my situation is to learn to rely on others sometimes. I learned that accepting help, physically or emotionally, does not make me weaker as a person. No! It only makes me a stronger person knowing that I have such a wonderful support system that is there to catch me when I fall and to love me no matter what.

"I mean, isn't that really the key to what living is all about? I realized that the important thing in life is our *honest* relationships with one another. I learned from you ladies at the Mommy Tree to finally allow someone else into my little inner protective circle filled with my deepest faults, darkest fears, and ugly secrets; and that by doing so I was actually releasing some of those fears and accepting those faults. By closing myself off for so long, I feel like I have missed out on really connecting with people. That's all going to change now, and I thank you, Missy, for helping me to see that finally."

Tears filled our eyes as we sat there silently for a moment. I reflected on what Gina had admitted and realized that she was so right in so many ways.

I asked gently when it seemed like the right time, "What about Ana and Tammy? When will you tell them about your move and plans?"

"I don't know yet. I'll tell them soon, but not right now. Look, Missy, I know this is hard to accept and I didn't mean to spill my guts out just then! But you have to understand that I need your support the most right now. All of this is happening so fast and I still have a hard time accepting it. You've got to know that this is my last chance. My *last chance*, Missy. There are no more options for me. So you see, I've got to take it."

I sat back down in the chair. I felt exhausted and my energy was drained. I still couldn't comprehend the fact that Gina was slowly dying and moving to Chicago for one last hope. The cruelty of a young mother and a beautiful woman dying was too much for me to bear. Tears streamed down my face.

Gina handed me a napkin. "Please don't cry, Missy. It's really not that bad. I don't want you to feel sorry for me. This is the hand life dealt me and I'm playing it the best I can. It will be fine really." Gina shakily got up from the table and hugged my shoulders. The irony of her trying to comfort me when it should have been me comforting her made me giggle uncontrollably. My giggling was infectious and pretty soon Gina was laughing, too.

"What in the world are we laughing at?" she asked in between giggles.

"I don't know!" I replied. I looked at her and took her hand in mine. Then I gravely said, "Oh, Gina, if I don't laugh I think I will go crazy with grief over this whole thing. I'm so sorry that I haven't been a better friend and helped you out more. I wish there was more I can do and say."

Gina gave me a warm smile. She sat down in her chair and looked at me straight in the eye. "Listen here, sister, and listen good. I don't want to see any guilt from you, okay? You have been the very best of friends to me and I will always cherish our friendship. I told you a long time ago that you were one of the strongest people I knew. Well, I meant it then and I mean it now. I need your strength, Missy. I need you to be strong for both of us. Knowing that I have your support and love is enough for me to go through with these treatments and the move and the whole thing."

I looked her back in the eye. "You got it. Anything."

Just then, Allen, Ray, and Ethan ran down the stairs. "Mom, I'm hungry!" Ethan exclaimed. I looked at the kitchen clock and realized it was almost dinnertime and that Eric would be home soon.

Gina grinned at me, "See, Missy? Life goes on!"

"Life goes on," I said sadly, but grinned back at her so she wouldn't see my sadness. I grabbed my purse and coat and herded the boys out to the car. At Gina's door, I turned and gave her the biggest hug I knew how to give. "Life goes on, but it won't be the same without you so close by. I love you, Gina."

"Love ya too, Missy." As I walked down the driveway, Gina called out, "Hey. Thanks."

I stopped and turned to her. "No," I said, "Thank you. We'll talk again soon. See you later." My heart was heavy as I got into the van and slowly drove away. I had no control over her situation, and worse, I couldn't help her. It was eating me up inside. I reached deep inside and pulled out my brave front once again. I had to be strong for Gina and able to fool Ana and Tammy so they wouldn't see my pain. I wanted to go home and crawl into bed and just cry. My friend was dying and there was nothing I could do to help her.

***

I did end up crawling into bed that night and crying myself to sleep but for other reasons than just my sadness over Gina's situation. When I got home from Gina's that afternoon, Eric was home early waiting to talk to me. After kissing the boys and me hello, he gently guided me into the kitchen. "We have to talk," he whispered.

Confused, I searched Eric's face and saw that he was trying to conceal his excitement over something. "What is it?" I whispered back. Eric looked over his shoulder and saw that Ray and Allen were glued to the TV watching their favorite afternoon programs. He pulled a piece of paper out of his right uniform pocket.

"This," he declared.

"What is that?" I asked but fear clenched my gut. Instinctively, I knew what that official looking piece of paper was.

"Now, Missy, just try and keep an open mind for a second, okay?" Eric teased.

"Oh, Eric! Just get on with it. What is that piece of paper?" I pleaded.

"Sit down for a second." I sat. Eric continued, "This piece of paper is my orders to our new duty station. We're moving this summer."

I exploded out of my chair. "Our *what?*" I asked in disbelief. My head was spinning. "How can we have new orders when we still have one more year here until we are tour complete? Why do we have to move this summer? I don't understand this, Eric. What in the world is going on?"

Eric said calmly, "Now, Missy, just take a breath for a second, okay? You know as well as I do that we are subject to move at the whim of the Air Force anytime that they see a need that I can fill. Well, a need that I can fill just popped up. I received special orders this afternoon."

I took a deep breath and blew it out. I ran my fingers through my hair and started to pace the kitchen floor. After a few minutes, I turned to Eric and said, "Okay, Eric, fine. I accept that you have a special need to fill blah, blah, blah. Fine. We have to move. I get it." I sat back down at the table. "So," I said, "where are we going to this time?"

Eric put his hands on my shoulder and stood behind me. "Well," he said slowly.

I turned around in my chair and grabbed his hand that was on my shoulder. "Well what? Just tell me. I'm a big girl I can handle it. Right?"

"Okay...here it goes. Missy, we are moving to Yakamoto Air Force Base which is just outside of Tokyo, Japan."

I was stunned. Speechless. Dumbstruck. Oh. My. God. Had he just said Tokyo, Japan? A whole new country? Whaaaat?

I was silent for a minute. Eric anxiously searched my face. I could see it in his eyes that he was actually excited about his orders. Tokyo. Japan. Oh. My. God.

"Say something, Missy. Anything. Are you mad, excited, what?" Eric asked.

I got up from the chair. "I don't know what to say, Eric. I mean, basically, I'm a little shocked. I'm not mad. I guess I am just a little scared. It is such a big move and so far away from our families. The whole 'living in another country' thing frightens me a bit."

Eric pulled me into a big bear hug. "I know how you feel, Missy. I felt the same way when I saw the message this morning." He pulled away and looked into my eyes. "But just think about what a great opportunity this is for us as a family. We're going to experience a whole new culture. The boys are at a perfect age where they will actually remember some of their experience. This really is a once-in-a-lifetime opportunity for us, and quite frankly, I'm pretty excited about the whole thing."

I smiled. "I guess you're right. It will be pretty cool living in a new culture, and I've heard the Japanese people are pretty friendly." My heart was starting to race. I was going to be moving to Tokyo, Japan, this summer! The gazillion things I had to do before the move spun around in my mind. For one brief second, I was so bogged down in my own situation that I momentarily forgot about my sadness over Gina.

Suddenly, I slumped back down in my chair and buried my face in my hands. Sobs wracked my body as I thought about Gina. Eric rushed over and put his arms around my heaving shoulders. "Honey, I know it's a shock to be moving so far away but it's going to be all right, you'll see. Don't cry, honey, don't cry."

I was crying so hard that I couldn't stop and explain to Eric the real reason for the tears. Deep down I knew that we were going to be all right with the move to Japan. All I could think about was my dear, sweet friend moving away to an uncertain future. Eric kept trying to comfort me and spin positive things about the move, but I wasn't listening.

I finally got myself together enough to explain to Eric the real reason for my tear-fest. He listened and I saw sympathy in his eyes. We held each other in the middle of the kitchen for a long time, each of us silently thanking God for our own personal blessings.

I was moving to a foreign country. My friend was dying and there was nothing I could do to help her. I was scared.

***

The next few weeks seem to fly by for each of us. Tammy was working extra shifts and was preparing for her new classes during the summer season. Gina had eventually told Ana and Tammy about her health situation. She was busy with her pending move and trying to keep her in-laws entertained after they had moved in to help her out. I frantically ran around trying to finish my "To-Do Move" lists. Ana was the only one who appeared calm that late spring. However, she had big news of her own to share, and she was going to actually be busier than all of us combined.

The four of us were sitting at the Mommy Tree one afternoon waiting for our children as usual. I noticed that Ana, who had been so calm the last few weeks, was very fidgety. She was rubbing her hands and her legs were bouncing up and down.

I laid my hand on one of her jiggly knees and asked, "What's the matter? You're as jumpy as an egg on a frying pan."

Ana appreciated my lame attempt at humor. She smiled and replied, "Well, nothing...*really*." Her eyes twinkled at me.

Tammy leaned over me and said, "What do you mean, 'nothing really?' Sounds like somethin' to me. Okay, sister, out with it!"

Ana shook her head, "Oh, ladies, you are not going to believe this when I tell you!"

"Tell us what?" Gina, Tammy, and I said in unison.

Ana took a deep breath and blew it out. "Okay, here it goes. I have a bun in the oven." She beamed.

Tammy's eyebrows shot up, and Gina and I looked shocked for a moment. Tammy said, "You're pregnant? Wow! That's awesome, Ana. Congratulations, girlfriend!"

The four of us leaped up and danced around in a tiny circle stomping our feet. Laughing, Ana pulled away. "I still can't believe it myself, amigas!" she exclaimed and cupped her cheeks with her hands. "This is so weird but so wonderful! I am very excited and very, very happy!" She was glowing and there was no way she could hide her joy. She briefly filled us in on all the important details—due date, how she was feeling, etc.

Out of the corner of my eye, I saw Gina's face cloud over with sadness for a brief second. She was thinking about the children she would never have. Then, as quickly as it had appeared, the sadness faded and Gina appeared normal and happy for Ana. She had officially put back on her brave front. I leaned over and gave her hand a small squeeze. She weakly smiled back as she fought the pool of tears in her eyes. I fought back tears, too, and adjusted my own brave front.

The school bell rang and the children rushed out of the gate. Allen ran up to Ray and gave him a big hug. My heart warmed at the sight of the two brothers giving each other affection. Ana watched Ray and Allen, too, and she turned and grinned at me. I knew that she was thinking of her own boy having a brother or sister to hug soon.

The children ran ahead of us as the four of us starting walking towards our cars. Ana, Gina, and I were walking in a straight line, and Tammy came up behind Ana and gently nudged me aside so that she could be next to her. She linked arms with Ana and me and Ana linked arms with Gina. The four of us looked like we were about to break out into song and skip down the yellow brick road like Dorothy and her friends in *The Wizard of Oz*.

Tammy spoke. "Hey ladies, you know what next week is?"

We all nodded yes. Next week was the last week of school. It was also the last week before Gina and I had to move and before Tammy started school herself.

Tammy continued, "This is also the last weekend that all four of us are going to be together. Did ya know that?" Our line stopped moving as Tammy's statement started to sink in. Our faces dropped. This was our last weekend together. Fresh tears sprung to all of our eyes. Oh my. Oh no.

"Okay, okay, let's not get all sappy right now," Tammy said as she rubbed a tear from her eye. "Ya know what? I think we should send Gina and Missy off with a bang. I mean a real good bang." She paused. I could see the wheels turning in her head. All I could think of was that the last time she had planned an evening we ended up with Dick Decker. I grimaced.

Tammy lightly tapped her index finger on her lips. She turned around and glanced at the schoolyard. "Yeeeaaahh," she said. "This just might do." I turned to see what Tammy was staring at and saw the Mommy Tree with her flower buds swaying in the gentle breeze. It was perfect.

I turned to Tammy. "Are you thinking what I'm thinking?" Tammy clicked her tongue and nodded her head up and down.

"Seems right, huh?" she asked.

"Yeah, it sure does," I agreed.

Gina faced us. "Just what are you two plotting over here? Hey, and just for the record, if you two are planning on any more nights in a club on the strip than you can count me out. Once a year is enough for me!"

Tammy and I smiled at each other and I nodded for Tammy to tell her the plan. "Gina, Ana," Tammy said, "Missy and I are thinking that we should have a little going away party at the Mommy Tree this weekend. Since Friday is the last day of school, we won't be meeting like this anymore." Tammy paused as we let the reality of that statement sink in. "So, I was thinkin' we could sneak into the schoolyard on Saturday night and just hang out under the Mommy Tree for one last time. Whadya say, girls?"

Ana was shocked for a moment. "What if we get caught on school property after hours? Won't we be in trouble?"

Tammy winked at me. "I think if we run into any trouble then Missy can handle Ol' Mr. Geary the principal. Right, Missy?"

I playfully punched her in the arm. Seriously, I said, "It is a little risky but that's kind of half the fun. We can bring blankets and just have a small picnic and we won't stay too long. I don't think we have to worry about getting caught. I mean, teenagers do this kind of stuff all the time!"

Gina hooked arms with Tammy and me. "I'm in."

Ana slowly hooked arms with Gina. "I'm a little nervous about this but count me in, too." Tammy shouted out a little whoop and punched the air with her fist. We quickly finalized our plans and agreed to meet Saturday night at midnight at the Mommy Tree for our "Super Secret Send-Off Goodbye Meeting." I couldn't wait!

***

The final week of school flew by for me. Ray's kindergarten graduation ceremony was very precious as his class sang songs and danced for the parents. Eric gently held my hand during the ceremony, and we were both emotional remembering our son as a tiny baby and the journey he had taken to reach this special moment. Our baby was an official first grader now, and we were very proud of him. I let the tears flow for the first time in public as Ray accepted his graduation certificate. I didn't worry so much about what people thought of me anymore. Thank you, Mommy Tree.

The next night was Saturday night and I ended up falling asleep at ten o'clock! What can I say? I'm a mom and I just don't stay up past ten o'clock anymore! I woke up to Eric gently shaking me and asking me if I was going to leave soon. I glanced at the clock and saw that it was eleven forty-five. I had fifteen minutes to change, grab my tote bag and comb my hair. Aagh!

I quickly changed into black jeans and the black turtleneck from my cat costume at Halloween. I slipped on a pair of black gloves and took one of Eric's black baseball caps. I was going to a Super Secret Send-Off Meeting, after all, so I had to dress appropriately for the part. I imagined myself as a slick robber or a cunning black ninja or even a super agent spy! Putting on the outfit made my heart beat a little faster. I was breaking into the schoolyard and breaking the rules! Yes, me, Missy Danvers, breaking another rule! I would never have done this a year ago, but things had changed for me. Whoopee! Off in our van I went with a huge smile on my face.

We had agreed to park our vehicles away from the playground fence so that we wouldn't draw attention to the fact that we were going to be breaking into the schoolyard. I knew that I was going to be late but for some reason I was okay with it. Maybe I had changed a little bit more than I realized. I quietly exited my van and grabbed my tote bag filled with blankets and snacks. Off to the schoolyard I crept like a cat on the prowl, as Ana would say.

I reached the fence of the schoolyard and threw my tote bag over the top. Awkwardly grasping the open holes of the chain link fence, I began my long climb. After a few moments, I grunted and groaned and broke out into a light sweat. Then my jeans belt loop got caught on a broken link. I was stuck! Oh no! I was the worse super agent spy ever!

I imagined being stuck to the fence with a huge spotlight illuminating my body and the voice of a nasally cop saying, "Stop where you are. Put your hands up. You are under arrest for breaking and entering on school property." I panicked and tried to free myself by tugging and pulling at my jeans, but it was to no avail. I was still stuck on the fence.

Then, to my horror, I heard a soft whistle and saw the dim light of the head of a flashlight coming my way. I tugged harder and harder on my pants but they would not budge. I was stuck, stuck, stuck! The whistler saw me and was shining a flashlight right on my face! Oh. My. God! The whistler slowly emerged from inside the schoolyard, softly whistling a tune that sounded like the theme from *Mission Impossible*. Duh, duh, duh, duh, duh, doodle dooo, doodle doo. I was stunned and scared and trapped like a caged animal! My heart felt like it was going to leap out of my chest!

Finally, the whistler revealed her identity by stepping under a streetlight next to the fence. The whistler was not a police officer. The whistler was just Tammy! I was glad to see her!

Tammy bent over laughing when she saw me hanging on the fence. "What in the hell are you doin', Missy, and what's with the black getup?"

"What does it look like I am doing, Tammy? I'm trying to break into the schoolyard, and keep your voice down for Pete's sake or we're going to get caught!" I hissed.

"Oh yeah, I forgot, I had better keep my voice down or every cop in Las Vegas is goin' come runnin' to bust us four moms at the schoolyard after dark! Ooooooooooh!" Tammy smiled. "Chill out, Missy, there's no one here but us chickens."

Tammy's comment relaxed me somewhat but I was still expecting the cops to show up any minute. I said, "And for your information, this is not a 'getup.' This is my official 'Breaking and Entering Super Spy Woman Wear.' You like?" I smiled and winked at her.

Tammy started laughing again. She slowly answered, "Yeeeaaah, right...whatever." She giggled, "Oh, by the way, Super Spy Woman, you may want to use the fence gate next time. It's always open." She swung the creaky gate open to demonstrate. "Do you need help getting down?"

I felt completely foolish as I feebly nodded yes. Tammy picked up my tote bag from the other side walked through the gate to the side where I was stuck. She stood on the tote bag and grabbed me around the waist, hoisting me up so that my belt loop would be freed from the jagged chain link. I slowly climbed down but my body was shaking with giggles.

Once we were both down, Tammy and I broke out into hysterical laughing. Tears were rolling down our faces as we picked up my tote bag. Tammy slung my bag around her shoulders and grabbed my black baseball hat that had fallen to the ground during my struggle with the fence. She put it on her head and hooked her arm through mine. We skipped like two little girls to the Mommy Tree where Ana and Gina were already waiting for us.

I gasped when I saw the Mommy Tree in the moonlight. The tree was so exquisite that it took my breath away. The Mommy Tree's mighty branches were glowing in the mellow light of the moon. Her massive trunk stood fervently absorbing the weight of her branch limbs. I stopped walking and just stared at the tree. I don't even know how to describe just exactly how I felt when I saw the Mommy Tree except to say that I was humbled.

Ana and Gina gave me a big hug when I reached where they were sitting under the tree. I took out my blankets and spread them out, and Tammy sat down on the blanket next to me. "Hey, ladies," she said while taking a bottle of champagne and four Styrofoam cups out of her enormous purse. "How about a little somethin' to get this party rollin?"

When Ana politely refused to take a cup, Tammy winked at her and pulled out a bottle of sparkling apple cider. We held our cups in a quick toast and each took a sip.

And then we sat. We sat there silently. Each of us was absorbing the moment. Reality was sinking in. Everything was changing. This was the last time we were going to be together like this under the Mommy Tree. Sadness crept over us like a thick blanket of fog.

Gina was the first to break the silence, "Okay, ladies. Is this a pity party or a *party* party?" She looked around at our grim faces shining in the moonlight. "Oh, I know how you all feel and I feel it, too, but we've got to snap out of it, sisters, and just enjoy the moment! Hey, I've got plenty of time to be sad in Chicago, but tonight I just want to have fun!"

"You're right, Gina," Ana agreed. "It's just that I don't know what I'm going to do next year without you and Missy at the tree everyday. It's going to be so weird, no?" Ana sniffed and was fighting back tears.

Tammy chimed in. "Yeah, it is going to be weird without you two here, but hey, there's always e-mail, the telephone, letters, ya know? It's not like we're not gonna still keep in touch, right?"

Gina and I nodded in unison and we both said, "Right."

"All right then, let's put on a little music and pour another round of drinks!" Tammy exclaimed. She leaned over and switched on her small portable radio. A nasal country singer's voice drifted through the air. Gina and I giggled at the twangy singer singing about loose lips, wide hips and cheap beer. That song ended and a new song started. It was Johnny Lee's song, "Looking for Love."

Ana nudged Tammy. "Hey, amiga. Sounds like your theme song, no?"

Tammy cocked her head and listened to the song for a minute. A slow grin spread across her face. "Yeah, Ana, I think you hit the nail on the head with this one as my theme song." Her grin faded and she somberly said, "What is it with me and my bad choices with men? I'm just like everyone else. I just want to find that one person to spend the rest of my life with, ya know? I don't want to end up alone. I know I have my boys, but they're gonna grow up and leave me someday. It just doesn't seem fair sometimes."

"Hang in there, Tammy. Your special someone is out there," Gina encouraged. "I think you are doing the right thing right now by just focusing on you and your goals. Get yourself straight first and everything else will fall into place. You'll see."

Tammy weakly smiled. "I think you're right, Gina. I need to get my life together first before I'm ready to share it with someone else."

Gina winked at Tammy, "Good for you, girlfriend. Just promise me that you'll stick with your classes and try to stay away from the Super Creeps and Ricks of this world, okay? You deserve so much better!"

I piped in, "Amen!"

Tammy stuck out her hand for a handshake with Gina. She said, "Okay, it's a deal! No more Super Creeps or Ricks, I promise. From now on it is hittin' the books time!" Gina and Tammy shook hands.

The song was still playing. I turned up the radio and started to sing along with the chorus. Ana, Tammy, and Gina joined in singing with me. We sounded like a wild pack of dogs baying at the moon as we sang. Our voices and spirits were joined for just a few brief seconds. We collapsed into a fit of giggles as soon as the song ended. I switched off the radio and wiped tears of laughter from my eyes.

The darkness of the night quickly swallowed us. We sat again deep in our own thoughts as the sadness of the occasion gripped our hearts. We knew it was getting late and it was almost time to go.

Gina cleared her throat and held her cup up for a toast. "I propose a toast to a new beginning in a foreign land. Sayonara, Missy!" She winked, wiped a tear away, and clicked my cup signaling my turn for a toast.

I held my cup and warmly said, "To new life and new attitudes. Congratulations, Ana." I sniffed and tried to hold my tears back.

Ana held her cup up, "To love and wisdom. Good luck in college. Bueno suerte, mi amiga, Tammy." A tear trickled down her face.

Tammy winked at Gina and as she held her cup up her voice cracked with emotion. "To good health and a brighter future. Stay strong, girlfriend."

The four of us stood up and formed a small circle. We looked up into the dark night sky and saw the powerful shadows of the Mommy Tree's branches. We lifted our cups and in unison shouted, "To the Mommy Tree!"

For a long time after our toast we just stood there rooted in our spots. None of us said a word as we let the tears silently fall down our faces. No words could capture what we were feeling.

Tammy was the first one to go. She picked up her blanket and put the radio in her enormous black purse. She gently threw my baseball hat back to me. Tammy went to us individually and gently took our hands in hers. I felt her put something in my palm but I couldn't tell what it was. Then Tammy quickly picked up her things and started to walk away, but she turned around and gave us a short wave goodbye. I watched as she faded into the darkness. Tammy was gone.

Ana, Gina and I slowly opened our hands. Tammy had given us each a Hershey's kiss. I squeezed my hand shut and smiled through my tears.

Ana slowly picked up her blanket. She grabbed Gina and me and gave us a huge bear hug. The three of us were sobbing into each other's shoulders. Ana pulled away and turned to walk away, but I gently grabbed her wrist.

"Adios mi amiga."

Ana nodded. She was unable to speak through her tears. She hugged Gina and me again. Then, she briskly walked away. Ana was gone.

Gina and I were the only ones left. Gina softly said, "Oh, I can't do this! I just can't say goodbye to you! This is so hard."

I sniffed. "I know. So let's not say goodbye. Let's just say 'see ya later.' I don't want any sappy speeches or any more crying, okay?"

"Okay."

I took a deep breath and tried to stop crying. "Okay, let's just get this over with and go together." I stooped and picked up my tote bag and blanket. Gina collected her things. We hooked arms and set off into the darkness together towards our cars.

I looked back one last time at the Mommy Tree. A soft breeze was blowing and I saw that the tree's branches were slightly swaying in the wind. It looked like the Mommy Tree was waving goodbye to us. I smiled.

Gina and I reached the gate. This was it. This was the point where we had to separate to go to our own cars. I inhaled deeply and looked Gina squarely in the eye. I said, "Gina, I know I said no sappy speeches but I want you to know that I love you. You have been the best of friends to me and I will really miss you. I want you to know that no matter where I am, I am always here for you if you need me. Thank you for being my friend."

Gina started to cry harder now. "Oh, Missy! I love you, too. You are the best friend I have ever had and I will really miss you, too." We hugged and neither of us wanted to let go. Finally, I pulled away and started to walk towards my van. Gina turned and walked in the opposite direction towards hers.

I stopped and turned to look at Gina. I called out, "Hey, Gina! See ya later!"

Gina stopped and grinned at me. "Yeah, see ya later, too!" Our eyes locked for the last time. Gina turned to go but for some unexplained reason, I couldn't move. I watched her as she got into her van and slowly drove away. Gina was gone.

I slid into the driver's seat and laid my head on the steering wheel. Then I wept until I felt hollow. Finally I pulled myself together and drove away from the schoolyard.

CHAPTER TEN

So there you have it. That's my story about my very special year with my friends and the Mommy Tree. I ended up moving to Japan a few days after school was over. I won't go into too many details right now about my years in Japan and my adventures with my new friends, the "Matcha Mamas", who were named after the powdered Japanese green tea that they drank together every morning. That's another story for another time. However, something happened in Japan on the first day of school that I think I need to tell you about.

***

The dust had finally settled from our move. All the boxes were opened and cleared and I finally found my children who had been lost and buried under all the paper wrapping! I hadn't really had the time to explore my new surroundings and our new base yet due to the whole moving-in process but that would come later. The first day of school arrived quickly and I was not sure that I was quite ready to start over again. But, summer vacation was over and it was time. So, off I went with Ray and Allen in tow to walk to our new school.

As I approached the school, standing boldly in front of the main gate was a big, beautiful cherry blossom tree surrounded by a wraparound bench. Tears welled in my eyes as I looked at the radiant tree standing tall and proud. I couldn't believe my eyes when I saw that this new school had its own Mommy Tree, too!

The tree's branches swayed gently in the wind, welcoming me to come over. As I walked, I saw some women standing off near the fence by themselves waiting for the main school gate to open. Apprehension and nervousness spread across their faces. They were not talking or smiling. I also saw a few women who were sitting on the tree's bench with their children. Those ladies were making small talk and smiling, and they reminded me of how Ana, Gina, Tammy, and I must have looked to others on the first day of school last year. I smiled and knew right away which group I was going to join.

I squeezed Ray's and Allen's hands tightly and added a bounce to my step as I confidently walked towards the school and broke out into a wide cheesy grin. I had a feeling that moving to Japan was going to work out just fine, after all. Hello, new Mommy Tree and hello "Matcha Mamas!

ACKNOWLEDGMENTS

A huge thank you to my husband, Yuri, for his patience, love and support during this project. Thank you for still believing in me even when I stopped believing in myself. I could not have done this project without you and I love you with all my heart. Thank you to my two sons, Reino and Austin, for their complete understanding when Mommy was "busy writing." You are the best boys and I love you both very, very much. Special thanks to Mom and Dad P for their sincere encouragement and unconditional love. You are the best parents and I'm lucky that you are mine. I love you both. Thank you Mom and Dad G for their enthusiasm and love and for listening to me "ramble on" about the project. I love you both too. Thanks to my family and friends. You are all special to me in so many ways. Many thanks to the publishing and editing teams at BookSurge for making my dream become a reality. Lastly, I want to thank my dear friend, Geodi - the wonderful woman who inspired me to write this story who is now the beautiful angel watching over me today. I miss you but I know we will see each other again someday.

EXTRA: I, the author, personally pledge to donate a proceed from each sale of this book to the National Multiple Sclerosis Society. Any additional donations can be sent directly to the National Multiple Sclerosis Society at:

National MS Society
P.O. Box 4527
New York, NY 10163

www.nationalmssociety.org
1-800-344-4867